KU-432-094

The Power Game

Slowed by alcohol, Luke staggers slightly, and I am half way across the room before he catches me again. But this time, he won't let me go, and he encloses me in a tight bear-hug.

'Luke. For Christ's sake! What are you doing?'

'Why? Don't you like it? Don't you like it when he pushes you around like this?' he says, tightening his grip further still.

'What are you talking about?' My question maddens him even more and he gives me a small, jarring shake.

'I know that bastard. I know this is what he does with women.'

Still advancing as he holds me, he bulldozes me against the wall, pinning me with his weight. He wraps his fingers around my wrist, and presses my hand against his cock.

'Does he want you this much?' he demands as he forces my palm up and down the length of his erection. 'Does he get this hard?'

As he rubs my hand over his wonderful prick, every instinct begs me to rip it from his trousers and impale myself on the solid, thick organ. I am ravenous for it. But he mustn't suspect. Wrenching myself from his grasp, I put up my hands and try to push him away. But as I struggle against him I am shocked by the strength of him. We are totally unequal.

The Power Game
Carrera Devonshire

BLACK LACE

Black Lace books contain sexual fantasies.
In real life, always practise safe sex.

First published in 2005 by
Black Lace
Thames Wharf Studios
Rainville Road
London W6 9HA

Copyright © Carrera Devonshire 2005

The right of Carrera Devonshire to be identified as the Author of
the Work has been asserted in accordance with the Copyright,
Designs and Patents Act 1988.

Design by Smith & Gilmour, London
Printed and bound by Mackays of Chatham PLC

ISBN 0 352 33990 X

*All characters in this publication are fictitious and any resemblance
to real persons, living or dead, is purely coincidental.*

This book is sold subject to the condition that it shall not, by way
of trade or otherwise, be lent, resold, hired out or otherwise
circulated without the publisher's prior written consent in any form
of binding or cover other than that in which it is published and
without a similar condition including this condition being imposed
on the subsequent purchaser.

In the General Election of 2010, the New Spectrum Party was swept to victory by an electorate impressed by its refreshingly radical policies and its charismatic young leaders. The personalities that walked the corridors of power were different. The envies and ambitions, the passions and the perversions of human nature, remained the same.

1

Luke's Story

'Fuck' is a word I use a lot. I don't usually let it slip out in front of the President of the United States of America. But that day I used it liberally.

The morning began well. The President delivered an impressive speech. The audience, crammed into a sports hall in a small town in New Jersey, had been appreciative. As the President's press secretary, I was gratified to see that a large number of journalists had turned up. They had been carefully briefed. They had asked no difficult questions. I was confident that the evening's TV coverage would be on-message. The President, always upbeat, was in an exceptionally good mood.

It was when we left that the trouble began. A few people, around a hundred or so, were gathered outside the building and, as the President crossed the pavement, they cheered and waved. The President, waving back, gave them a broad and very genuine smile. A posse of photographers vied for his attention.

'Hey, Paul,' they heckled. 'This way, Mister President.' Paul paused briefly, giving them time to take the shots they needed. Just as he was about to get into his car, I heard a commotion behind us. A security guard shouted something and I turned to see a man emerging from the crowd. Later I would be unable to remember what he was wearing or what he said. I don't remember seeing the gun. But I would never forget the expression on his face. It wasn't right.

What I did next was later described by some as brave. It was nothing of the sort. Bravery implies some awareness of danger. But I sincerely (and, as it turned out, stupidly) didn't think the stranger would harm me. I stepped back towards the President, my body shielding his. I managed to shout just one word. 'Paul!' It was enough.

I heard nothing. All I registered was the pain. It ripped through me, crushing the breath from my chest. I slumped forwards, gasping as I tried to drag some air into my lungs. 'Fuck,' I said. 'Fuck. Fuck.'

Around me, people were moving quickly. The bodyguards nearest to the President bundled him into the car and it sped off. Police outriders followed, raising a cloud of dust from the hot road. The man with the gun was swept away by a sea of security staff. A policeman was yelling into his radio. 'The President's fine, but the bastard shot the English guy.'

One of the President's personal assistants passed me. 'Great job, Luke,' he shouted. Someone offered to take the briefcase I was still holding in my left hand, but for some reason I couldn't let it go.

Serena, the First Lady, was running towards me. She looked concerned and I didn't know why. 'Luke! Are you OK?'

'I'm fine,' I said. I smiled at Serena. She was wearing a cream suit, and her hair was twisted into its usual elegant chignon. Not for the first time I thought how gorgeous she was. She took the briefcase from my hand and placed it carefully at her feet.

A security man was trying to make her leave the area. 'It might be dangerous, Ma'am.' She dismissed him with a perfunctory wave of her hand. No one told Serena what to do.

Her face looked different. It floated, disembodied, lovely, in front of me. I forced myself to focus, but sweat was running into my eyes. I couldn't see. As I raised my arm to run my hand across my face, I saw that it was smeared with red. Someone was bleeding.

'You sit down,' she said. 'The medics will be with you in a moment to look at that shoulder.'

I glanced down. A deep red stain was spreading down my right arm, soaking the fabric of my Italian suit. 'Oh,' I said.

Serena placed a hand on my back and I sank to the ground, grateful not to be standing. There was a large hole in the arm of my jacket, the torn fabric hung from my elbow.

'You won't be wearing this again,' said Serena, smiling kindly. I frowned. She bent down to ease my jacket off my shoulders. 'Before your arm swells,' she explained. Her hands were gentle against my chest. My arm wasn't the only thing that was about to start swelling.

As she leaned over me a sleek lock of blonde hair escaped and I reached up to brush it out of her face. She gave me a look I didn't understand. My face was level with her thighs. I wanted to reach out and slip my hand up under her skirt. To know what her fabulously long legs felt like.

Behind her I saw an ambulance, moving slowly towards us through the crowd. But it was Serena who held my attention. I was certain she would be wearing satin underwear. Very soft and very silky. Pink, or maybe lilac. Ivory would look stunning against her golden skin. Whatever the colour, it would be very expensive.

'Bloody expensive,' I said. Serena smiled. Sitting down

beside me, she folded my jacket, and pressed it against my arm.

'Don't worry,' she said, looking down at the torn material. 'After what you just did I'm sure Paul will be happy to buy you a new one – a whole wardrobeful of new ones.' I had no idea what she was talking about.

I watched as the pale grey cashmere turned crimson. But I didn't care. I couldn't stop thinking about Serena's knickers. French knickers, trimmed with deep lace. I imagined running one finger inside them, feeling soft tufts of fair pubic hair against my skin. I groaned.

'Poor Luke. Does it hurt very badly?'

'Yes.' Suddenly giddy, I couldn't sit up any more, and I flopped onto my back. Above me, dark clouds drifted across a wide sky.

Serena was looking into my face. She reached forwards and placed a cool hand on my forehead. I wanted to sit up and kiss her, but I was too tired. The clouds were getting lower.

'Serena,' I said. 'I don't suppose you fancy a fuck?'

Then I passed out.

Cassandra's Story

I'm waiting in the spacious reception area of one of London's grandest hotels when I first notice him. He wears the same black trousers and white shirt as the other hotel staff, but he has a confident swagger that makes him stand out from the crowd. He's stationed behind a large linen-covered table, pouring champagne into row after row of sparkling glasses.

The champagne looks inviting. And so does he.

I glance at my watch. I have a few minutes to kill

before my party arrives, and I never leave spare time unfilled. I saunter over to the table of wine.

'Hi,' he says. He has a strong Australian accent. It figures. With his surf-bum sunburn and streaky blond hair, he could have come from no other country. 'Can I get you some champagne?'

'Thank you.' I wait for him to pass me a glass, and when I lean across the table to take it from him, I let my hand brush against his fingers. He looks at me with a hint of surprised amusement. I move away to sip my drink alone, satisfied that I have made an impression.

Tonight the hotel is the venue for the Golden Flame PR Industry Awards. The great and the good of the PR business are gathered to take the credit for other people's work and tell each other how fab they are. I am here to join a table of ten from my agency. And as one of the lower forms of life at Renshaw Winterman, I'm well aware that I have only been invited to make up the numbers. My heart sinks as I study the table plans and see that I have been placed next to Brian from finance. I'm just about to switch the name cards and swap Brian for possibly the brightest and certainly the best looking of our account executives, when Brian descends upon me.

'Hello, love,' he bellows. 'I see you've found the champagne.' And judging by the way he is swaying, so has he.

Three hours later, I'm rigid with boredom. PR people never need a reason to enjoy themselves, and this dinner is one of the best excuses of the year. But surrounded by people having a good time, I'm having no fun at all. Across the room, the party hats, streamers and disposable cameras the organisers have placed on all the tables are being put to good use. Fuelled by too many complimentary drinks, some of the bright young things of the PR world have started a wine fight, dunking the streamers into their glasses and using them to send puddles of Chateau-bottled claret into the laps of rival agency staff.

In the corridor earlier, I had seen one leading London consultancy owner having her bare bottom photographed by one of her account managers. She'll regret it in the morning. If she remembers it.

As political specialists, we at Renshaw Winterman are supposed to regard ourselves as a cut above the fluff heads in the lighter weight areas of the PR business. Personally I would rather write press releases about brown being the new black than White Papers. But while political PR does not excite me, I am not overburdened with alternative career options.

After spending three years at Cambridge, I managed to give up partying just long enough to leave with a reasonable degree. My father provides me with a substantial private income, but the deal is that I have to put my costly education to good use, and I must at least make a token effort to finance my very expensive shoe habit. Following numerous unsuccessful periods of employment, my father introduced me to Marcus Renshaw, who offered me a job at Renshaw Winterman. I surprised everyone by not cocking it up. So sadly I'm stuck in it.

And tonight I feel I am earning every penny of my risibly small salary. Brian, who has trotted after me like a devoted puppy all evening, is not good company. A big man, with hair as thin as the windows in the envelopes he uses to post our payslips, Brian thinks integrated accounting systems are a fascinating topic of conversation. He has yet to realise that no one else agrees with him. I watch him scribble endless columns of figures that are supposed to illustrate his tedious point on a napkin and stifle a yawn.

Renshaw Winterman has bagged a brace of prizes so far. The plastic gold torches set in rectangular slabs of clear acrylic are of no monetary value, but they will keep Marcus off our backs for a day or two. And our success has prompted Marcus to order more champagne, for which I am grateful. I fill my glass and gulp down a mouthful, hoping that excessive alcohol consumption will do something to alleviate the ennui.

When I feel Brian's large, hamlike hand crash down onto my knee, I can't help stiffening. I only manage to wriggle out of his clutches by reaching for a party hat and plonking it on his ugly head. Before he has a chance to take it off, I snatch up one of the cameras and snap a shot.

'Oh dear,' he says. 'You've caught me looking daft.' You never look anything else, Brian, I think.

It is with difficulty that I force myself to listen to the less than compelling tale of how Brian managed to lower his golf handicap. And as I strain to follow the story, I can feel my focus slipping.

The Australian waiter is at our table. I watch him weaving between the guests. As he steps forwards to serve a plate of food I catch his eye. There is a mischief in his expression that I like. I like it very much. As he moves towards me, I lean back in my chair slightly, giving him more room, and, more importantly, a better view of my breasts. I arch my back, just enough to catch his eye, and see his smile broaden. This man is easily distracted.

'And so by two thousand and four I was already down to thirteen,' Brian is saying. The waiter and I exchange glances. Then he moves away, and I watch him disappear into the crowd. I refill my glass again and Marcus shoots me a warning look, which I choose to ignore. 'And I hope I'm not being immodest when I say I'm likely to be playing off ten next year.'

The waiter returns to clear plates from the table. He leans over me and, as he does so, I feel his leg brush against mine. The gesture passes almost unnoticed, but to me the invitation is obvious. My eyes drop to the front of his trousers, and I am pleasantly surprised by what I see. The trousers are not tight, but beneath the black material the swelling of his cock is obvious. It's a magnificent, and delightfully unexpected, sight.

It's funny how arousal works. A few minutes ago, my mood could have been lightly flirtatious. But now the sight of that cock and the inappropriate context plunge me instantly into a state of heavy, grinding need. I wonder what has induced the burgeoning erection. Has the waiter been touching himself? Thinking about my tits as he slips his hand into his uniform and gives himself a surreptitious grope in between serving courses? Across the table, Marcus is telling politically correct jokes to his adoring staff who all oblige him by laughing uproariously. But I don't hear any of the punchlines.

The waiter is standing close to me. The fabulous prick is within my reach. I could so easily touch him. It would take almost nothing to grab a handful of tempting, stiffening cock. He could so easily bend and touch me. Slide his fingers down the front of my dress. Take my tits into his hands. I shudder and feel my face start to burn.

Brian taps me on the shoulder, startling me from my erotic daydream, but this time I struggle to banish my dirty thoughts from my mind. My excitement, like a pang of hunger, is difficult to ignore. Brian is talking, but I can't listen any more.

The waiter now has plates of puddings balanced on his arm. His face gives nothing away, and his self-control both irritates and excites me. With one hand, he arranges the plates on the table. But the other slips down the back of my dress. Just as I had fantasised. I freeze as he slowly caresses me, his warm fingers drifting from one shoulder to the other. I stare down into my lap; cross my legs. The movement pinches delightfully. Brian is still talking. If only he knew. I picture myself standing and lifting my dress, showing myself to Brian and the others at the table. I imagine their eyes on me, on my swelling clit between the lips of my sex. I imagine their shock at the true extent of my arousal. As the waiter leans forwards to lower the final plate, his hand presses more firmly into my shoulder and my flesh tingles beneath his touch.

Then he is gone, but on the table in front of me is a folded scrap of paper. I pick it up and read: 'Do something about it. Scott.'

And as I watch Scott walk away, I know exactly what I want to do. I want to use his lovely prick to bring myself off. I imagine it inside me, stretching me, filling me. I don't just want it. I need it. Brian drones on, and I try to ignore the pulse that beats between my legs. But I can't. I need to come. Oh God, soon. I wonder how I can do it. I could dash to the loo – a few quick strokes and it would be over. Maybe, if I squeeze my thighs together, I could come at the table. I'm so horny, I'm sure I can get there very quickly. But it's Scott I want.

I look up and see him standing on the other side of the room. He smiles at me, and then turns to disappear into the kitchens. I can do nothing but follow.

'Please excuse me,' I say to Brian, and I slip out of my seat. I can feel Brian's eyes on me as I cross the room, and hope that my glowing cheeks and shaking hands have not given me away.

The editor of the UK's best-selling quality daily is about to deliver what promises to be a highly entertaining speech, but I will hear none of it. As the country's most famous journalist starts to address a captivated audience, I leave the room, my mind on baser issues.

Behind the kitchen door, Scott is waiting for me. He takes hold of my hand and leads me across the bustling kitchen and out through a side exit. The hotel is thronging with guests and staff, but the service yard outside is deserted.

Fragments of the speech reach us via the hotel's PA system. But as Scott motions me to a darkened corner behind a parked delivery van, I can't concentrate on anything but him. With sweat running between my breasts, and my breath already coming in hoarse little gasps, I am thinking about something far more interesting than who has been voted the industry's most promising new graduate.

There is no time for courtship. I lean against the wall and lift up my dress. The champagne has made me reckless, and I don't care that I'm behaving like a whore. I gather up my skirt to bunch it high around my waist. I stand with my legs apart as Scott runs his eyes up my thighs to my panties. There is a greedy longing on his face as he looks at my underwear. His admiration makes me smile. Beneath my expensive dress, I'm wearing the cheapest possible red and black lingerie. Tiny lace knickers and a matching suspender belt trimmed with cute satin bows. It's the sort of underwear that scratches; that never lets you forget you are wearing it. It's my little private joke. I love the contrast between the immaculate exterior and the sleazy slut underneath. And clearly Scott shares my fondness for the low-class porn look.

He says nothing. And neither do I. But the fact that

we don't speak makes the encounter more thrillingly sordid. We're going to fuck. Nothing more – and nothing less. I watch him unzip his trousers and take out a thick rigid cock. I stand still as he advances. For Christ's sake, I wish he would hurry. There's no foreplay. He simply pulls my panties down to the tops of my thighs and pushes inside me. The assault excites me, and I know I'm going to come quickly.

Scott thrusts hard, forcing my legs further apart, and the panties tear away, slithering down my legs to the floor. He slips his hand between our bodies, and traces tiny circles around my clit. An exquisitely pleasurable shudder runs through my limbs as his finger swirls around and around, the pressure increasing until I know I can't hold back much longer. Clinging to his shoulders, I stiffen and climax.

My satisfaction doesn't slow him. He takes my hips into his hands and buries himself deeper inside me. Too aroused to care about my feelings, he plunges deep. I help him, reaching down to press my hands against the back of his thighs and jerking his hips towards me.

I feel him shaking as he strains towards his end. I look up. His head is thrown back, his mouth open as his breath rasps past his lips. He is ready. Then, at last, I feel a final shiver run through him. His fingers press into my hips and he gyrates against me, intent on nothing but his own orgasm.

Inside the hotel, the winner of the night's big prize is being announced.

'And this year's Best Consultancy award goes to ... Renshaw Winterman!'

Later, back at the table, Scott serves coffee. With impressive calm, he leans over me as he lays a plate of petits fours on the table, looking as if nothing has happened. I pop a chocolate into my mouth and smile benignly at Marcus.

I wonder if there is an award for the best fuck in a car park.

2

Luke's Story

Washington is a hard city, but even at the height of its hot and humid summer, I love it. I love its people, its vibrancy, its place in history. And most of all I love its politics. Here politics is not just an occupation, it's a reason for existence, and that suits me fine. Washington has been my home; I've lived and worked here for four years. It seems a lot longer.

It's six thirty in the morning. I hadn't planned to be working so early, but the habit of waking at dawn is hard to break. I had got up at five and, after my usual run, found myself sitting at my desk not long after sunrise. Just as I am every day.

As I go to reach across my desk for a file, a sharp pain shoots through my right shoulder. It's been a few months since the assassination attempt. Fortunately, I was still unconscious when the President came to visit me in hospital. A number of people had witnessed my totally inappropriate pass at Serena, and Paul had been informed of all the details. The gun-shot wound healed well enough for me to leave hospital after just a few days. It will take me considerably longer to recover from the embarrassment of having to explain my crush on his wife.

Abandoning my attempt to reach the papers, I sit back in my chair and glance out of the window. A heat haze is already shimmering from the paths and terraces around the West Wing. It's going to be another warm day.

I look around my room. Later the corridors outside my office will be teaming with people as journalists, technical teams and White House staff begin to fill the cramped quarters of the press briefing room for the morning off-camera session. But this is my own private space. It's sparsely furnished. The dark wood of the filing cabinets and desk contrasts starkly with the white walls and the floor is covered in a carpet of an unremarkable grey. Above my desk hangs a somewhat grim picture of the martyrdom of Saint Sebastian. It had been a rather unwelcome birthday present many years ago, and at first I had hated it. But its dark passion had eventually seduced me and I'm now very fond of it. It's the only decoration on the plain plaster. The room is not luxurious, but I've been happy here.

Outside I can hear the drone of vacuum cleaners and the faint beat of a Mexican radio station. Over the cacophony, I hear one of the cleaners singing along in a loud and tuneless soprano. I smile to myself as I recognise the voice. It's Rocío. A great girl. A terrible singer. I yawn and stretch in an attempt to ease my aching shoulder. I'm just about to carry on with my work when there's a quiet knock at the door. Rocío never passes my office without calling in for a gossip.

'*Venga,*' I call.

The door opens and in she walks, carrying a tray laden with coffee and pastries. She pushes the door closed behind her with a curvaceous hip.

'*Hola guapo,*' she says. 'I've been to the coffee shop and brought you a leaving present.'

'*Hola Rocío.* Breakfast!' The move is classic Rocío. Feeding people is her shorthand for affection. I'm deeply flattered. Sweeping aside what are actually rather important papers, she places the tray in front of me, and perches on the edge of my desk. 'Thank you so much. This is lovely.'

'Ah yes. *Sooo* lovely,' she says, aping my English accent and sounding like a freakishly Hispanic Audrey Hepburn at the end of *My Fair Lady*. The way I speak always causes her much hilarity.

'Don't take the piss. Remember I'm a national hero.' I try to extract a dossier I'm preparing for the President from under her backside. 'You're working late today. Shouldn't you be leaving?'

Her strong hands flip the lid off a cup of very black coffee. 'No.' She gives a little shrug and helps herself to a Danish. 'I waited for you.' Her heavily accented voice is soft and lilting – Washington drawl overlaying the roll of her native Mexican. Her English is far worse than my Spanish, but I like to hear her struggling with my language. Just as she is fascinated by mine, I find her pronunciation fabulously sexy.

I realise I'm hungry, and I eat heartily. While we eat, she chats merrily, and then, when I've finished, she polishes off the rest of the food, still talking with her mouth full.

Rocío has Latin beauty that is almost a cliché. Her flawless skin is the colour of creamy coffee, and her midnight-dark hair falls down her back in a glossy thick plait. Her full lips are always painted in deep red. Her body is plump and voluptuous and this morning her blue uniform gapes a little at the front where her rounded breasts strain against a row of small buttons. I watch as she leans forwards to take the last crumbs from the plate and the buttons yield further. It won't take much for her to fall out of the dress completely.

When she stands up and takes the tray away, I assume she's heading home.

'Thank you for my leaving present. It was very nice.'

She puts the tray down on a chair, crosses the room to lock my office door, and then turns to me with a wicked smile on her face.

'Oh no,' she says. 'That was not your present.'

Her fingers move to her top button and she begins to undo her dress. I hold my breath as her gloriously deep cleavage comes into view. She pushes the dress down to her hips and for a moment she stands still, letting me admire her wonderful shape. Her white bra is perhaps a tiny bit too small and her breasts spill out over its sides and top. It's a good look. I wonder if she notices as my cock begins to come to life under the desk. I feel it, steadily unfurling, lengthening against my thigh.

Moving with the casual grace of the truly sensual, she walks towards me and, sitting on the desk in front of me, reaches forwards to open my jacket. I wince slightly as her hand touches my injured shoulder.

'Still sore?'

'A bit.'

'Ah, poor baby,' she purrs. Her sympathy is only half genuine. I know she's highly impressed by my role as saviour of the President, no matter how many times I try to tell her that it was a complete fluke that I was the one who got shot. When we fucked for the first time after the attack, she came quickly and loudly.

'Let me rub it better for you,' she says sweetly. She reaches inside my jacket and slips it off. I don't move as she undoes my tie and, one by one, unfastens the buttons on my shirt. She eases it from my shoulders and drops it on the floor. Then she sweeps her hands over my arms, and I sigh in appreciation as she soothes the tension in my muscles. Rocío's touch is far more healing than any of Paul's expensive physiotherapists. As she works, her hands inch slowly further away from my shoulders and down my chest. The massage becomes less and less about my injury. I see her trying not to smile as she glances down at the growing bulge in my trousers. And then, I feel the side of her hand brush against the tip of my erection. The touch is light and could pass for an accident.

'Oops, sorry,' she says. But she isn't. She is the naughtiest little physio ever. Her hand slides, deftly flicks open the button on my trousers and slips inside. I see her eyes sparkle as she registers the full extent of my hardness.

'Mister Luke, you are a terrible patient,' she scolds. 'How can I treat your injuries if you keep getting an erection?'

She gives my cock a gentle squeeze, and I know that I'm beaten. My eyes close as she teases me. Blood rushes to my groin. My trousers become intolerably tight. Then she lets me go and reaches behind her back to undo her bra. I marvel as her breasts fall towards me and I reach out to trace the magnificent curves with one finger. I take them into my hands, gently lifting one and then the other, luxuriating in their weight.

'You like them?' she asks, thrusting back her shoulders, proudly displaying herself for my approval.

'I love them.' I smile. 'You know I do.'

I lean forwards and, still holding each breast, I bury my lips between them, slowly running my tongue the length of the crease that divides them. I could lose myself forever in her splendid flesh. My erection stiffens further as I move to her nipples. Dark as ripe cherries, they are large and prominent, sticking out from her soft breasts like bullets. As I lick and suck each in turn, I feel them harden beneath my lips. She's too tempting, and I can't resist letting my teeth graze against her flesh. With her fingers in my hair she leans against me, mewing like a kitten as my mouth wanders over her.

Slipping off the edge of the desk, she moves her body down mine and I feel her lovely nipples brush the length of my chest. My stomach tightens as she torments me with tiny butterfly kisses, her lips travelling leisurely over my torso, smearing red streaks of lipstick over my skin. She pauses to caress my navel with a slow swirl of her tongue that makes my breath catch in my chest. Then she carries on her downward path.

When she is level with my hips, she reaches down to finish undoing my trousers. I groan with relief, as, finally, she slides the zip and I am at last released. She pushes the trousers down, just far enough to reveal my prick jutting up towards my ribs. With her eyes fixed on my cock, she lets out a low whistle between her teeth.

'*Que magnifico*,' she mutters.

I laugh. 'Rocío, you've seen it before.'

She scowls. 'And Michaelangelo's *David* looks like shit just because you've seen him more than once?'

I can't argue with her logic.

She is still moving. Down and down. Taking my cock in her hand, she wraps her breasts around me. She presses herself tight against my erection and rubs herself up and down, wanking me with her tits. I look down, and see the engorged tip of my cock poking out from between her breasts. It's almost enough to make me lose it and, with another groan, I close my eyes.

'*Dios mío*,' I mutter. 'That's pretty *magnifico*, too.'

'I know,' she says, looking up into my face and grinning lasciviously.

Then I feel her warm breath against my shaft. At first she teases me, licking me like a lollipop. It won't do. Lifting my hips slightly, I strain towards her, keen to feel all of her talented mouth.

'*Rocío. Por favor. Estas jugando*,' I whisper, lapsing into Spanish because I'm no longer in the mood for linguistic games. But she needs no encouragement. I can't help but sigh as she takes me slowly into her mouth. Her lips, tight around me, slip down the length of my prick. Inside her, I can feel her tongue pressing against the base of me, pushing me up against the roof of her mouth. As she takes me deeper still, I feel the very back of her delicious throat. It's fantastic.

Her head bobs in my lap, and she works me, faster and faster, harder and harder. My cock wrecks her make-up and her hair loosens, silky curls trailing over my stomach and thighs. A glow of pleasure spreads from my balls through my stomach and to my spine. Shit. I can't come yet. I try to think about anything but the feel of her. My fingernails curl into my palms as I struggle to control myself, but I know that soon she'll take me too far. It will not be long before I empty myself into her, and if my cock's going to be any use to her at all, it's now or never. Using every ounce of self-discipline I possess, I reach down and gently lift her off me. Rocío sits back on her heels and looks up at me. Sweaty and dishevelled, she looks eminently fuckable. My sacrifice is not great.

I bend down to lift her dress and slip one hand into her white cotton panties. I know how she likes to be touched. I know how to whip her into a frenzy of passion. I still have the scars from where she once sunk her teeth into my wrist when she came, and many times I've had to put my hand over her mouth to stop her terrifying the White House security guards with her shrieks of delight. But now as my fingers move towards the dark triangle of her sex, she pulls my hand away.

'Rocío?'

She leans forwards and presses her finger to my lips. And I understand. This move is also classic Rocío.

Sometimes Rocío is the mistress, and she will lie on

the floor in my office for lazy hours, her legs spread wide for me to lick her to countless orgasms. Afterwards she will get up and go, leaving me hard and helpless until hours – occasionally days – later, she will surprise me in the car park or in a corridor, sneaking up behind me and stretching around my waist to masturbate me to a climax that is almost embarrassingly easy to reach but so much better for the wait.

And sometimes she is the servant.

'No,' she says, her black eyes twinkling. 'This one is just for you.'

As she bends over me once more, I smile, lie back against my chair and put my hands behind my head. I am in no position to argue.

Later, long after Rocío has gone, I empty my in-tray, send the last of my emails and close down my computer. One of my press assistants bangs on my door.

'Hey, Luke,' he shouts. 'The guys are waiting for you to come and join them for a farewell drink.'

'Great. I'll be with you in just a minute.'

I clear the last of my personal belongings from the filing cabinets, stuffing the usual collection of photos, letters and trinkets that builds over time in a job into an aged brown leather case. Finally, I lift Saint Sebastian down from the wall and drop him into the bag.

I'm going home.

3

Cassandra's Story

Lord Fenwick Jones of Railton Lea is not a happy man.

'I've managed to get you that job, Cassandra.'

'Wonderful.' I put on my 'professional but enthusiastic' voice.

Recently elevated to the Upper House, Charles Fenwick Jones does not have much to do with the day-to-day comings and goings at the Commons any more. But as a former Chancellor of the Exchequer, he is not without influence and can still pull a few strings. This latest tweak has got me out of a difficult situation. Following the incident in the car park at the awards ceremony, which, I later found out Brian had been watching from the shadows, rumours about my behaviour had inevitably reached Marcus. With similar inevitability my P45 reached me. In a speech that began something like: 'This hurts me as much as it hurts you.' Marcus banged on about how I am wasting my talent. I couldn't be bothered to listen.

The new job is a rather menial role in the government's recently reorganised communications department. My degree and my PR experience at Renshaw Winterman gave me a veneer of credibility necessary to apply. My charm and Charles's influence have done the rest. I'm not sure that I'm cut out for the serious world of big-boys' politics, but Charles points out very forcefully that I am being offered a drink in 'the last-chance saloon', and turning it down isn't an option.

'I've gone out on a limb for this one, Cassandra.' Then he adds, rather unnecessarily I feel: 'Again.'

'I know, and I am really grateful.'

'So you should be. Don't let me down this time, eh?'

'I won't. Really I won't. I promise, Daddy.' And so my future is decided. It looks like I've landed on my Jimmy Choos again.

At the end of the first week in my new job, I join my new colleagues and some older friends in our well-established after-work watering hole, the Ship and Anchor.

Among the crowd is William De Courcy, a razor-sharp political journalist who'd been a regular sparring partner during my time at Renshaw Winterman. Standing well over six feet tall with a mop of dark curly hair, there is a bearlike quality about William. His generous nature and impeccable public-school manners mean that everybody likes him. Including me. In the two years that I've known him, William has become a dear friend.

With William is Simon Moore MP. Holder of a rock-solid safe seat, Simon is one of a new generation of politicians that took the country by storm in the last election. His moderate good looks and his job as host of the hugely influential TV programme *Moore From The House* have made him something of a household name. Married to a constantly smiling wife and father of two constantly smiling children, Simon has an appearance of respectability that Middle England loves. Those who know him well know that he's not as squeaky clean as his publicity material would suggest. Right now he's addressing the cleavage of Camilla, who works in the party press office and has, without doubt, been employed for her decorative value as much as her intellect.

As alcohol flows, earnest conversations about transparency of government and the question of university funding are replaced by slightly less intelligent debate punctuated with increasingly ribald jokes at the expense of political rivals.

Inevitably, the conversation turns to the arrival of the government's new director of communications, and my new boss, Luke Weston. I know Luke by reputation only. By all accounts his career in political journalism had been brief but dazzlingly successful. It was followed by a stint in the US, but after getting himself rather publicly shot, Luke has packed in his role as an American super-hero and has been taken on by the PM to bring some States-style pizzazz to dull little Westminster. He's due to start his new job on Monday morning. I won't be sur-prised if he arrives by parachute.

'You're his best mate, William. What's he really like?' Camilla asks.

William smiles almost secretively. 'He's OK.'

'Is he really such a master of spin?' Camilla's question is greeted by much ooing and ahing. The 's' word is rather unfashionable these days and one we try to avoid.

'If he can spin you lot he'll be some circus act,' says Lucy, a young and ferociously ambitious journalist from a Sunday broadsheet, not renowned for her support of our party. William laughs heartily.

'Lucy, he could spin a double-decker bus on his little fingertip.'

The rest of the team roars its agreement.

'Well, I hear he's a complete babe,' I mutter to William. 'So if he's hung like a horse as well – he's my kind of man.' As I speak, the conversation dies away unexpec-tedly, and my comments, meant only for William, are heard by everyone. Over the titters of my audience, I hear another voice behind me. It's deeper. Softer.

'I'm glad to hear it.'

I turn around to face the most beautiful man I have ever seen.

'Hi,' he says. 'I'm Luke Weston.'

'Oh shit!' I say, my hands flying up to cover my mouth.

Revelling in my embarrassment, the rest of the party bursts into shrieks of laughter. I know that I should shake Luke's offered hand but, paralysed by shame, I just stand staring at his lovely face. Fortunately, William steps in to spare my blushes.

'Luke!' he exclaims, giving Luke an enthusiastic hug. 'Welcome back. This is Cassandra Jones. As you just heard, she already thinks very highly of you.'

I shake Luke's hand at last, trying, and failing, to think of an amusing response. Luke looks as though he's about to smile. But he doesn't.

'It's good to meet you, Cassandra.' He pronounces my name with care, as if the word is important. 'You must be Charles Fenwick Jones's daughter.' His tone is hard to gauge. I can't tell if he is scornful or approving of my connections.

'Yes. Well, no.' I don't want him to think my father is the only reason why I'd been given my job.

Now he does smile. A slow-burning killer of a smile that lights up his eyes before it lifts one and then the other corner of his mouth.

'A mysterious parentage. How very interesting.' There's only the tiniest hint of sarcasm in his voice, but it's enough to make me cringe. William interrupts just in time.

'Luke, come and meet some of the others.'

With his arm around Luke's shoulders, William guides the new comms director around the bar, introducing him to journalists, lobbyists and party staff.

'This is Camilla,' says William. 'And Lucy. Simon of course you know.'

'Yes,' says Luke, and for a moment his smile freezes on his face. I notice he doesn't shake Simon's hand.

'I'd offer to buy you a drink. But you don't, do you?' Simon says, sneering at the can of Diet Coke in Luke's left hand. Luke says nothing, and, smoothly, William moves Luke away to introduce him to the rest of the team.

As the conversation sweeps on, I take the time to examine my new boss. He's tall, but there is nothing gangly or awkward about him – he's comfortable with his height. His thick blond hair is slightly longer than is conventional, and he has a habit of running his fingers through it to push it out of his face. His skin is lightly tanned to the colour of warmed honey, his dark-green eyes have the fathomless depth of perfect emeralds. The jacket of his obviously expensive suit is draped elegantly over one shoulder in that after-work casual style English men so rarely pull off, and an impossibly white shirt reveals just a suggestion of a lithe, fit body beneath. I allow my eyes to travel to the front of his trousers. They're far too well cut to give many clues as to what's underneath the beautifully woven fabric, but the hint of a bulge looks promising.

But it's not only his looks that are compelling. With the careless confidence of the naturally charismatic, he holds court over the rest of the group, entertaining them with witty stories about his departure from the US political scene and his return home. Used to impressive speakers, the team gathers around him, hanging on his every word. I'm amused to see the women fidgeting nervously and fiddling with their hair as he addresses them. Even the men can't take their eyes off him.

As he speaks, he takes a packet of cigarettes from his pocket. When he opens it, I notice his hands are strong yet graceful. They're hands that are capable. Hands that could coax, thrill or soothe. He leans forwards slightly and takes one of the cigarettes between his teeth, his lip curling against the tip. Then he lights up, those amazing eyes closing a little against the smoke. I don't usually like men who smoke, but now, watching the pale plume he exhales drift up from his sensual mouth, I find I can't look away. If my life depended on it, I cannot look away.

'Cassandra! Another beer?' William calls from across the bar.

'Please, William,' I shout back, with an attempt at levity.

Anxious to regain some dignity after the embarrassment of our introduction, I leave the little circle huddled around Luke and cross the room to feign interest in a list of 'specials' chalked up on a menu board. As I try to concentrate on making a decision about a sandwich, I can't stop myself listening to him. The merest hint of a Yorkshire accent sets him apart from my usual social set. His voice is earthy. Masculine. His laugh is big and unselfconscious.

I look up to see William walking towards me, two beers in his hands.

'Whoops,' he says, handing me a bottle.

I scowl. Making dodgy comments in front of my friends could have been dismissed as a mistake caused by rather too many Buds. Making the same comments in front of my new director was a catastrophe.

'Yeah, OK. He must think I'm a prat.'

'Well, let me see.' William frowns as his journalist's mind weighs up the evidence. 'First you made a crude comment about the size of his knob. And then you couldn't remember the name of your own father. I would say "prat" was the only fair description.'

I giggle and give William a shove. Across the room Camilla is chatting to Luke, running her tongue over her glossed lips and looking at him from beneath lowered lashes. I nod towards them.

'Check out Camilla,' I say. 'She looks as if she wants to sling him up against that wall and shag him right now.'

'And you don't?'

I can't bring myself to answer and laugh off the question.

'Cassandra,' says William, 'Luke is rather ... complicated.'

'Looks pretty straightforward to me,' I say, swigging a mouthful of beer and watching Luke smiling seductively at Camilla. Wriggling with almost visible sexual arousal, Camilla thrusts out her silicon chest at him and blushes beguilingly.

'No really, Cas –' William is trying to be serious, '– He's had a tough couple of years.' I give a snort of derisive laughter. I assume William is talking about the shooting. Having bits of your arm blown off must be something of a nuisance.

'Don't worry. I'll be gentle with him. Anyway,' I say to alter the direction of the conversation, 'what's he like to work for?'

'Great. You'll get along fine.'

'Yes.' I watch Luke lean towards Camilla and lightly touch her arm as he laughs at some private joke. 'I think we will.'

A week later, I arrive at party HQ at a quarter to ten. Still wearing my jacket and carrying my briefcase, I stroll up the stairs to our office, confident that Luke, who so far has spent most of his time at Downing Street, will not be around to witness my late arrival.

As I walk down the corridor to the communications department offices, I see the door of the ladies' loo open and a red-faced Camilla emerge. Making a pretence of getting a coffee from a vending machine, I watch as Camilla scuttles away, smoothing her hands over her dishevelled hair. I wonder whether to shout to tell her that she has her V-necked sweater on back to front, but then unkindly decide to leave it to somebody else to point out the mistake. Moments later Luke saunters out of the ladies', nonchalantly tucking his shirt into his suit trousers. On his face is the furtive, hazily post-coital smile of man who has just enjoyed a profoundly satisfying fuck.

Envy is an ugly emotion, and one unfamiliar to me. But as I watch Luke stride towards his office, I feel an unpleasant twisting in my stomach at the thought of Camilla claiming his lovely body and I recognise the bitter sentiment as pure jealousy. Explicit and unwelcome images of what they had been doing in the loo spring into my mind. I see her sitting with her legs spread on the seat. I see him, watching her pee. Then her, coming against his mouth. The thoughts disturb me deeply.

Forcing my mind to the day ahead, I turn back down the corridor towards my desk. I flash my electronic security card at the entry scanner on the main door to the department, but it refuses to open. Then I jiggle the handle. The door remains obstinately locked.

'Here. Let me help you.' Luke stands at my shoulder looking down into my eyes with a disarmingly frank intensity. As he reaches over to take the card from my hand, I catch the scent of him – a heady mixture of expensive aftershave and the fresh sweat of sex. It connects with something primeval deep inside me. My briefcase crashes to the floor, sending papers, discs and stationery skidding across the carpet. Oh great. Now he can add 'terminally clumsy' to 'vulgar' and 'intellectually defective'. We both crouch to pick up the debris and, moving too quickly, I wobble slightly. Luke puts down the discs and files he had been carrying, and reaches out to steady me, taking a firm hold of the top of my arm. Our eyes meet again, and I see a trace of amusement cross his lips.

'I'm sorry I haven't been able to spend much time with you yet,' he says. I don't point out that if he spent less time screwing during working hours he might have had more opportunity to introduce himself properly. 'And it's a shame you had to leave so early last Friday night. I didn't get the chance to talk to you much.'

I hope my heart is thumping because I'm flustered at dropping my bag. But I'm not sure. 'I had to come back to the office to finish some work,' I lie.

With my palm on the floor, I've clearly regained my balance, but still Luke doesn't move his hand. I want to ask him to take it away. I want to remind him that a sexual harassment charge does not look good on a CV and in the twenty-first century a man can't just slap his hand on a woman's body any time he wants. But Luke's touch is assured. Unrepentant. Luke's is the touch of a man who is not used to rejection. Perhaps I imagine it, but I half believe I feel his thumb graze the side of my breast. My mouth grows dry. I should tell him to fuck off. Instead I hear myself say: 'Are you settling in OK?'

'Yes. Thanks. But with the party conference coming up, I've got a lot of work to do.'

He's turning on the look that I had seen him use on Camilla in the bar. I feel its full strength boring into me. Then he glances away and begins to pick up the rest of my belongings as if he felt nothing spark between us.

When he raises his eyes again, the look has been switched off. He probably doesn't even realise he was doing it. Damn him.

Irritated, I hastily scoop up the remaining files from the floor, and ram them back into my case. We both stand up. Calmly, Luke swipes my card through the scanner again, and the door clicks open

'Will you be coming to the conference?' he asks, handing me back my card.

'Oh yes,' I say brightly. 'Just try keeping me away.' I force a smile, and he smiles back. He looks as if he's going to say something else. Then his expression changes and the silence is suddenly awkward.

'Well,' he says. 'Have a nice day.' The Americanism sounds strained in his very English accent.

'Thank you,' I reply. 'I will.' And I slip quickly through the door and slam it shut, leaving Luke standing in the corridor.

Nine hours later, I'm relieved to be back at my flat. I kick off my shoes and drop my jacket onto a chair. I strip off the rest of my clothes, shower and pull on a T-shirt and soft cotton trousers. Then I close the curtains and light a few candles around the sitting room. Finally, I settle in front of the TV with a bottle of Chablis and a chicken salad from my favourite deli to enjoy a DVD of a new film I'd bought on my way to work. But when I open the case, the disc I take out is clearly not mine. The words 'Press Briefings – Jan. to March' are written on its face in Luke's refined hand.

Curious, I pop the disc into the player, and see Luke, fronting a series of press conferences at the White House. I watch him command the room, explaining complex points in clear, effective words, parrying difficult questions with tact and diplomacy, and lightening the atmosphere between serious discussions with gentle humour. His conviction, his honesty and his level-headed reasoning are impossible to resist. He's stunningly good.

I notice that he smiles more readily than he has done since his return to the UK – even, white teeth flashing. He looks easy. Relaxed. And heartbreakingly desirable.

The film ends, and the screen goes blank. But as I fumble with the remote to turn off the TV, I notice another disc concealed in the bottom of the case. I swap it with the first and press Play.

This scene is very different. In the middle of a large and beautiful bed writhe two semi-naked women. I smile as I realise that I'm watching someone's very private home movie. Then I laugh out loud when I recognise press officer Camilla and the journalist Lucy.

But there's another person. The person who is circling the bed with the camera. He's out of the shot, but I hear his voice as he directs the girls. The soft, husky tone and the faint accent are unmistakable. It's Luke. I'm not smiling any more.

Lucy is kneeling on the bed facing the camera wearing a silky white camisole and white lace panties. Camilla, her knees either side of Lucy's lean body, is crouched behind her wearing nothing but a black bra and G-string.

On Luke's command, Camilla reaches up to sweep Lucy's bobbed, chestnut hair from her shoulder and bends to kiss her neck. Lucy sighs and, as she turns her face, the two women kiss. At first the kiss is tentative, and I see Camilla's eyes flick to the camera. Luke urges her on with reassuring words. The girls' tongues touch, their lips part, and lightly they nibble and nip. Doubts fade. Slowly, the kiss deepens, and their mouths lock together.

I take a forkful of food but, as I watch the action, I suddenly find I'm not hungry and push my unfinished

31

supper to one side. It feels strange to be watching two women, and my hand closes on my remote control to turn off the TV. But I can't bring myself to press the button.

Camilla's hesitant hands run up Lucy's belly to circle briefly around Lucy's breasts. Then they dive to the bottom of the camisole. Camilla raises her face, and looks into the camera again, seeking encouragement.

'That's right,' prompts Luke. 'Lift it up.'

I lean forwards towards the screen as, slowly, Lucy's breasts are revealed. Lucy's nipples are the most delicate shade of pink, and they jut from the plains of her small breasts, erect and aroused. Camilla lifts the top higher and, almost lazily, Lucy raises her arms so that it can be removed. Slowly, Camilla's hands travel over the curves of Lucy's body in a trembling quest of discovery. She takes the two tips of Lucy's nipples between her fingers, twisting and tweaking until the pink deepens to a darker shade. Lucy stretches back against Camilla, giving herself up, allowing Camilla to do what she has to do.

'God, that looks good,' I hear Luke whisper. I can only agree. It looks so good I feel giddy. I find myself slipping my hands under my T-shirt to rub my equally aroused nipples. It's not difficult to imagine the swell of Lucy's tits, and how they would feel beneath my palms. And judging by Camillia's purr of pleasure, they feel good. Neither woman needs encouragement now. As Camilla continues to caress Lucy's breasts, Lucy's hips begin to rock as she gives way to pleasure and arousal overcomes her. Camilla strokes down Lucy's flat stomach, and then stretches further to sweep sensuous circles over Lucy's spread thighs.

'Touch her,' says Luke.

When Lucy raises her head from Camilla's shoulder to smile at Luke, her glazed eyes are unfocused. She's intoxicated with pleasure. 'Yes,' she says to Camilla. 'I want you to touch me.'

But Camilla does not need to be told. She pulls down the front of Lucy's knickers, and her other hand slips inside. Beneath the lace, I see her fingers moving in a rippling caress. Lucy's eyes close, and she leans back against the other woman once more. Whatever Camilla is doing, it's obvious that Lucy is enjoying it very much indeed. But we can't see it, and it frustrates Luke as well me.

'Hey,' he says with a laugh in his voice. 'Let me see.'

Lucy lifts her bottom from the bed, and Camilla slips the knickers down her legs, tossing the scrap of fabric to one side. Then with one hand on each of her legs, Camilla spreads Lucy's thighs wide.

'Oh Jeez,' mutters Luke, as the inner folds of Lucy's sex are exposed for his camera. Camilla's finger buzzes against Lucy's clit, and we see the little organ swell beneath Camilla's touch. My own hand in my knickers copies the skilled movements. When Camilla pushes a finger up into Lucy, I do the same to myself.

Camilla's finger slides and Lucy thrusts against it as if she can't get enough. Her movements become almost desperate, and she groans and grunts. When Camilla withdraws and replaces one finger with two, the sounds smooth to a steady, low wail. I wonder how long Lucy can bear what the other woman is doing without coming. A small cry answers my question, and I know she can't be far away. Lucy throws back her head and arches her spine, sending her lovely little tits skywards. As she gyrates against Camilla's hand, they jiggle rhythmically. They look so divinely pretty, I wonder how Camilla is managing to stop herself from reaching up again to touch them.

'Yes,' says Lucy. Her body tenses, and she flings her

legs even wider to press herself against Camilla. Camilla holds her hand still as Lucy orgasms, letting her lover finish herself exactly as she wants. I've seen women faking spectacular orgasms in movies, but this so very genuine paroxysm is something I've never witnessed before. Its beauty leaves me breathless.

When she's done, Lucy sinks against the other woman. With her full lips parted in post-orgasmic bliss and her hair clinging to her face in sweaty tendrils, she looks wonderfully, wantonly sexy, and for the first time ever, I see how good a woman looks after she's come.

But Lucy isn't still for long. As she regains her breath, her hand moves up Camilla's body, and she cups one full breast. Camilla is clearly going to get her reward.

Slipping the firm flesh from the top of the bra, Lucy lowers her head to suckle a dark, dusky nipple. Camilla groans, pushing herself towards her lover, trying to fill more of Lucy's mouth with her tits. It's not enough and, with an impatient shrug, Camilla snaps off her bra and releases her breasts, which tumble, heavy and luscious, into Lucy's waiting hands. Lucy's earlier inhibition has gone, and she massages the proffered breasts with unfettered enthusiasm. I'm painfully envious. Camilla's tits may owe more to the skill of a surgeon than the blessings of nature, but my excitement now turns my scorn for their unnatural size and over-perfect shape into pure lust. I want to touch them too. I really, really want to touch them.

Lucy slips further down Camilla's body. As Camilla falls back against the bed, Lucy eases the other woman's legs apart, drops between the spread thighs and plants a tender kiss on Camilla's satin-covered mound. I'm thrillingly shocked when Lucy moves the G-string to one side, and a plump lip bulges from the fabric. Lucy moves the panties the other way, and we see more of Camilla's plump sex protrude rudely from the tight garment. Luke is obviously enjoying this disgusting display too, and on the soundtrack, I hear the rasp of his breath as he inhales sharply.

Against the edge of the satin Camilla's clit is visible. Delicately holding the G-string to one side, Lucy lowers her head and, with the tip of her tongue, dabs at the nub, causing Camilla to growl with pleasure. For a glorious time, Luke films Lucy lapping and licking at the other woman's sex. Then, as Camilla writhes, lost in her building ecstasy, Lucy sits up and looks directly into the camera.

'Luke,' she whispers. 'She's ready for you.'

Luke needs no more persuasion. I hear his voice off camera. 'Lucy – take this. I want you to film me fucking her.' The camera is exchanged, and Luke walks into the shot. He has already stripped and, as I watch him walking towards the bed, I'm gripped by a pang of longing. His body is as fabulous naked as it is clothed. He's in an advanced state of sexual arousal, and I wonder if just the sight of the girls has stiffened his cock or if he has been playing with himself as he filmed them. The thought of him, the camera in one hand, his prick in the other, makes my stomach clench with desire.

He wastes no time. He yanks off the G-string and, placing his hands on Camilla's thighs, he thrusts his cock into her in one smooth movement – the master claiming his harem. But Camilla is happy to be taken. Gripping onto the edge of the bed, she raises her legs, her toes curling with delight.

'Oh, Luke. You're the best,' she moans in true pornstar style. But I'm sure she is not exaggerating. He arches away from her so that he can kiss her, his mouth travelling sensually over her lips, her eyes, her neck, and then slowly down the curve of her collarbone to her

35

breasts. And all the time he fucks her, sliding with calculated strokes in and then just as carefully out. The muscles in his arms, his chest, his thighs, bunch and swell as he moves. His hand is against her mound, and I watch him finger her, knowing that what he's doing would feel wonderful.

'You're nearly there aren't you.' It's a statement, not a question.

Camilla gives a little whimper in reply, her eyes closing in a recognisable ecstasy.

'Move in closer,' says Luke to Lucy. 'Film her face as she comes.' The shot narrows, and Lucy homes in on Camilla. Even though I can no longer see Luke, I can tell by the way Camilla's breasts are moving and her shoulders are sliding against the bed that he's still thrusting into her. She moans and whines, laughing and crying, as if unable to decide which of the whirling emotions is stronger.

'That's it,' says Luke. Camilla's mouth opens wide and her body shudders as she climaxes.

Now Lucy focuses on Luke. She moves in tightly to film his prick in startling close-up. Watching Luke's thick cock as it continues to plunge into Camilla, my own fingers suddenly feel inadequate and I look around in a panting need for something else to fill me. My eyes fall on one of the candles beside the sofa, and I lean forward to blow out the flame.

As I turn the candle over, hot wax drips onto the inside of my thighs. But I'm indifferent to the pain. I'm oblivious to any sensation but my howling need for gratification. I bring the candle down and press the thick tip against the entrance to my empty, needy body.

I hear Luke's breath quicken. Then he does something that makes me gasp. He takes his cock out of Camilla and, just as in a porn film, holds it in his hand so I can see him come. I watch him pump himself with steady, firm strokes, sending jet after powerful jet of semen streaking across Camilla's stomach and breasts. My own hand works in time with his as I rub at my clit, frantic for my own orgasm.

By the time I slowly push the candle into myself I have already started to climax. As I watch Luke's come slide down Camilla's body, my sex contracts in delicious spasms against the hard, cold wax. My orgasm ripples through my body to the ends of my fingers and the very tips of my toes, bringing blissful relief.

As the last wave of my climax ebbs away, I lie still on the sofa, staring dreamily at the screen. The film ends, and for a while I watch fuzzy snowflakes.

'I will have you, Luke Weston,' I whisper to myself. 'I will have you.'

4

Cassandra's Story

But Luke's not mine for the taking. Occasionally our paths cross, but he's never anything more than polite. After watching him spectacularly naked on the DVD, the nearest I get to seeing him undressed is when I catch him on his way back to the office from one of his almost obsessively regular lunch-time runs.

As preparations for the party conference hot up, he's slick, efficient and always totally in control. But he's a mystery that fascinates me more as each day passes. I want to crack the riddle of the teetotal fitness freak who eats junk food and chain-smokes. I want to decode the spell that can turn this consummate professional into the insanely uninhibited man of the DVD who risks filming himself having sex with a national newspaper journalist and a junior member of his department.

The disc, now safely back in its correct case in Luke's office, remains as evidence of what he can be. But as time goes on, I find it increasingly hard to believe that the Luke I saw on the film and the Luke who is my boss are the same person. His coldness towards me seems to deepen.

And the more dismissive he becomes, the more I want him. Since seeing him on the DVD, raw and graphic images keep ambushing my thoughts, making me gasp out loud. Even at work, the memories had overwhelmed me on more than one occasion. Locking myself in the loo, I had yanked up my skirt and thrust my hands between my thighs to bring myself to a hurried and unsatisfying orgasm.

In the week before the conference, I am at party HQ when a researcher who works on *Moore From The House* calls with a request to appear on the show. I go to Luke's office with the details scribbled on the back of one of Camilla's press releases.

'Luke, Simon Moore was wondering if –'

'No.' Luke does not look up from the pile of letters he is signing.

'But –'

'I won't help him. And let me know if he approaches any of the ministries directly. I don't want any of our people on his programme.'

I know that favours are granted to tame journalists. Useful snippets of information are carefully leaked to those who will run stories that show the party in the best light. And those who cross us are frozen out. That's the way it works. But I'm surprised at Luke's decision to blacklist one of the most influential shows on TV. There's an irrationality about it that's out of character.

'But you don't know who he wants.'

'I don't care who he wants.'

'He wants you.' Finally, I have Luke's attention. He looks up, and chews the end of his pen thoughtfully.

'Jesus,' he says as much to himself as to me. Then he says: 'The answer is an even bigger no.' Simon's production company will be disappointed. Luke's high-profile position and the exotic end to his career in the US would make him a fascinating guest, even without his telegenic looks.

'So what shall I tell him?'

Luke shrugs, and turns his attention back to his paperwork. 'Tell him I don't need the wank.'

I go back to my desk and pick up the phone, trying to think of a slightly more tactful way to phrase Luke's regrets at having to decline the kind invitation.

That night, walking across Westminster Bridge in search of a taxi, I see him on the other side of the road. He's leaning against the wall of the bridge and staring down into the black water of the Thames. I slow down to shout goodnight. But there's a strange stillness about him, and I can't bring myself to disturb him. I wonder what thoughts occupy his mind.

I'm not at my best at our morning team meeting on Friday. Luke is out, and there is no one else I want to impress. The meeting rooms are busy, so we camp in Luke's office.

The room is clinically ordered. The single personal touch he has added since his arrival is a horrible picture of a man being crucified, his face twisted by a pang of deathly agony that verges on the orgasmic.

Camilla, who has decided to promote herself to the position of Luke's deputy in his absence, is monopolising the meeting. She sits on Luke's desk, her trim bum slithering around on his papers. For some reason it irritates the hell out of me. Her inane comments are soporific, and I find myself yawning so regularly I'm sure even she must take the hint. She doesn't.

I turn my attention to the other members of the department. Toby, a junior press officer, is by far the most interesting. Not yet 21, Toby is completely unaware of his dark good looks. I, however, have registered every detail, and I can tell that beneath his slightly geeky clothes there is a good body.

I stare at him hard, lower my gaze, and then lift my lashes to look at him again. I feel a small surge of satisfaction as I see his face colour and he looks away quickly. Shifting on my chair, I slump slightly, allowing my skirt to ride slightly too high up my legs. It's cheesy – but it works every time. Toby, a helpless victim, looks down at my exposed thighs. Perhaps I'm not the only person who finds boredom a highly effective aphrodisiac. Idly, I wonder if I should suggest finding a quiet corner of the office to follow the little game through to its logical conclusion. It would provide a welcome diversion to lock him in an empty office, pull down my knickers and let him rub me off with his young, and doubtless inexperienced, fingers. But timid Toby would never dare.

Crashing through my daydreams, Camilla is asking me a question. She has been explaining a new campaign evaluation system she is planning to introduce.

'What do you think, Cassandra?' I can't tell Camilla that I haven't been listening to a word she says, but I don't have the energy to lie. Instead I smile bountifully and say, 'That's as fascinating as I'd expect from you, Camilla.'

'Exactly,' says Camilla, looking smug. 'I thought you'd be impressed.'

Golden sunshine streams across the room and I long to be outside. William has invited me to his house in the country for the weekend, but I'm not due to leave for another four hours. The weekend seems a very long way away. I try to concentrate on the rest of Camilla's presentation, but it's hopeless. I decide it's time to bring the meeting to a close.

Reaching down under my chair, I fumble in my handbag. A few minutes later, the whine of Camilla's voice is drowned out by the ringing of my mobile phone.

'I'm sorry, everyone,' I say, reaching into my bag to take the call. 'I thought I'd switched it off.'

'That's five pounds in the charity box,' says Camilla accusingly.

The others turn to look at me as I say into the phone, 'Yes ... This is Cassandra ... Oh, hello, Mrs Bannister. Oh my God. No.' I let my eyes widen dramatically. 'Yes, of course,' I go on. 'I'll be right there.' I close my phone and say: 'You'll have to excuse me, I'm afraid I have to leave you. That was my cleaning lady. I've been burgled.'

'That's dreadful,' says Toby. 'Does she think much has been taken?'

'A Lucian Freud drawing and a Faberge egg apparently. But the awful thing is my little Jack Russell was in the flat at the time. He'll be terrified. I ... I must go.'

'Yes,' says one of the research assistants, standing up and giving my hand a reassuring squeeze.

'You run along,' says someone else. 'I hope everything's OK.'

'Thank you,' I say, my voice breaking very slightly. 'Thank you.'

And giving a brave smile, I turn to go, leaving them staring after me in shocked silence. Camilla, who has been to my flat and knows that I own neither a Lucian Freud, a Faberge egg nor a dog, looks the most shocked of all.

Later, I ease my Saab convertible out of Westminster and head towards the M4. I punch a number into my phone.

'William! Hi. Is it OK if I arrive a bit early? My meeting ended sooner than I expected,' I say, almost truthfully.

'Of course, darling. I won't be down until this evening, but I'm sure there'll be someone there to let you in.'

Unpinning my hair, I turn my face to the sun and take a deep breath. The weekend has arrived.

* * *

I have never been to William's house before, but it's not difficult to find. A landmark in picture-postcard pretty Berkshire countryside, it's impossible to miss the huge iron gates flanked by a pair of matching lodge houses that mark the entrance to Temworth Manor. I swing off the road and edge slowly up a tree-lined drive, until finally I turn a corner to see the house, rising up from spectacularly beautiful parkland. It is film-location lovely.

Constructed from mellow cream-coloured stone, it glows in the fading sunlight. In front of the house, a broad path circles an elegant fountain and sweeps up to a set of wide stone steps which lead to a large and imposing double doorway. Tall, sparkling windows are ranged with Georgian symmetry on either side of the entrance. I look higher, and see that the house is constructed in three storeys, topped by a smart grey slate roof.

I pull up outside, and haul my bags from the car. When I walk to the door, gravel crunches reassuringly beneath my feet – a heart-warming sound of England. As I wait for my knock to be answered, I take another look at the fabulous grounds. Ancient cedar trees punctuate rolling lawns and, in the distance, I can see a herd of grazing deer. The whole scene is like something out of a Jane Austen novel, and I half expect Mr Darcy to come riding up the drive. But the person who answers the door gives me just as much of a shock.

'Luke!'

He looks as confused as me. 'Cassandra!'

'Hi,' I stammer. 'I'm here for the weekend. I didn't know William had invited you too.'

'No.' He hesitates. 'No he didn't. I'm here because . . .' He stutters, and then stops talking. Clearly Luke doesn't feel that he needs to explain what he is doing in William's house. Just about remembering his manners, he opens the door for me and stands to one side to let me in. 'William won't be here till later. But come in.'

Luke is wearing a pair of jeans that hang loosely from his lean hips and a casual cotton shirt, but maddeningly looks just as lovely in these as he does in everything else. For someone who embodies city-chic during the week, he does country-weekend very well. Unlike me. As I follow Luke into a magnificent entrance hall, I look down at my feet and notice that the Temworth gravel has gouged a hole in the toe of my left shoe.

The manor is just as grand inside as it is outside, with high, ornately painted ceilings and tall, elaborately carved fireplaces.

'This is a gorgeous house.'

Luke looks around with a vaguely disinterested air. 'Yes. It is.' His dismissive reply verges on rude. 'D'you know what room William's put you in?'

'He didn't say.'

'Well, I guess you'd better have the blue room. It's got one of the nicer views.'

He does bother to help me with my luggage, but I'm in left in no doubt that he has better things to do. He leads me up a broad staircase and along a corridor furnished with carefully placed antiques. On the walls hangs a mouth-watering collection of art and, as we walk down the corridor I spot a Lily and a Sargent. William's family must have an abundance of good taste. And money.

'And these pictures are fantastic.'

Luke marches past a sublime little Constable landscape without even a sideways glance. 'Um? Oh. Yes.'

Finally, he opens the door to a pretty bedroom with walls that are covered in a blue toile, and dumps my bags on a chintz-laden bed. As he lifts a case, I notice an expensive-looking Cartier watch on his wrist. Much grander than the Japanese number he usually wears to the office, it looks out of place on his arm.

'Nice watch,' I say.

Luke looks uneasy and tugs the cuff of his shirt down over the watch's face. 'Thanks.'

'Was it a present?'

'Yeah. It was a present.' He scratches the side of his nose, his discomfort betrayed by body language he, as a professional communicator, should be able to control. I want to ask more, but I don't dare probe further.

I stand and look at him, waiting for the bollocking I know I'm owed for skiving off. It doesn't come. Nothing comes.

'So,' I say, ignoring his ill humour and fixing my brightest smile on my face. 'What's the plan?'

'Plan?'

'What are we doing this afternoon?'

'Oh, I'm working on the PM's speech for the conference next week. I came down here so I could get on with it in some peace and quiet.'

The barbed rebuke is not lost on me. I must amuse myself. I look out of the window in search of inspiration. Luke's right. The view is lovely. Beyond a series of terraced lawns, I spot a stable block, and horses idling in neatly fenced fields.

'Perhaps I'll go and look at those horses.'

'Er ... Yes. If you want. You'd better get changed though,' he says, eyeing my suit and strappy shoes.

'I've come prepared,' I reply, nodding to the pile of bags on the bed.

'Good. Have fun.' Without saying anything else, he turns and leaves the room, shutting the door behind him just firmly enough to convey his irritation.

'And thanks so much for your help,' I add under my breath.

Feeling slightly out of place in Wellington boots that are too new and a red jacket that makes it very obvious that the country is not my natural habitat, I head for the stables, following a wide path from the house and finally ending up in an immaculately maintained Victorian courtyard. The heads of well-bred horses poke out from brick stables, and between freshly painted stable doors swing hanging baskets groaning beneath the weight of tastefully coloured late summer flowers. A handful of stable staff busy themselves with their evening duties, clanking buckets of feed across the yard and nipping in and out of boxes to straighten rugs.

I wander through an arched exit, and see a dark-coloured thoroughbred ambling across a glossy green paddock. His beauty is so spectacular, even I can't fail to be impressed. I pause to admire him.

'He's handsome, isn't he?'

I turn to see Luke standing behind me. 'He's lovely. I didn't know William was into horses.'

'William isn't. He's mine.'

'Oh. What's his name?'

'Aplauso.'

It is a name I recognise, and I try to impress Luke by saying: 'After the famous flat racer?'

Luke laughs. 'No. He *is* the famous flat racer.'

I gulp in an effort not to say something uncool in response to this revelation.

'He doesn't race any more,' Luke continues. 'We retired him a couple of years ago. All he does now is eat and shag.'

For a while, we lean on the paddock fence, in a slightly hostile silence.

'Do you ride?' I ask.

'When I get the time. I grew up on a farm. We always had horses at home. I expect you were a fully paid-up member of the Pony Club.' There's a bitter edge to his voice.

'Wasn't everybody?' I respond, with an equally icy tone. The truth is that horses terrify me. But if Luke's going to play the working-class hero, I'm entitled to be the rich bitch. Luke doesn't rise to the bait, but instead turns his attention back to the horse.

Aplauso pauses to lift his head, filling his nostrils with the scent of his master. He trots towards us. His tail is high, his neck raised into a powerful crest. He's showing off. Letting us see what a fine creature he is.

Luke steps a little closer. I feel the heat of his breath against my neck. He is wearing a slightly battered Barbour, and the rich oily fragrance of it reaches me. He produces a handful of feed from his pocket and takes hold of my hand to press a few grains into my palm.

I shiver at the contact. When I glance up at Luke again, I see the ghost of a knowing smile on his lips. Aplauso stretches his strong, regal head towards me, and Luke lifts my hand.

'He won't hurt you,' he says softly. Aplauso takes the corn from my hand and crunches it thoughtfully, whickering gently.

Suddenly faint, I sway slightly. For a moment, Luke returns the pressure and I feel his firm body supporting mine. As Aplauso nudges me for more corn, Luke's hand curls around my waist. I turn my head and our mouths are inches apart. I take another handful of food, and this time I feed it to the horse without Luke's help. I'm thrilled at my bravery.

I turn to Luke, wanting his praise. But he's gone.

I don't see him again that weekend.

5

Cassandra's Story

I normally break out in a rash as soon as I venture outside the M25, but Brighton I like. As the venue for this year's New Spectrum Party conference, it's heaving. Politicians, press and hangers-on swell the crowds in every bar, cafe and restaurant. All the hotels for miles around are fully booked. And as part of the government team, I'm staying in one of Brighton's finest. As I walk through the grand doors, a porter wheeling a trolley stacked with my Louis Vuitton luggage behind me, Toby, the junior press officer, arrives, carrying an overloaded sports bag. He waves me a hesitant greeting.

'Hi, Toby,' I call.

Shy, quiet Toby looks at his feet as he says: 'Hi, Cassandra.'

We check in together and, while Toby orders the morning papers, I order a manicure. We exchange a quick 'see you later', and go to our rooms.

I stroll over to my window, and fling back the curtains to see that my room overlooks a courtyard. As I examine the rather uninspiring view, I feel a sulk coming on. I bet the PM can see the sea from his suite. Oh well. I raise my arms above my head and roll my shoulders, feeling the stress of the journey drop away as I stretch. Without turning away from the window, I shrug off my jacket and I'm about to take off my blouse, when I notice a curtain twitch in a window of a room opposite. Wearing a red sweatshirt and black jeans, the dark-haired figure behind the voile is clearly recognisable. As I begin to unbutton my top, the person retreats slightly, and then freezes. Sweet little Toby is obviously hoping to get a peek at me getting changed. I could be outraged. I could cause a scene. But the thought of being watched holds some appeal. I lower my head and smile to myself. OK. I'll give him something worth looking at.

I slowly unfasten my blouse, lingering over each button as if undecided about taking my clothes off. Then I ease the blouse open, leaning forwards slightly to show off my breasts in their satin bra. I unzip my skirt and, turning round so that my admirer can see the contours of my backside as I bend over, I push the garment down my hips and step out of it, still in my high-heeled shoes. As I unpin my hair, it tumbles down over my shoulders and I arch my back slightly so that the ends brush against the upper curve of my bottom. Watch and weep, Toby.

In my underwear, I pretend to carry on stretching out and easing my muscles. I put my arms behind my head and fake a yawn, knowing that it will show off my breasts beautifully. As I bend and turn, I make sure that all my body is displayed to maximum effect. I smile with satisfaction as Toby's partly concealed hand slides down to his crotch and I see him fumble with the front of his trousers. His arm begins to move in a steady rhythm.

Crossing the room to the bed, I swing my hips provocatively, enjoying the thought of Toby's avaricious eyes on my figure. With a sigh, I lie back against the covers, as if I have all the time in the world and getting dressed is just too much of a chore. Slipping my hands into my bra, I hitch out both breasts from the cups. Bound by the confines of unyielding satin, they cleave and bulge voluptuously over the top of the fabric. It's easy to imagine how I am stoking Toby's desire as I lick one fingertip and trace a little wet circle around each deep-pink nipple. Dropping my chin, I blow on one and then the other and they harden as my breath chills my skin. Then I cup my breasts in my hands and lift them up to him, tempting him with my flesh. As I gently pinch each nipple between the tips of my fingers, they grow harder still and seem to strain towards him. I'm starting to really enjoy this game.

And so is Toby. Throwing up my head, I admire the shape of his growing erection faintly visible behind the sheer curtain. Distorted by the shadows, it is huge, standing out from his body as he rubs it vigorously.

Reaching behind my back, I look down to watch my tits jut forwards as I stretch to unfasten the bra. They are a pleasing sight, and I'm not surprised when I see Toby's hand moving at a more urgent speed. I think of the things he must be wanting to do to them. Stroke them. Bite them. Come over them. Undoing the clip, I toss the bra onto the floor, but decide to leave on my French knickers, shoes and stockings to add to the erotic effect.

While I lie on the bed, I run my hands slowly over my satin-clad stomach and hips, up and down my thighs, dreaming of just how much Toby would love to do the same. I can almost hear his groans of desire. Lazily, I let one finger run the length of my sex, pausing to caress my clit as it pushes up, swollen and aroused beneath the fabric of my knickers. I let the very tip of my fingernail rake across it, teasing myself deliciously. The sensation is wonderfully pleasurable, and now I groan out loud. It would be easy to carry on, but I decide it might be even more fun to let my peeping Tom in on the joke.

I reach for my mobile and dial a number. The figure

in the window jumps as the phone rings. Then he picks up the call.

'Yes?' His voice is thin on the end of the line.

'Toby,' I whisper, 'does this look good?' I part my legs, and pull my damp knickers to one side so that he can see me clearly. There's an almighty crash as Toby drops his phone. I stifle a smile. He picks up the handset again and I hear his heavy breath. 'Toby, why don't you join me? You'll get a better view from in here.'

For a moment there is silence. Then I hear him say: 'Yes,' and the phone goes dead. I settle back on the bed, and I pass the time by gently stroking my nicely warming clit. My wait is not a long one. In what feels like a matter of seconds, there is a soft knock on my door, and I open it, flinging it wide to shock him with the sight of my almost naked body. The gesture has the desired effect, and Toby stands transfixed by the vision before him. I move aside and beckon him into the room. He has done up his trousers, but his erection is almost bursting through the fabric. Despite his obvious embarrassment, he can't keep his hands off his helplessly aroused cock and he gropes at his trousers like a little boy needing the loo.

'I'm sorry,' he stammers. 'I didn't think you could see me.'

'It's OK, Toby.' I walk towards him, letting my body sway slowly and languidly as I cover the space between us. Standing in front of him, I press a wet finger against the full curve of his bottom lip. I feel a frisson of pleasure when I see him put out the tip of his tongue to lick where I've touched him. He's desperate to taste me. 'And surely,' I continue, 'it's better to jerk off while looking at the real thing rather than some silly girl in a porn mag.' It's then that I remember the camera still in my bag from the PR awards dinner and an idea dawns.

'But maybe,' I say, 'you can do both.' I go to my piled luggage and take out the camera. 'Why don't we make you your very own personal wank-mag?'

For a moment Toby looks nonplussed as I shove the camera into his hand, but when I lie back against the bed and ask him what he wants me to do, his condition of extreme arousal means that he is more than willing to join in the fun.

'Tell me how you'd like me, Toby,' I say softly.

Toby, his face flushed, says nothing.

I reach down to run my hands over the curves of my bare breasts.

'Oh, come on, Toby, surely you can think of something.' I sigh ostentatiously. 'Or shall I just get dressed?'

'No!' exclaims Toby. 'I'd love to see you holding your tits. Like you were earlier.' Obligingly, I cup my breasts and, squashing them together in true top-shelf fashion, I lean forwards to let him photograph me. With shaking hands, Toby takes the first shot.

His confidence building, Toby says: 'And I'd like to take a picture of you on all fours. Please.'

'Like this?' On the bed on my hands and knees with my bottom towards him, I look back over my shoulder and smile into his camera.

'Yes. That's fine.' The camera clicks.

'But I'd like to see more . . .' His voice trails off, unable to express his sinful thoughts.

'More of this?'

He whimpers again as I slip my knickers down over my bottom, hollowing my back slightly to make sure he gets a clear sight of my sex between the tops of my thighs. As I look back over my shoulder, I see that he has taken his prick in his hand and is sliding his palm up and down its length. I open my legs slightly wider and feel my lips part, exposing the wet core of me to his camera. I feel his lustful eyes on me, penetrating me. He sighs in admiration.

'Good?' I ask.

'Oh yes.'

Slowly, heavy with arousal, I stand up and wriggle my hips so that the knickers fall right down to my ankles. Toby stares at the little pile of fabric as I step out of the underwear. Almost naked now, I glide over to Toby and stand in front of him. He drops his eyes to my naked tits.

'Lie down and let me show you another angle,' I say softly. With my hand on his shoulder, I gently push him to the ground.

His eyes widening in greedy anticipation, he lies on his back on the carpet while I step over him to stand astride his shoulders, giving him a fine view up the insides of my stockings to my sex.

'Wow,' he says, eyeing the baby-soft down of my pubes. 'You really are beautiful.'

'Oh yes, Toby. I certainly am.' I let my fingers drift up my thighs, and I see his hand twitch as he fights the urge to reach up and touch me. But touching isn't allowed, and poor Toby knows it.

As I lower myself into a squat over his face, he groans and closes his eyes. I know I've hit a nerve.

'What is it, Toby? Is that too much?' I lean forwards to look at his face between my thighs.

He opens his eyes again. 'Yes. I mean no.'

'So take your picture then.' I'm so aroused now and I know I'm glistening wonderfully for his camera. I tip forwards further so that the lower curve of my breasts will come into the shot. With shaking hands, he raises the camera and takes the picture he wants so badly.

His task completed, he grits his teeth and reaches down to grab himself again, his hand moving at too rapid a pace as he hurtles towards his orgasm.

'No,' I say, reaching back to still his arm. 'Not yet. There must be something else you want for your photo album?' Toby looks at me, and I see him hesitate. 'Surely you can think of something.'

His face colours again as he says quietly: 'Well, I'd like you to do what you were doing earlier.'

'What do you mean?'

'I'd like to see you ...'

'Go on.' I want to hear him say it.

'I'd like to watch you masturbate.'

'Oh really?'

Toby swallows hard and nods. 'Yes. All the way.'

I'm not one to turn down a challenge. Smiling seductively, I move back to the bed and lie against the pillows, spreading my legs to caress myself. At first, I act for his camera, arching my back and thrusting my breasts at him. I rub myself with just the tips of my fingers so that I don't obscure his view when he comes in close. But masturbating while a man photographs me is so very kinky that it isn't long before my need for satisfaction takes over. Stabbing my spiky heels into the bed to brace my legs apart, I thrust one finger inside my sex while my other hand rubs at my clit. Through half-closed eyes I watch Toby taking his pictures. And I'm going to give him something more than the digitally enhanced and sterile sexuality of a glossy magazine to photograph. I will let him capture the steaming, panting reality of me.

Pushing myself up onto my knees, I thrust my hips towards my outstretched finger, moving against it as if it were an offered erection. My breasts wobble and leap as I bounce up and down on my hand. I don't have to fake it now. The frenzy is real, and nothing matters but the finger I'm jabbing up into myself. Now, more than anything else, I want to bring myself to orgasm.

When I look at Toby again, I see that he has taken the last picture. The camera drops from his fingers and, bending his knees, he begins to climax into his hand. He grunts and thrusts his hips with each convulsion of his ejaculation as if he is pouring himself into a real lover and not just thin air. His come spurts, landing on the carpet in a succession of soft little splashes. The sight is enough to send me over the top and, hunched over my juddering hands, I come too, with a deep sigh of satisfaction.

When I've recovered, I stand up and shrug on one of the hotel's robes. I go to pick up my discarded clothes, but looking down at the lace and satin of my panties I pause. Extracting them from the tangle of garments, I press them into Toby's hand.

'Here,' I say. 'A souvenir.'

Then I pick up the camera and toss it to Toby who, clinging tightly onto the knickers, is struggling to zip up his jeans.

'Pity that's not a digital camera. You'll have to be on very friendly terms with the staff of the photo shop where you get those developed.' And, as Toby battles to untangle his sweatshirt from his flies, I leave him to treat myself to a leisurely bath.

It is Thursday night and the communications team is in high spirits. The Prime Minister's speech – the highlight of the conference – was delivered this morning and succeeded in delighting the party faithful. As it had been every day of the event, coverage of the conference was positive in today's TV and radio news bulletins, and we're expecting tomorrow's papers to be just as good. In the hotel bar, the party's press officers have gathered for a drink, but I am in no mood to celebrate and I sip my white wine in morose silence.

My little bit of fun with Toby has done nothing to solve my problem – my growing obsession with Luke.

He had put in an appearance earlier in the evening, and had thanked each member of the press team in turn for their efforts during the conference with carefully chosen and obviously heart-felt words. Having worked round the clock for three nights running, Luke is clearly exhausted and, after checking the last TV news coverage and the next day's first editions, he had gone to bed. It was like the sun going in.

This is not how the game goes. I'm supposed to whistle and he's supposed to come running. But Luke clearly hasn't read the rules and needs some guidance on how to play. And in the crowded hotel bar, I suddenly decide that if he isn't going to make the first move, I'll just have to make it myself.

I down the remainder of my drink, make my excuses and take the lift to Luke's floor. Light still streams from beneath the doors of many of the rooms, but the end room – Luke's room – is in darkness.

I spot a housekeeper, moving slowly down the corridor behind a trolley laden with freshly laundered towels. The housekeeper, I quickly discover, speaks little English, and is easily convinced by my story of how I locked myself out of my husband's room. A cursory glance at her room list and a quick flash of my conference pass is enough to persuade her to open the door to suite 348 for 'Mrs Weston' and I slip inside, closing the door softly behind me.

I find myself in a vestibule from which leads a number of doors. I open the nearest and it brings me into a spacious sitting room. I pause, letting my eyes adjust to the darkness so that I can make out my surroundings.

There is evidence of his presence: a PC open on a desk, a suit jacket thrown over a sofa, an empty coffee cup on a table. A tie has been discarded on the back of a chair. I pick it up and run the smooth silk through my hand.

Then I notice something that makes my heart miss a beat. On a small table by the window, is a silver-framed photo of a woman. A woman who looks just like me. I pick up the picture to study it more closely. Judging by the cut of the suit and slightly dated make-up, the photo had probably been taken a few years ago. But there is my streaky blonde hair, my full mouth, my cornflower-blue eyes, my sloping and, I must say, rather elegant nose. The resemblance is decidedly spooky. Sounds of laughter drift from the corridor and I jerk up my head, startled by the noise. But in Luke's suite all is quiet. With a slight shudder, I replace the picture on the table.

Putting my fears aside, I cross the room, my feet sliding noiselessly over the deep carpet. I move to a second door, open it, and peek inside. It's Luke's bathroom. Easing the door wider, I step inside.

The room is strangely tidy. On a shelf next to the white sink, I see an array of toiletries, and I move closer to examine the bottles and tubes – an intimate collection not meant for my eyes. Picking up his razor, I press my thumb against the blade, enjoying the sting of the cold steel. Then, I squeeze some of his toothpaste onto my finger and rub it across my teeth. I might as well taste nice for him. Spitting into his sink, I wipe my mouth on his towel. A packet of condoms is open on a window sill. I help myself to a handful, tucking them into the pocket of my jacket. Finally I reach for his bottle of aftershave, unscrew the lid, raise the bottle to my nose and inhale deeply. As I breathe in the sharp, familiar scent, a bolt of excitement goes through me – as sure and as strong as if he had touched me.

Silently, I put the bottle down. Treading carefully, I leave the bathroom and return to the vestibule. My heart is beating wildly as I slowly open the final door.

And there he is. Stretched across a large bed, he is asleep, his arms flung above his head. His body is covered by a sheet, but beneath the starched cotton I can dimly make out the contours of his strong frame. I cross to the bed and lean over to look at him more closely. A shaft of moonlight streaks across the room, highlighting the perfect angles of his face. His hair is silvered by the pale glow. He hasn't shaved this evening, and there's a trace of fair stubble on his upper lip and jawline. His head is turned to one side, exposing his throat and the column of his neck. As I admire him spread out before me, I feel a familiar tug of longing deep inside my sex. I'm once again amazed by his incredible beauty.

His lips are slightly parted as he breathes – deep and slow – and the urge to press my mouth against his is almost irresistible. Almost, but not quite irresistible. I want to take my time and enjoy every minute of this invasion of his privacy. I'm not ready to wake him yet.

With infinite care, I pick up the sheet that covers him between my index finger and thumb and lift it from his skin. As I move it slowly down his body, I'm gratified to see that he's completely naked. He stirs, and mumbles something unintelligible. I freeze.

'No,' I whisper. 'Not yet.'

Almost as if he is obeying my command, he stretches languidly, and then settles again into a sound sleep. Dropping the sheet at his feet, I back away a little so that I can look at the whole of his exposed body. I remember what he looks like only too clearly from the disc the previous week. But this flesh and blood Luke is even more lovely than his video facsimile.

His long legs reach almost to the very end of the bed.

They're not smooth, nor are the hairs so dense that they mask the shape of his solid calves and thighs. One leg is slightly bent, and here the tension in the muscles makes them bulge into fuller curves.

His chest is broad, and around each dark nipple is a circle of fine golden hairs. Below his ribs, the slope of his stomach is firm and flat, but even now when he's relaxed, the muscles are clearly defined. His skin is sleek and even toned. My fingers ache to reach out and touch it. To feel its warmth against my hand. But still I hold back.

His arms are powerful but well-proportioned. Here there is one imperfection – a fresh and jagged scar on his right shoulder, just above the swell of his bicep. A souvenir from the famous assassination attempt I guess. Somehow the fault only serves to underscore the perfection of the rest of him.

I've saved the best till last, but now I allow my eyes to wander back down his body to where his cock rests against his thigh. Even limp and still, it's pleasingly large. I burn to rouse it out of its quiet pliancy. Over his heavy balls the wrinkling of the skin contrasts superbly with the firmness of his flesh elsewhere. Around his penis, tapering slightly towards his stomach, the hairs are darker, but still not coarse – the curls are soft and invite me to touch.

I don't take my eyes from his body as silently I undress, stripping off my clothes and dropping them in a pile on the floor. For a long time, I merely stand watching him, enjoying the luxury of studying him without self-consciousness. I stare. The most narcissistic of my previous lovers would have blanched in the glare of such scrutiny, but right now Luke is powerless and can do nothing to avoid me. The strength of my position is thrilling.

I'm torn. I want to pause and enjoy. Stalling, stretching out my pleasure, I slip my fingers between my legs, sliding them through the sticky folds. I'm already so turned on I know I could come easily, standing in front of him.

But this time it isn't enough. A building need is driving me on, and soon I will have to touch him. Choice is not an issue. I tiptoe back to the bed, and climb onto the end to kneel between his feet.

'I want to look at you,' I whisper, easing his thighs further apart.

Crouching down low on the bed, I lift my eyes. He shifts again and, as he moves, his cock rolls against his leg. Beneath it, his balls settle between his bulky thighs. I follow the line down to where I can just see the beginning of the curve of his buttocks.

'Beautiful,' I say. 'But you know that, don't you?'

I push my hands underneath him, delighting in the feel of his muscular, neat bum against my palms. As I move my fingers upwards between his legs, I hear him let out his breath in a soft sigh. When I reach his balls, I take them gently into my hands to feel them move and shift beneath my touch. For a while, I hold him, savouring the weight of him in my cupped hand.

I lower my face over his groin. Close to him now, I breathe the musky, male scent of him. I examine his cock minutely, taking in the subtle differences in the colour of his skin, the changes in texture created by bruised-purple veins just visible beneath its surface. He's circumcised, and I can see all of the deep pink head and the dark eye at its very tip. I've never seen anything I desire more.

Not wanting to shock him out of sleep, I blow gently on his prick, letting my breath travel up and down its length. He responds. Beneath my lips, his cock twitches and starts to lengthen, and encouraged I lower my mouth to tease him with light kisses.

He murmurs again and I pause over him. But he's still speaking in the strange, incomprehensible language of the unconscious. He shifts his hips, anxious for more. Oh yes, he's aware of me now, but on some dream level that still doesn't quite connect with the reality of what I'm doing to him.

I flatten my tongue and run it the whole length of him, keeping my eyes wide open so that I can see, as well as feel, the lovely cock against my lips. He tastes as good as he looks. I lick him steadily, satisfied with my magic as his cock fills and swells further. I hear him mutter something and, uncertain, I raise my head to catch his words. He says it again, and this time there is no doubt.

'Liz, please. Lizzy.'

Suppressing a smile, I turn my attention back to his cock. He'll get my name right by the time I've finished with him.

Closing my fist around him, I begin to slowly wank him, watching closely as the fine skin slides over the contours of his now turgid flesh. Bending over him again, I hold his rigid member in my hand and I press my lips to the tip. I push against him, letting his shaft force my mouth open. Down and down I go, taking inch after glorious inch of him into my mouth until I feel him nudging against the back of my throat. Then I slide back up, keeping my eyes on his cock, which is now glistening with my saliva. With long, slow strokes I ravish him, my mouth sliding from the tender end to the dark base of him.

He's half awake now, and I feel him reach down to push his fingers into my hair, eager to pull me further onto him, quick to try and take the lead. But I've not forgotten his arrogance when he touched me at party HQ. I've not forgotten how mercilessly he had dominated Lucy and Camilla. Luke needs to be taught a lesson. And I'm the one to teach him.

I slip off the bed. Bending down to my clothes I pull my belt from the loops of my trousers and carefully wind it round one of his wrists. I move his arms closer together to repeat the procedure with his other wrist. Then, with trembling fingers, I fasten the belt to the bedstead above his head.

'Cassandra?' His voice breaks into the silence. 'What are you doing?' He looks down at me through eyes still heavy with sleep.

I smile and say nothing. Then, as I take him into my mouth again, he doesn't seem interested in an answer. He throws back his head and lets out a low moan of pleasure.

It is now that he realises he is tied up. He looks up at his bound arms and I see a twinge of panic cross his face.

'Shit, Cassandra! What the hell's going on?' He struggles to raise himself onto his elbows. 'Untie me!'

'No.' Crawling up his body I press my hand into his shoulder, pinning him back down on the bed. 'I'm in charge here.' And to reinforce my words I lean over him and nip his left nipple with my front teeth.

'Ow,' he says. 'That hurt.'

But his body belies his words, and as I pinch and roll the tiny tips between my forefinger and thumb, his nipples harden and grow. He arches his back, straining towards me. If I'm hurting him, he's enjoying it.

'Come on, Cassandra,' he mutters. 'Untie me.' But his protest sounds feeble and he makes no further attempt to struggle. His compliance sends a surge of desire through me.

He sighs as I trail my fingers down his stomach

towards his cock, and I know he won't complain any more. My hands drift idly over him, and I pause, uncertain how best to enjoy the lovely treat I've prepared for myself. Then I know what I want. Straddling his body, I climb up the bed towards his face.

'Lick me,' I order. 'I want you to lick me.'

But he already knows, and he lifts his head from the bed to meet me. I watch, dizzy with excitement as my mound nears him. Edging towards him, I reach down and spread the lips of my sex with my fingers. I want him close to me. When finally I feel his lips against me it's almost too much, and I take a deep breath to calm myself. My hips begin to move, and I curse him softly as I slide myself across his open and willing mouth. Then, as he swirls his tongue around my clit, I'm frozen by the pulses of delight that shoot through me. With my hips jutting forwards to reach his mouth, I hold myself perfectly still. I give a sigh as, slowly, he pushes his tongue into me.

I can hardly bear to move away from the source of so much pleasure, but I don't want him to make me come like this. I want to be in control. I want to use his splendid body, and I won't give him the satisfaction of thinking that I'm another one of his conquests, reduced to helpless desire by his pretty face and his practised technique.

I ease my knees back down his body and reach for a condom. Tearing the packet open with my teeth, I slip the condom into my mouth, and then, bending over his erection, roll it down the length of his shaft with my lips. It's a trick he obviously enjoys, and I feel his cock jerk in my mouth.

Astride his hips, I take him in my hand and guide him to the entrance of my sex. Eager to reach me, he strains up towards me, but I reprimand him by pulling away.

'No. Don't move.' He is stilled by my harsh words, and I move towards him again.

Slowly, lengthening the moment, I settle onto him, feeling myself opening up to him until he's buried deep inside me, the base of his solid shaft nestling tightly against me. It's exquisitely pleasurable. For a while I'm still, allowing my body to grow used to the sensation of deep, delicious penetration. Then, I rise up and feel him leaving me. But I won't let him go. I sink down, growling with lust as he fills me again. Picking up a divinely slow rhythm, I begin to rock gently backwards and forwards, pressing my clit against him as I move. The pace is unhurried. I'm enjoying myself too much to rush. I feel him try to push with his hips underneath me, but again I stop him; this time my warning is more severe.

'I said don't move. You must learn that you can't always have your own way.'

Cupping my breasts in my hands I lean forwards to brush my stiffened nipples against his dry lips. Then, cruelly, I pull away. Staring at my tits as they swing towards his face, he watches the curves filling and flattening as I rock against him. I know he wants to lean forwards, to take my breasts into his mouth, but I keep myself tantalisingly out of range.

As he struggles to stay still, I see him bite into his bottom lip. But if he's finding it too much of a strain, it's just too bad. With a groan he closes his eyes, and that won't do either. I will force him to watch me.

'Look at me, Luke, I want you to see me come.' Obediently he opens his eyes again as I slip one hand between my legs and begin to massage my clit, while my other hand rotates slowly against the nipple of first one breast and then the other. I work his cock in and out of myself, using him like a dildo.

But I've gone too far. Lightheaded with desire, my

breath grows deeper and more urgent. I'm spinning out of control as the pressure begins to mount and hot pleasure seeps through my limbs. I cling to his arms, my nails raking against his flesh as I strain towards my climax. Every nerve in my body is singing. Then I feel the first vicious spasm grip me, and I push my body down towards him as, with a low moan of satisfaction, I come.

When it's over, he clearly thinks it's his chance to take charge, and he tries to push himself up again. With a strength that surprises us both, I shove him back down onto the bed.

'No,' I say sternly. 'If you move it's finished.'

'OK.' His voice is hoarse with desire. 'OK.'

With his cock buried inside me, I take up the tempo once again. Moving gently, I flex the muscles deep inside my sex to grip him with a rippling caress. I look down into his face and see that his teeth are clenched. He's trembling with passion. Just in time, I slow and then stop. He groans in frustration – an inarticulate plea for the orgasm I've snatched from him.

'Cas. Please –'

'Shh.' I brush the tip of one finger against his mouth. 'You must be patient.'

His cock is now so huge it fills me completely, pressing against the very top of me. He's penetrating me so deeply it's almost painful. His darkened eyes are fixed on mine. Silently, he begs. But I won't move.

'I can't do this, Cas,' he gasps.

'Yes, you can. You don't have any choice.' He can't argue. My supremacy is affirmed by the inertia that costs him dearly. Smiling in triumph, I lift myself nearly off him, then slide back down, engulfing him slowly, at last giving him a small reward for his acquiescence. I hear his murmur of gratitude.

I reach backwards to stroke his balls. Beneath the soft skin they are taut with arousal, rammed up hard against the base of his cock. He can't last much longer.

But I haven't finished with him yet. Moving my hand further down the crease of his buttocks, I find his anus and press my little finger against the forbidden opening. I look into his face. Questioning. Challenging. Luke stares back at me in wide-eyed anticipation. He can say or do nothing. I feel him shudder with delight as slowly, so slowly, I slip the tip of my finger into him. He likes that. Oh God, does he like that. I move gently – probing, pushing, finding the tiniest places that give him most sensation, feeling the delicate pressure as his muscles tense involuntarily against my finger.

'Christ,' he sobs. He thrashes his head to one side, and I see his face begin to contort. He's shaking uncontrollably, sweat beading on his face and chest. My victory is complete. I've found the little perversion that is the key to his most profound pleasure. But still I won't allow him release.

Withdrawing my hand, I climb off him and snap off the condom. Then I order him to turn over.

'What?' His eyes are full of fear, but other emotions are stronger. He can't fight them. He's lost to an irrepressible curiosity coupled with deep and consuming lust.

'You heard me. Turn over.'

He glances up at his tethered wrists and for a moment he hesitates, but he dares not disobey. He won't offend the mistress who's giving him so much pleasure. He must go on. He can't stop, even if he wants to. He turns his body and his arms twist painfully, but he manages to arrange himself so that he is face down. He shivers as he waits for me, his big shoulders heaving as he breathes heavily. On my knees behind him, I push his legs apart.

Then, bending down, I press my lips against the tender swelling of his balls, licking him in a teasing caress. He whimpers in anguish, but I hold the slow pace for a while longer. Denial makes the prize all the more desirable. I want him to want it more than life itself.

When I move my tongue up the column of flesh above his balls to circle the rose of his anus he writhes in a fever of need. I show him no mercy and, parting the cheeks of his lovely bum, I stiffen my tongue and push into him. I lap at him as deeply as I can in leisurely strokes. He groans again and I know he's ready. Sitting up, I spit on my fingers. It's all the lubrication I will use – I don't want it to be easy for him. Then he gasps as I ram two fingers high into his arse.

'No!' he yells. 'Oh God, no.'

He claws at the pillows, his features creased in agony as his body adjusts to the sudden and unexpected fullness. I see pain and pleasure vie for domination as sensation blisters through him.

Tears stream down his face, but he can't deceive me. I know what he really wants. I move my fingers in and out, fucking him for all the world as if I have a prick. In desperation, he grinds himself into the sheets, seeking the friction his swollen cock so badly needs.

'No,' I scold again. 'You must leave it to me.'

But it is time. I want him to see him come. I want to see his squirming, orgasming body dance to my tune. He's my puppet and I'm going to jerk his strings. Leaning forwards, I reach underneath him to grasp his cock. When he realises that I'm going to allow it to be over, his relief is palpable and he cries out, pathetically grateful for my touch. I wank him hard, my hand on his penis moving in the same rhythm as the fingers in his anus. It's more than he can take.

'I'm going to come.'

'I know you are,' I whisper and I fuck him harder still, my fingers thrusting into him to the hilt. 'Let it happen. Now.'

There's nothing else he can do. Snarling an obscenity, he begins to climax. In the throes of orgasm he's strong and I can't force him to be still any longer. Ignoring my instructions he pushes into my hand – one last lunge to finish himself off. He opens his mouth in a silent howl as the convulsions swamp him and, for what seems like an eternity, he's locked into his orgasm. His seed gushes from him, soaking my hand and pooling on the sheets.

At last he finishes, and I let myself sink down onto his back. Sprawled beneath me, he lies very still as he regains his breath. I can feel the frantic hammering of his pulse against my breasts. I can feel the scorching heat in his sweat-sticky skin. I have wrecked him. I think of the way his first touch had turned my knees to jelly. I think of how watching him on the DVD had reduced me to masturbation so frenzied I blush every time I remember it.

And now, Luke Weston. We're even.

6

Luke's Story

On Friday afternoon, the conference is winding down and we prepare to head back to London. With the main business of the week behind us, Cassandra and I change into casual clothes. I usually work on Saturday and Sunday, but Cassandra is clearly looking forward to two days off and, as we get ready to leave the hotel, her pre-weekend larky mood is contagious.

Cassandra had planned to drive home, and I bin my train ticket to go with her. We take a slow route, and she coaxes her car down the country lanes with the caution of a born townie. We chat with the ease that comes with growing familiarity, beginning the slow process of getting to know each other.

We swap lists of favourites. She likes Frank Sinatra, which is good, and tolerates Mozart, which is surprising. I like the country. She says it smells of shit and that she loathes the colour green. Her favourite film is *Singin' in the Rain*, and she isn't too rude when I tell her I've not seen it. She's never heard of *The Draughtsman's Contract*, so I tell her that my second favourite movie is *The Incredible Journey*.

'I always cry at the bit where the cat falls in the river,' I say.

She laughs, but I'm not certain that she believes me.

Sitting beside her, I watch a curtain of pale hair blowing across her face. I love the way it drifts over her lips. Sometimes she leaves it in front of her eyes and I can't tell if she's watching me from beneath the silky waterfall. Sometimes she shoves it away impatiently, flipping it from her face with her forearm. I know some-day soon I will have to feel it against my cock. To know what it's like to be wrapped in it and leisurely wanked.

'Oh, look,' she cries pointing across a field. 'Cows.'

'Yes,' I say, without interest. I watch her hands, mes-merised by the fluid gestures she uses to highlight her words. I glance down at the crescent-shaped welts her long glossy talons have left on my forearms and shudder. Last night, Cassandra's nails against my skin had given me an unexpected and unfamiliar thrill.

She is wearing tight jeans tucked into ridiculously high-heeled boots that gave me an instant hard-on when I first saw them. Beneath her white cotton shirt, her breasts are naked and they ripple slightly as she moves to change gear. She is wearing the shirt unbut-toned quite low and, all afternoon, tantalising glimpses of her tits have been driving me wild. As she leaned forwards to throw her bags into the boot of the car, I was certain I caught a glimpse of a rosy nipple and I struggled not to stare. It's hard to tear your eyes from perfection and, like the rest of her, her breasts are per-fect. I remember them cramming into my face as she climaxed for the first time last night and I feel my cock begin to harden again.

She catches me looking at her.

'What?' she asks.

'Nothing. I was just thinking your breasts look great in that shirt.'

She glances down at herself, her lips pursed in concen-tration. Then she looks up again and says, 'They do, don't they.'

I laugh. 'Cassandra, you are the vainest woman I know.'

Taking one hand off the wheel, she presses the tip of her index finger to her cheek and raises her eyes skyward. It's an irritating little gesture and I can't decide if it makes me want to slap her or fuck her.

'Perhaps,' she says, 'that's because I'm the best-looking woman you know.'

As I laugh again the slap-her-fuck-her question is resolving itself in my mind. Last night, after that first insane time, the sex had gradually mellowed into something less frantic but equally as thrilling. We had made love, something I had not done for a long time.

We hardly slept at all. Falling away from her, reeling with pleasure, I had occasionally drifted into a light doze. But soon the feel of her body next to me had roused me once more and, hopelessly excited, I'd reached for her again and again. I can hardly believe I'm still capable of wanting her. But want her I do.

'Pull over,' I say. 'There.' I point to the bramble-choked drive of a derelict farm building.

'What?' Cassandra looks surprised, but she obeys me, swinging the car off the main road. We bump a few yards up the track, and into a patch of dense woodland.

'OK, stop.'

'Why?'

'Because I have to fuck you. And I have to fuck you now.'

A slight smile plays about her lips and she turns her head away as she comes to a halt and yanks on the handbrake. But she says nothing.

We get out of the car. The spot is quiet. We won't be disturbed. I turn to Cassandra. She is leaning against the car door, looking at me with such a seductive glint in her eye that it's as much as I can do to stop myself from tearing her clothes off and ramming my cock into her straight away. But I will wait; I want to make the best of every moment.

I stand in front of her and look into her face. Her pupils are dark and wide, reflecting nothing but desire. I can feel her shallow, irregular breath against my lips. Taking my time, I bend to kiss her, letting my tongue explore the curve of her lips, tasting every part of her delicious mouth. Kissing doesn't usually turn me on much, but as Cassandra kisses me back, her tongue sliding over mine, I feel as randy as a schoolboy.

Not taking my eyes from hers, I tug her shirt out of her jeans and lift it slowly.

'Luke, this is crazy.' Yes, it is crazy to be undressing her just yards from a busy road, but I don't care. And she doesn't care either. Despite her protest, she smiles invitingly, and while her words try to stop me, her eyes will me to go on.

'Are you questioning my decision, Miss Jones?' The shirt continues its upward path.

'That depends on whether you made it with your head or your dick. Sir.'

'And that's the kind of insubordinate remark that will get you sacked.'

She looks at me with the arrogant, laughing expression that was one of the first things that attracted me to her. 'No. It's the kind of insubordinate remark that will get me fucked.' She is so right.

Dropping my gaze I see the taut, toned stomach and, lifting the shirt higher still, the lower curve of her firm breasts. Teasing myself, I pause before pulling the shirt right up to reveal the candy-pink nipples I've been desperate to look at. Her heart is beating hard, and beneath her fine skin I can see her pulse. When she gives a little sigh, her breasts sway slightly.

'Do that again,' I order. And there it is. The sigh. The sway. I could eat her.

I bend to nuzzle against her soft flesh. She's hot, and her skin is slightly damp. She smells sublime. She tastes even better. I run my tongue slowly around each cute nipple, letting the hardening buds slip into my mouth. She gasps as I take one gently between my teeth and flick my tongue against the tip. As I slowly increase the pressure, she pushes against me. She is so sensitive to my touch, I wonder if I can make her come just by playing with her breasts. But right now I want to play with all of her. I hear her let out her breath in a low hiss as I release her.

I unfasten her belt and unzip her jeans. Slipping my hand inside, I discover she is wearing no underwear. The feel of flesh-warmed denim and the thought of the thick seam pressing against her naked sex send an erotic charge through me. I ease my fingers through the down of her pubes to the lips of her sex. Gently, I probe between the petals of her labia. Christ, she's wet. It thrills me to know that she wants me as much as I want her. With both hands inside her jeans, I ease them over her hips, letting my palms slide over her smooth, tight bottom.

I drop to my knees in front of her and pull off her boots, then lift one foot and kiss the soft instep. It must tickle because she giggles and I feel her tremble as she fights the urge to pull away. But then, as I gently push my tongue between each of her pretty toes, the giggle turns into a low purr of delight. Placing her bare foot on the ground, I reach up to slide her jeans down her legs, and she lifts one foot and then the other as I tug them off her.

I let my fingers run down the outside of her thighs and she sighs as I slowly caress the backs of her knees. Then, as I move back up her legs to trace the lovely line between the top of her thighs and her bottom, the sigh becomes a groan of a more serious pleasure. She won't argue with me now.

In front of me, her sex tempts me. Between the plump folds, her clit peeks out at me. I can't resist any longer. I lean forwards and, with the very tip of my tongue, I nudge the delicate lips apart so I can look at her properly. Sitting back on my heels, I gaze at her, captivated by the sight of her silky pink sex.

Many women would have been embarrassed by such close examination, but Cassandra has no doubts about her beauty, and she stands unflinching, clutching her shirt above her bare breasts. As I regard her, she opens her legs wider still and presses her back against the car, exposing herself to me. Her juices, mixed with my own saliva, trickle from her, leaving sparkling trails on the insides of her thighs. She looks incredible. The burning in my groin suddenly flares. If I'm not careful I'm going to come in my trousers before my cock even touches her. She is fucking incredible.

'Cassandra,' I whisper. 'Oh, Cas. You're so lovely.'

I lean forwards again. I draw her clit between my lips, sucking on it as if it were a tiny cock. I reach up and place my hands on the delicious swell of her bottom. Pulling her towards my face, I rock her gently against me, enjoying her moans as she sways in front of me. Her hips gyrate to an ancient beat. She grasps her breasts, twisting her nipples between her fingers, handling herself much more roughly than I would ever dare. I groan too as I watch her abuse her fantastic body.

I slide one hand round to the insides of her parted

thighs and find her entrance. In response she bends her knees slightly, pushing, begging me to penetrate her. I feel her twitch with desire as I circle the damp, hot opening. She is so ready to be filled. Slowly and with infinite care I push a finger up into her.

I move inside her, enjoying the velvet softness. I stroke, knead, probe, press, while all the time my mouth never leaves her clit. I swirl my tongue around the tiny tip and hear her whimper.

'Oh. Oh. Please, don't stop.'

As if. Pleasuring her is just too good.

She begins to mumble, a stream of half-finished sentences pouring from her lips. Adorable, loving nonsense is punctuated with filthy and shocking phrases that are almost too erotic. I hear the words 'fuck' and 'shaft' and 'cunt' and I know that her dirty talk could excite me too much. I force myself not to think about what she is saying. What is it about this woman that makes the urge to come so irresistible?

She is so exquisitely aroused now and I want to keep her there, poised on the precipice of her orgasm. But when I change the pace, pressing the hard bud between my lips and my tongue she shudders briefly and is suddenly still. I recognise the pause, knowing it is the calm before the storm.

And then she's coming over my mouth. I put a hand to the ground to steady myself as she flings one thigh across my shoulder and thrusts against me. She groans as the agony of her sexual tension mounts and then screams one single unintelligible word as her joy peaks. Knowing how sensitive she will be now, I let her choose the pace and the pressure. I want her to use me – to milk every last drop of pleasure from her climax. I want to give her all that I can.

And she takes. Pushing her fingers into my hair, she

holds me close, pressing me hard against her spasming sex. Then her grip slowly loosens, and her movements slow as her tremor subsides. With a deep sigh of content-ment, she leans back against the car, her eyes closed as she floats down from her high. I smile to myself as I look up at her face. It's the face of a totally sated woman.

But now it's time for my own satisfaction. I stand in front of her and rip open the studs that fasten my jeans. As I take my cock into my hand it jumps against my palm. My climax won't be far away. Gently parting her legs with my knee, I ease into her as the last contractions of her orgasm flutter deep inside her. I move my hips quietly, enjoying every small sensation. I feel as if I'm melting into her, like a warm knife sliding through butter. It's very sweet and very powerful. She pushes towards me, easing me closer, taking more and more of me until I can't tell where I end and she begins. She rocks with me, instinctively following my lead.

I want it to last. I want to go on and on burying myself deep inside the wonderful wetness of her. But as she brushes her lips against my ear and breathes my name, I can stand no more. Turning my head against her shoulder, I tense and come.

Cassandra's Story

As we join the queue of traffic crawling up the M23, he says: 'The PM's hosting a reception for the press at The House on Friday night. There'll be some people there you might like to meet. Do you want to come with me?'

'I'd love to,' I reply, 'but I've already said I'd go with Simon Moore.'

'Simon's going?' Luke frowns. 'I didn't know.'

'Yes,' I laugh. 'Are you worried about the competition?'

Luke does not smile. 'How come he asked you to go with him? I didn't realise you were that –'

'Important?' I ask, a note of irritation sounding in my voice. But I have to admit that I too had wondered why Simon had invited me. Simon isn't one to waste his time on people that don't matter, and there are plenty of people in the government press office who are more influential than me. I have never been on Simon's guest list before.

'No. I was going to say friendly.'

I am slightly taken aback. Surely it's a little early in our relationship for Luke to start going all possessive on me. Well, I'm not going to play that game, and I'm damned if I am going to admit that I can't stand Simon. 'Oh yes,' I bluff. 'We're great mates.'

'I see.'

'You see what?' I ask, lifting my chin and regarding him with haughty defiance. He stares back at me, and for a moment I can't read his expression.

'Nothing.'

I pout. One night of (admittedly great) sex does not allow him to be jealous. He has no right to be stroppy about other men.

'Does it bother you?' I ask.

'Does what bother me?' He leans forwards, picks up a couple of my CDs, and pretends to read the covers. I'm not convinced by his feigned indifference.

'My friendship with Simon.' I want him to look at me but he studiously avoids eye contact.

'Of course not,' he says. 'It's nothing to do with me.'

'That's right. It isn't.'

And we fall into a sulky silence. He reaches round to the back of the car, and hauls his briefcase onto his lap. I glance across to see him take out some papers.

'Luke, I –'

'Do you mind if we don't talk. I've got a lot of reading to do before we get back to London.'

I concentrate on my driving, a vague sense of unease swelling in my stomach.

7

Cassandra's Story

Luke arrives at the reception with the Prime Minister. As usual, the PM's entrance creates a frisson of excitement. But it's Luke I find myself staring at. Simon Moore hands me a glass of wine and I'm slightly taken aback when following my line of vision he says: 'I hear you're quite friendly with the PM's new poodle these days.'

His description of someone who is possibly the second most important person in the country is rude, but I don't pull him up. I know that Simon is far too certain of his own opinions to be challenged by mine.

'Luke? I work for him, that's all.' I don't want to talk about Luke.

Simon smiles. 'I see.'

I wonder if he does.

'I didn't think you'd be impressed by someone like him. He's not really our sort, is he?'

I watch Luke moving through the crowd, charming and confident as he shakes hands and chats with the assembled journalists. 'What do you mean?' I ask.

Simon smirks. 'He comes from Ripon, for God's sake. It's a miracle he can use a knife and fork.'

'He's a good comms director.'

'He's a cunt.'

Disloyally, I say nothing.

Simon looks around the room and yawns without covering his mouth.

'God, this is boring. Do you fancy going on somewhere a bit more lively?'

Luke is talking to the editor of the *Telegraph*. Suddenly, he glances up and, without a flicker of a smile, looks directly at me. I turn away.

'Yes,' I say to Simon. 'I'll get my coat.' I finish my wine and we head towards the door. Luke watches us leave.

'Where are we going?' We speed out of Parliament Square, heading west.

'To see a show.'

'Great. A musical?'

'Sort of. But this entertainment isn't designed for a West End audience. The productions my friend Caroline puts on are for invited guests only.'

Our journey ends in Mayfair, and we pull up outside a smart town house just off Curzon Street. The door is opened by a well-groomed lady I assume to be Caroline. She is wearing a dress of deep crimson that plunges almost to her waist to reveal much of her well-preserved breasts. Her hands are gloved in satin that rises nearly to her shoulders. Her make-up is heavy but well applied. And if her full lips have had some synthetic help, and her forehead has been artificially smoothed, her surgeon has done a good job. She oozes glamour.

'Hi, Caro,' purrs Simon. 'This is Cassandra. A . . . friend of mine.'

Caroline looks me up and down. Appraising me. 'Very nice.' She leans forwards and kisses my cheek, and I'm enveloped in a cloud of her heady perfume. Her embrace is initially no more than friendly, but before she releases me she lifts a hand and gives my right breast a gentle squeeze. The contact is brief, but long enough. To my horror, I feel my nipple stiffen into her palm. Caro's lip curls. She feels it too.

Simon smiles but doesn't comment. 'The Rubens room as usual?' he asks.

'Yes,' says Caroline. 'You know the way. Some of the others are already seated and waiting for Act One. See you later.' She stands aside and, as Simon leads me on, I only just manage not to squeal as Caroline pats my bottom.

'She likes you,' whispers Simon as we move from the entrance hall, but I'm not sure that I want the approval of a woman like Caroline. I wonder what she would have tried to do to me if Simon hadn't led me away. Would she have tried to kiss me? I know I would have let her. The thought of her vermillion lips on my mouth excites me more than I care to admit. Would she have carried on touching me? I know I would have let her do that too. I know I wanted to unbutton my blouse and feel those gloved hands on my naked breasts.

In a tastefully furnished ante-room, Simon pauses beside a small inlaid rosewood table and catches hold of my arm to stop me. He takes a small silver phial from his jacket pocket and empties a little pile of white powder onto the polished surface. With a platinum credit card, he chops the pile into a neat line. Then he rolls a £50 note and hands it to me.

'Something to liven up your ice cream and popcorn.' He gestures towards the table. 'Help yourself.' I take the note from him and lower my head over the table.

When I've finished, I turn to Simon and ask: 'What is this place?' Simon's smile is dark. He puts a finger to my lips and, to my shame, I feel my mouth open, letting his finger brush against the wetness of my tongue.

'Shhh. You'll find out soon enough.'

Simon picks up a bottle of champagne from a selection arranged in a giant cooler together with two glasses. Then he opens a pair of double doors, and we enter a darkened room. Inside are a dozen or so guests, sitting in silence on gilded chairs arranged in rows, facing a small raised area that serves as a makeshift stage.

Above the stage is a large painting that occupies practically all of one wall. Thrown into stark relief by a small spotlight, it dominates the room. My art history isn't good enough to date the painting, but I understand the subject clearly. It's a rape scene. A generously curvaceous woman is spread against a rock, her clothes ripped away to reveal one luscious breast and a white thigh. Above her looms her assailant. He is naked. His back to the viewer, we cannot see if he is aroused, but the tension in his firm buttocks and taut thighs leaves the audience in no doubt. This man is ready.

His gaze holds that of his victim. But there is no fear in her face. Her lips are moist and parted – we can almost hear her breath panting through them. Her eyes sparkle with excited anticipation. At her shoulders and at her feet, frolics a trio of nymphs. It is obvious by the wicked delight on their faces that they are looking forward to a thrilling show.

And so are we. As Simon and I take our seats in the back row, I am certain that Caroline's idea of an amusing performance is the same as mine.

A troupe of wigged and powdered musicians in golden brocade breeches arrange themselves in front of the stage and begin to play. The sweet and soothing notes of Schubert's 'Trout' Quintet are a striking counterpoint to the charged atmosphere in the room. Conversation falters, and the audience is stilled into silence.

The spot is dimmed briefly, and when the stage is lit once more, the area in front of the painting is occupied by a cast of five posed in exactly the same positions as the characters in the image.

The hero of the scene stands as naked as the man in the picture. His pneumatic limbs are those of a dedicated bodybuilder. It's not a look I normally admire, but for this little tableau he is ideally cast. Dark and oiled, his skin glistens, making the pale complexion of his intended partner look even more delicate.

But like her painted inspiration, there is nothing vulnerable about our female star. She is radiant with confidence in her feminine strength. Plumper than is fashionable, her breasts are more rounded, her belly more domed, her hips more womanly. There is more of everything about her. This is a woman who denies herself nothing. She is draped in a fine voile and, like the woman in the picture, her dress covers little of her body. One breast is fully exposed, and her shaved mons is only partly hidden. A slit, ruffled with the deep pink of her labia, is clearly visible beneath the sheer material.

Her nymphs, three blondes of super-model beauty, are dressed in the same diaphanous fabric. It lifts over their erect nipples, highlighting more than it conceals and, as they move around their mistress, we see curves and hollows that are more intriguing because they are partly hidden. Standing to the side of their mistress, they slowly lift the veil that covers her, to let it sink, billowing, around her hips. They caress her breasts and our hero watches her ample flesh rippling as hands circle over her. When he's seen enough, he arches over her, suckling each nipple in turn as the nymphs lift them to him.

Simon leans towards me. 'Very pretty,' he murmurs.

'Oh yes.' And very arousing. The coke and the show are having an effect. My clit feels tingly and hard between my crossed legs.

The hero turns and at last we see the full magnificence of him in glorious profile. His cock is so long and thick that it makes me catch my breath. I wonder if any human orifice can contain it.

But our leading lady clearly has no such doubts. With a soft sigh, she abandons herself into the arms of her entourage, her legs spread wide, her sex open and ready to be ravished. Her nymphs hold her still, offering her to their god.

The hero accepts the sacrifice. We see him close in, that splendid penis sinking slowly into his victim. We see it all – the cock plunging, and then retreating, her sex, gripping him at each thrust. His body rises over hers and falls in a smooth rhythm. He is as beautiful in action as the still god of the painting.

'Now that really does it for me,' says Simon, nodding towards the action on the stage. 'Is it floating your boat, Cassandra?'

I can't answer him.

Our female lead moans, arching her back, her arms raised in a graceful curve above her head as she pushes her breasts up for her ladies to pleasure. They tweak and tease, pull and lap, covering her with kisses and long licks, probing between the bodies of their mistress and her lover into dark shadows hidden from the audience. There is no part of her that is not pampered and petted. Her hips begin to jerk, her body possessed by a force she can't control. As the god thrusts just once more, she is pushed into a loud and long climax.

The nymphs tickle and tease each other at her feet. Their breasts are stroked; fingers are pushed into their pink pussies. One by one, they also reach the end of their performance, shuddering and sighing as they orgasm.

But the leading man has more to show his house. Withdrawing, he turns to face us and, grasping his cock firmly in one hand, begins an elaborate show of pleasuring himself. In extravagant sweeps, he caresses his erection, his hands running smoothly from base to end, squeezing a sparkling drop from the tip.

I can hardly bear to watch any more. My own need to masturbate is overwhelming. I contemplate making my excuses and going to the loo to relieve myself. But the show is so good, I really want to come while I am still watching it. It won't be difficult.

My eyes fix on our hero masturbating his big black cock, and I concentrate on the relentless rhythm of his movements, imagining my fingers keeping the same insistent beat against my own body.

As I lean forwards, I think again of Caroline's hands. I feel her satin-covered fingers slipping into my sex. And then, more shamefully, up my bottom. The rude thought takes me closer. With my legs tightly clamped against each other, I squeeze my thighs together. The slight friction is enough, and suddenly I am climaxing. I press myself hard against the chair to stop myself from moving as my orgasm ripples between my legs, spreading up through my belly until it forces out my breath in a sigh.

Concerned that I might have been rumbled, I turn and flash a quick smile at Simon. He smiles back. If he has noticed my climax he says nothing. It is then that I realise that I am not alone in seeking relief. An elegantly dressed woman two seats away from me has her partner's hand between her thighs. She is clinging to his arm and rubbing his hand vigorously up and down. I hear her whimpering softly.

Then Simon shifts in his chair. He parts his legs slightly and unzips his trousers to take out his bulging erection. He slides one hand up and down the swollen knob, thrusting the other into his trousers to knead his balls. And, without a trace of self-consciousness, he masturbates himself to orgasm, his spunk spilling down his cock and onto his trousers.

On stage, the hero comes too, his orgasm spurting over his supporting cast in a truly spectacular finale.

Much later, I fling myself into the back of a cab and shout my address to the driver. Leaning back against the seat, I watch late night revellers thronging the pavements. It's nearly one in the morning, but the traffic is heavy, the lights of London are still burning brightly. I'm too awake, too excited to go home.

I lean forwards and tap on the glass that separates me from the driver.

'You're not going to like this, but can I change my mind?'

Luke stands in the doorway, wearing nothing but a pair of jeans. I eye his naked chest, and feel a sudden urge to lean forwards and press my mouth against his golden skin.

'Hello, Cassandra.' There is no welcome in his tone. He raises an arm to rake his fringe out of his eyes and, as he does so, a flash of pale armpit triggers a spasm of lust between my legs.

'Hi. I was passing . . .' He looks at me strangely. I can't believe I came out with such a crap line either. 'And I wondered if you were still up.' My voice sounds artificially bright.

'Right,' he says. I peer over his shoulder into his flat. It's artfully modern – white walls, pale floors, funky lighting and expensive, fashionable furniture – a bland style that looks as if it was copied from a book. The silver-framed picture of the girl that I'd seen in Brighton is prominently displayed on a side table.

'And you are,' I bluster. 'Up, I mean.'

'I am now.'

I start to laugh, and then I can't stop. Our eyes meet, and as he regards me, I see his expression change. Suddenly I find I have to lower my gaze.

'Look at me, Cassandra,' he commands. 'Look at me.'

I raise my head and his features swim in and out of focus.

'Shit. You're loaded. What are you on?' I try to say 'nothing', but the word won't come. Gripping hold of the top my arms, he shakes me hard. 'Tell me what you've taken.'

'Nothing, I've just had too much to drink.'

'You took something. What did you take?' He's still peering into my eyes.

'I dunno. Just a teeny bit of coke Simon gave me.' I watch the colour drain from his face, and I'm genuinely puzzled. He doesn't seem the type to be shocked at a bit of recreational drug use.

'How much?'

'Just a little.' I drop my eyes and look down at his bare feet. His toes are long and straight and tanned. Jesus, even his feet are sexy.

'How much?' He is shouting at me, and inexplicably I feel hot tears welling in my eyes.

'I don't know,' I wail. I really can't remember. And I don't want to talk. I want to fuck. I want him to take me to his inevitably huge designer bed and fuck me senseless.

'And you've been drinking?'

'Oh yes.' I'm smiling. Grinning stupidly.

'Shit,' he says again, pulling me into the flat.

With a tight hold on my hand, he leads me to a caramel-coloured leather sofa and sits me down. I am horribly disappointed when he reaches for a shirt that had been discarded on a chair, and pulls it on, covering his perfect torso. Then he goes to the kitchen and returns with a glass in his hand. He props me up in his arms and raises it to my lips. I lean forwards to drink and then begin to gag as I swallow the foul liquid.

'Yuck! What's that?'

'Salt water.'

I struggle to get up, but he pulls me back towards him. Lifting the glass again he says: 'Drink it. We've got to get what's left of the booze out of your stomach. And then you can try to sleep the rest off.' He forces my mouth open and makes me finish the drink.

I have only taken a few more mouthfuls when I'm swamped by a wave of nausea.

'Oh no!' I cry. 'Where's the loo?' I push him out of my way and stumble across the hallway to the bathroom. I make it just in time.

Standing beside me, he holds my hair out of my face as I am violently sick.

I wake with a start. The first thing I am aware of is a thumping headache. The second is that I'm in Luke's bed. For a while I lie still, waiting for the room to stop yo-yoing, then I push myself up onto an elbow. Through the one eye that will open, I see Luke, sitting in a chair on the other side of the room. With one leg slung over the other and his arm draped across the back of the chair, he is watching me silently.

'Hi.' My voice is croaky.

'Hi,' he says. 'How are you feeling?'

'Not great.' I reach up and rub my swollen eyes. 'But I don't deserve any sympathy.'

'No. You don't.' He runs a hand through untidy hair. 'Can I get you anything? Are you up to some breakfast?'

I clamp my hand over my mouth. 'Christ, no,' I manage to reply. I still feel horribly nauseous, but I doubt that I have anything left to throw up. I am also aware that vomiting is not attractive and I decide that Luke has already seen enough of me doubled over his lav.

'Suit yourself.'

While I do remember being very sick, I have no memory of Luke putting me to bed. I run my hand down my body and am disappointed to find I am still wearing my panties. I notice he is still wearing the same jeans and shirt he had on last night.

'And you look pretty terrible too,' I say. 'Did you sleep in those clothes?'

'I didn't sleep.'

He stands up and pads, barefooted, across the bleached oak floor to his bathroom. He doesn't bother to close the door. I hear him lift the loo seat, and carefully, holding on to my throbbing head, I roll onto my side to watch him. I can see his back as he unzips his flies and pees noisily. A curiosity is roused. I feel a desire to go and stand behind him. To look over his shoulder. I wonder how he handles himself. What his cock looks like in his hands.

When he's finished, he says: 'I need to get ready for work. Are you sure you're not going to puke any more?'

'No. I'm fine.' I try to sound convincing.

'Good.'

With his back still towards me, he undresses, stripping off with out self-consciousness. It's easy to be uninhibited when you're beautiful. I watch the muscles in his arms and shoulders ripple and relax as he yanks off his shirt. Then he bends to pull down his jeans. When he shoves his boxers down his thighs, I catch a brief glimpse of his inert cock as it flops forwards against his leg. The sight sends a dart of desire through my belly. He steps into the shower and I watch the shadow of his body through the opaque glass bricks of the shower screen as he washes. Finally he emerges, wraps a towel around his hips and moves to the sink to shave. For a moment he is absorbed in this very masculine, very personal ritual. The scents of costly shaving foam and shampoo that drift from the bathroom are intoxicating, but what I really crave is the smell of him. I look away, furious at how much I want him.

A large and colourful picture above the bed catches my eye. Kneeling up, I lean nearer to get a closer view.

'Hey, nice print,' I shout, peering at the signature in the bottom corner. 'Is it a Degas?'

As I reach forwards to lift the picture from the wall, Luke's reaction is instant. He drops his razor into the sink and hurls himself across the bedroom to grab my wrist.

'Don't!' he yells. I recoil, startled. 'Don't touch it. It's alarmed.'

'Shit,' I mutter. 'It's not a print?'

Luke shakes his head. 'No,' he says. Slowly, cautiously, he releases my hand. 'It's an original. If you move it the alarm will deafen the whole building.'

I am flabbergasted. 'You own a Degas?'

'Yes'

'How come?'

'It's a long story.' He turns away from me, wiping shaving foam from his face with the towel.

'But a Degas? Hidden in your bedroom?'

'It's not hidden. I look at it a lot.'

I roll onto my stomach and gaze at him with renewed fascination. 'Oh, go on, tell me where it came from?'

'I will. Sometime.'

I'm intrigued, but I sense there is no point in pressing him further. As far as he is concerned, the conversation is over.

He opens a wardrobe and takes out his clothes. I watch him dress, buttoning a crisply laundered shirt, fastening stylish and unobtrusive cufflinks, selecting from a row of expensively tailored suits. Slowly he changes from Luke Weston, the testosterone-soaked hunk that had opened the door last night into Luke Weston, the most powerful man in our business. He turns to me again as he flips his tie into a neat knot.

'Your things are there,' he says, nodding towards a pile of tidily folded clothes on a chair. 'There's coffee on in the kitchen if you want it. Help yourself to a bath or whatever and let yourself out. I must go. I've got a breakfast meeting.'

And without another word he turns on his heel and walks out of the room. I hear the click of his well-shod feet as he strides across the hallway, and then the slam of the door as he leaves me alone in the flat.

Forcing myself to sit up, I wince as a band of pain contracts around my head. I catch sight of my reflection in an artistically down-lit mirror. My hair is standing up at an alarming angle on one side and my mascara is smeared down my face in dark streaks. My skin has taken on a jaundiced-yellow tinge. Forget heroin chic – I look cocaine crap. I have definitely overdone it – big time. Never again, I vow to myself.

I look around the room. Like the rest of the flat, it is decorated in impeccable taste. Along with the Degas, there are other good paintings, well arranged on chicly plain walls. The morning light is filtered by blinds and the furniture is cutting edge. But there is something missing. Luke's bedroom is as soulless as the rest of the flat.

Beside his bed there is a wide chest of drawers. I know I'm being unforgivably nosey, but I can't resist easing open the top drawer and taking a peek. Inside there is an ordered pile of clothes. I lift out a jumper and press it to my face. It still carries his sexy scent.

The rugged wool scratches my skin. I let it stroke my neck, then I move the jumper further down my body and rub it against my naked breasts. They pucker and point at the touch. My free hand drifts down over the curve of my belly, and I inch my fingers into the top of my panties. I push further down. After watching him in the bathroom, I'm already wet, and my fingers slide in delectably. For a while, I lie quite still, my hand inside my knickers, gently stroking my tingling clit. And all the time I keep the jumper moving against my breasts, enjoying the manly texture.

I turn onto my side and rock myself against my own hand, dipping one finger into my sex. I move smoothly, imitating his cock when he is at his most languid. His jumper is between my thighs, coarse and harsh against my delicate flesh. It feels splendidly dirty to be abusing myself in his bed, using his neatly folded clothes as an aid to my indulgence. I wonder what he would think if he came back and caught me masturbating with his jumper, and the thought of being interrupted excites me. I picture him standing at the door, watching me. I experience the humiliation. The rubbing between my legs becomes more fevered, and I drag the wool roughly between my thighs with one hand while I use the other to palm my mound. I couldn't stop now, even if he wanted me too.

'I'm sorry,' I hear myself moan. 'But I'm such a filthy slut. Such a fucking filthy slut.' My climax is swift but satisfying. I lie back against his bed, leaving my fingers inside myself to feel the final quivers of my orgasm.

It is then that I notice a pack of photographs in the open drawer beside the bed. I push myself back up, reach for the envelope and take out the prints. Each one is of the blonde girl.

But these pictures are very different. In most of the shots she is naked, posing provocatively for his camera. In the first she's leaning against a wall, her legs spread wide, her pert breasts thrust forwards. In another, she is facing away, bending over to reveal a prettily shaped bottom. Between her long, lean thighs, the faint shadow of her down-covered sex is dimly visible. Like a flower in bud, the rounded swelling hints at beauty still concealed, the picture all the more erotic because of what is unseen.

In the last image, she's wearing nothing but high-heeled black shoes, long black gloves and a set of spectacular costume jewellery. A stunning necklace glints at her throat and from her ears dangle huge clusters of diamanté. One wrist is bound in more glittering jewels. She stands with her hands on her hips, her head thrown back, laughing into his camera. It's the pose of a woman who knows she is beautiful. A woman who knows she is loved. Flicking through the pictures, my stomach knots with envy once again.

Shaking my head, I quickly slip the photos into their envelope and stuff them back under the clothes. As I replace the pictures, my fingers brush against smooth fabric at the bottom of the drawer. I reach further inside and take out a small blue velvet case. When I open it a collection of jewellery cascades onto the bed – diamonds, sapphires and rubies of breathtaking beauty. In the pile of jewels I recognise the diamonds worn by the girl in the picture. I'm no expert, but they no longer look like fakes to me. These jewels look very authentic indeed. Hurriedly, I scoop them into the case, and push them back to the bottom of Luke's drawer.

And as I lie back on his bed, I can't get the image of the mysterious woman out of my mind. If she's Luke's girlfriend, where is she now? If she's an ex, why does he still have her pictures? But if he is in a relationship, it hasn't stopped him from sleeping with me, Camilla, Lucy and countless other women, for all I know. None of it makes sense. Who the hell is she?

8

Cassandra's Story

Late the next evening, unusually, I am one of the last in the office. I had done the unforgivable and kept my diary clear in anticipation of an invitation from Luke. Of course it never came. Now, sitting alone at my desk, I decide I need cheering up, and one person who can always lift my spirits is William. I fire off an email.

'How R U?'

His reply arrives straight away. 'Pissed off!!!!!'

'Why?'

'Deadlines. Editors. Usual shit. U?'

'Bored. Fed up. Fancy sharing a bottle of Chianti L8r?'

'OK. But where's Mr Spin?'

'Luke? Fuck knows.'

'But U do know what he's like to fuck.'

I giggle and bash back: 'O yes.'

It takes a little while before he responds: 'What was he like?'

'William!!!!!'

'Tell.'

His rather wicked invitation tempts me, and I type: 'OK. Lovely.'

'Regular? Large? Party-sized?'

I laugh again as I write: 'You've never seen?'

'No. Luke – three years careering round rugby pitches at university – still came out with a double first. Me – 22 hour shifts in the library to get mine. No time for sport.

No time for after-sport lads-together baths. Not a clue how big he is . . .'

'Big enough. And very, very beautiful.' Typing the words makes my knickers feel warm and wet.

'And how did he treat you?'

'Like a princess.' I pause and then add: 'And sometimes a whore!!!!'

'Rough?'

'Sometimes. Just enough.' A tingle runs through me as I think about how he handled me – the masterful way he made me yield to his touch. And yes, he could be rough. I remember him taking me against the tiles in his bathroom at Brighton, a fistful of my hair in his hand. I type: 'But sometimes very gentle. Always very nice.'

Quick as a flash, William sends: 'What nicest?'

I know what I want to say, but I wonder if I dare. Then I decide that I will. I write: 'His face. When he came.' And it was true. The moment of climax, so intensely personal, is something I don't always want to share. But I had watched Luke. I had watched the way his orgasms darkened his eyes and parted his lips. I had watched every flicker of pleasure cross his face. And he had looked so much better than merely 'nice'.

'Do tell more!!!'

'I shouldn't.'

'No. U shouldn't. But want to hear it. Tell me.'

William's obvious interest makes me regret writing so intimately. I don't want to lead him on. Maddeningly, Luke has wiped out my ability to fancy any other man but him. 'Don't get the wrong impression.'

'I won't. Only want to hear about it. Tell me.'

I feel a flush of arousal creeping from my neck as I type: 'And watching him.'

'????'

'U know.'

'Tell me.'

'His cock in his hand.' I have watched men masturbate before, but there had always been a barrier, as if I was witnessing an exhibitionistic display and not sharing a private act. With Luke, it was very different. At first he had been reluctant. Almost shy. But then he had relented and relaxed. I was invited into his inner world. The honesty had taken the experience to a totally new level.

I'm slightly shocked when William sends back: 'U watch him cum?'

'Oh yes.' I pause to catch my breath, the vivid memory of Luke's body suddenly makes it difficult to type.

But William won't allow me to stop. He sends: 'How? Where?'

'Over me. Over my tits. My face.'

'Putting you in your place!'

'Yes. And I loved it.' No reply comes. I write: 'What u doing?'

'Sexy conversation. Wot U think?'

I picture William, unzipping his flies to release his straining cock. I see him, his hand cupping his balls, his fist jerking up and down the length of his prick, enjoying his masturbation just as Luke had enjoyed his.

I sigh as I slip one hand under my skirt and with the other I type: 'Me 2.'

And it feels good to be giving myself the wank I now so badly need.

For a moment, we're each absorbed in the gentle pleasure we are giving our own bodies and no messages pass.

Then he sends me: 'Wot you thinking about?'

'His prick. Inside me. Pushing inside me. Making me scream.' In my knickers, my hand moves quickly as the memory warms me.

'That sounds so good.'

'Oh he is. Beautiful, and hard, and so, so good.' Against my clit, my finger works in a more desperate manner.

'And what's he doing?'

'He's underneath me. Heaving me over him.' I remember squatting above him on that bathroom floor, my clit scraping against him as he thrust up into me, fucking me from every angle until there wasn't an inch of my sex that wasn't raw with arousal. It sent me, and I came, clinging to him like a drowning woman.

The orgasm that flutters through my sex now is less intense but equally as sweet.

Seconds pass. And then William's reply arrives. I shudder as I read the words: 'I'm going to cum.' I think of William at his desk, trying not to cry out as his orgasm builds. And when he comes, that stifled cry turning into a sigh of pure pleasure. I know his orgasm will be long and he'll enjoy every tiny second.

A little later he sends: 'Thanx. Thanx so much.'

The phone call comes through on my mobile at just after 9 a.m. Greg Jones of the *Daily Mercury* begins the conversation with an innocuous question about the PM's holiday plans. He ends it with a veiled reference to a corruption scandal in the US. I key Luke's extension from my desk.

'Luke? I've had a strange phone call this morning from Greg on the *Mercury*. I think there's something we need to discuss.' I hear the tension in his silence. I don't need to explain what I'm talking about.

'Luke?'

'Can you come to my office?'

'Of course.'

As I walk down the corridor, my stomach churns. I don't want to believe what I've heard – but it answers too many questions. I've often wondered why Luke is so cagey about money. Why he was so embarrassed about the watch. How he could afford the champion racehorse and the Degas. And how he came by the secret stash of jewellery. But if he had been taking money in exchange for influence with the President, it explained everything.

When I reach Luke's office, he is sitting at his desk looking pensive.

'Come in,' he says, waving me forwards. I close the door and cross his office to lower myself carefully into a chair opposite his desk.

'You've had a call too?'

'Not directly. William emailed this morning and warned me that Jones was on to something. Could you do me a favour? I'd like you to do some asking around. Can you try to find out if the press teams in any of the other departments have been asked awkward questions? If they have, can you find out what they've said and then I'll sort it. These are the people Jones normally talks to.' Luke has compiled a list, handwritten on lined paper. He skids it across his desk to me. 'It might be a good idea to start with these first.'

'Sure. Do you want me to try and find out where the story is coming from?' I ask. He almost laughs.

'Oh no. I know exactly where it's coming from,' he says. 'Thanks. And now I've got to speak to the PM so that I can explain what's happening. I think I'd rather he hears it from me before he gets it from anyone else.' He loosens his tie before punching a number into his phone.

'Hi,' he says after a very brief pause. 'It's Luke. Can you put me through to Martin?'

As I go to leave the room, my mobile rings. I step out into the corridor to take the call. William's voice on the line is breathless.

'I can't get through to Luke. What the fuck's going on?'

'I'm not really sure.' The coolness of my voice contrasts with the hysteria in William's.

'This is nasty, Cassandra. Tell him I'm doing everything I can. Is he OK?'

I look through the door back into Luke's office and see him hunched over his desk, his phone pressed to an ear, a cigarette clamped between his lips. The top button of his shirt is undone and a lock of blond hair flops over one eye. He looks uncharacteristically dishevelled. And very handsome.

'He's fine,' I lie.

'Get him to call me as soon as he can. And tell him –' William is suddenly silent.

'Tell him what?'

'Nothing.'

'I'll ask him to phone you.'

Carefully, I close the door and go back to my desk. I begin the process of gathering information, putting in calls to press people in other government departments. Most have no idea what I'm talking about, and I end the calls quickly before I arouse too much suspicion. A few others admit that yes, now I mention it, Greg Jones has asked some funny questions about Luke.

Luke spends the rest of morning on the phone, and as I go in and out of his office with the details of Greg's questions and the answers he was given, I catch disjointed fragments of conversations. He explains, reassures, coaxes – wiping the trail left by Greg.

Just before lunch, he calls Greg and I hear a little of what he says. He is convincing. He knows how to kill a story as well as build one. His tone is polite, but beneath the warmth there is a steely determination that is almost frightening. Greg Jones is left in no doubt that running the story would not be a good idea. And by the time the first edition of the *Mercury* goes to print, I'm certain the story is dead.

As the streets begin to darken, the press staff start to pack up for the day. After checking to see if Luke needs any more help, one by one they bid him goodnight, each with a word of encouragement or support. At last he and I are alone in the office. As Luke hangs up on one last call, our eyes meet and I venture a smile. He does not smile back.

'We really didn't need that today,' he says.

'Who ever decided to dish the dirt has very bad timing.' We're just about to announce the date for the next general election – a fight that will be difficult to start with a disgraced comms director.

Luke snorts. 'Not at all. If this story makes the papers this week, it couldn't do me more damage. The timing was perfect. Anyway, thanks for your help. I wouldn't have managed without you.'

'Yes, you would.' He says nothing. I take a deep breath. 'Simon Moore's having a party tonight,' I say. 'Would you like to come?'

'I don't think that would be a good idea.'

'But –'

'No really, Cassandra. Thanks for thinking of me but I won't be good company tonight.' There's a softness in his voice and I dare to hope.

I brave the question that I've been dying to ask all day. 'Luke? What did you give Greg?'

There were many stories Luke could have fed to Greg Jones in exchange for pulling the corruption piece. Three weeks ago, on the day of his son's funeral, a well-known and popular back-bencher called David Thompson had been arrested on a drink-driving charge. So far the story had been kept out of the papers, but it would have made a nice little exclusive for the *Mercury*.

'What do you mean?'

'I wondered if you'd let him have David Thompson.'

Luke looks appalled. 'Shit. No.'

'So what did you tell him?'

'The truth.'

I'm in a hole, but I don't stop digging. 'You mean you didn't take the money?'

The pain that flashes briefly across his features makes me regret my words immediately. 'Of course I didn't,' he says, very quietly.

'No,' I say, suddenly knowing that it's true. 'I'm sorry.'

He looks at me for a moment, and then just shakes his head. The rest of the press team had worked tirelessly all day to help him clear his name, and obviously no one doubted him. I'm disgusted that I'm the one who didn't have faith. I cross the office and go to put my arm around him. But as I touch him, I feel his shoulders stiffen beneath my hand. I take my arm away.

'Luke, you said you knew where the story came from. Is there something you haven't told me?'

Luke's contemptuous glare reminds me of my position. I'm the office girl. The junior who doesn't need to know.

'There's a lot I haven't told you.'

'Right.'

'Anyway, I don't think there's any more we can do today. You might as well go now,' he says, leaning over his desk to pick up a file of papers in what looks like an attempt to end the conversation and show me that I'm no longer needed. I am dismissed.

'Yes. Will you be OK?' I ask.

When he looks up again, his eyes sparkle unnaturally. 'Yeah.' He draws a slightly unsteady breath.

'You don't look OK.'

'It's not been a good day. What do you expect me to look like?' It's a fair point.

'Well if there's anything I can –'

'Please, Cassandra. Please just leave me alone.'

I do as I'm told.

9

Cassandra's Story

Later, at Simon and Fiona Moore's party, I am having a miserable time. I sit on the steps leading down to Simon's floodlit courtyard garden and light a cigarette. Inhaling deeply, I look around at the golden couple's fashionable slice of London and sigh.

I can't blame my bad mood on the party. Fiona has learned that if a job's worth doing, it's worth paying someone else to do it. A team of expensive caterers, musicians and decorators has been employed to ensure the party is a great success. A new-style political wife whose intelligence and career success matches that of her husband, Fiona is now busy working the room, making sure that she has exchanged witty pleasantries with everyone who matters. She hasn't bothered to talk to me. But half a decade of marriage to Simon would be enough to make anyone lose the plot – Fiona deserves my sympathy not my contempt.

'Life and soul' are my middle names, but tonight I'm the party pooper, not the party-popper. I can't rid my mind of Luke, and the image of his ashen face earlier today is burned into my consciousness.

The sound of footsteps breaks into my thoughts, and I look round to see William walking towards me. A bottle of champagne dangles from his hand. He sits down beside me and offers me the bottle.

'Drown your sorrows?'

'Yes, please, William.' I take a swig, offering him a drag on my cigarette in return. For a while we sit in companionable silence, and then I ask: 'Do you think he pulled it off today?'

'Yeah. There was nothing in the first editions.'

'How did he do it?'

William laughs. 'Magic powers. People have to believe him, even if they don't want to.'

I feel uncomfortable mentioning it, but I want to sound out William's opinion. 'I did think he must have given Greg something else instead.' William looks at me curiously. 'Like what?'

I shrug. 'If someone else had made a mistake, he might not try too hard to cover it up for them.'

William's wide eyes make it clear that he does not share my suspicions. Now I really do feel like a shit. 'Not Mister whiter-than-white Weston. He always plays by the rules. Stupid bastard.'

I try to smile, but somehow I fail. 'I wouldn't call him stupid, but I'd agree with the bastard bit.'

'Ah,' says William quietly. 'Things not going so well with you and the lovely Luke?'

'Things are fine.' William gives me a strange look. 'Well, no. Things are crap right now. One minute everything was great. The next he's treating me like I'm a pork chop at a bar mitzvah. I just don't know what's going on.'

'Well, if it's any consolation, I don't suppose he does either.'

'No, but I don't go for the mean and moody Bronte-hero type. I just think he's behaving like a complete tosser.'

'A tosser, perhaps. But you still want to bonk his brains out. Right?'

I pause and then laughing say: 'Yeah. Right.'

'But he's not a tosser,' says William thoughtfully. 'He just comes with a lot of baggage.'

What sort of baggage? If I'm ever going to understand Luke, I need to know. I turn to face William. Plucking up my courage, I ask: 'William, who's that girl in the picture at his flat?'

'He hasn't told you about her?'

'No.'

'And you never asked?'

'No. I figured if he wanted to tell me, he would.'

'Oh, boy.'

'Tell me, William.'

'Her name was Elizabeth. She was his wife.'

'Luke was married!' I splutter, choking on a mouthful of champagne. 'So what happened? Is he divorced?'

William shakes his head. 'No. She died.'

'Oh, Christ. How?'

'Heroin overdose. Luke found her dead on the bathroom floor.'

'My God, that's awful. So when you told me he's had a bad time, you weren't talking about the shooting?'

'Nope.'

'How did he handle it?'

'He was all right.' William can't look me in the eye, and I sense that somehow he isn't telling the truth. 'He went away for a while as you know. I think that helped.' William pauses to take a long drink from the bottle. 'I expect you noticed. You look a lot like her.'

'Yes,' I say, 'I noticed.' I'm saddened by the story, but also relieved. At last I have an explanation for Luke's ambivalent attitude. 'Is that why you tried to warn me off him?'

'I just didn't want to see him hurt again. I know he has a weakness for girls with long fair hair and boarding-school accents.'

I smile. 'And of course great tits.'

A gang of Young New Spectrum Party boys staggers past us into Simon's garden, doubtless having dropped in on their way home from a wild night in some pricey bar. I catch a drift of a bawdy rugby song, boomed out in raucous, drunken voices. It's the sound of lads having a laugh.

Their high spirits makes me think about fun-loving, carefree, surfer-dude Scott. Sweet, innocent Toby. Both barely out of their teens, they have no past. Tonight they feel like an appealing alternative to a proper grown-up man with proper grown-up problems. But my situation is hopeless. I'm hooked. I need advice. Badly.

'What should I do, William?'

'I don't know. I just don't know.'

'Oh, come on. You're supposed to be his best mate. Give me a steer.'

'No really. I'd be the worst person to advise you.'

'But I need help. I just can't get him out of my mind. I'm becoming obsessed with the bloody man. I can't look at his hands without imagining them on my body. I can't stop thinking about the way his eyes sparkle when he smiles. That cute way he bites his bottom lip when he's concentrating.'

'The way his suits always fit him perfectly?' chips in William, helpfully.

'And how sexy he looks driving that divine Aston Martin of his.'

William nods in agreement. 'The way he laughs at his own jokes,' he says. 'The smell of him.'

I shoot William a puzzled glance. 'William?' William smiles sheepishly. The penny drops with an almost audible clang. 'Oh my God!'

I remember the terror in William's voice on the phone earlier that day. I remember how he had held Luke that little bit too long the evening he arrived back in Westminster.

'That's right,' he says. 'You've guessed it.'

'You? You and Luke?' It's too much to take in.

William shakes his head again. 'No. Sadly not me *and* Luke. Just me.'

'I had no idea. How long?'

'How long have I been gay? Or how long have I been in love with Luke?'

'Both.'

'I've been gay all my life. And I've been in love with Luke from the moment I saw him.'

'Christ. Time for another cigarette, I think.' I fumble in my bag for the packet and light up again, this time one for each of us. 'So in those emails, when I told you about what happened in Brighton, it was thinking about Luke, not me, that turned you on.'

William has the courtesy to look embarrassed. ''Fraid so.'

'But Luke's not ... Is he?'

'No. That's the problem. Luke hasn't got a gay cell in his body. Just my rotten luck to fall for a straight guy.'

'But does he know how you feel about him?' I ask, handing William the cigarette.

William gives a wry laugh. 'No. It's difficult to say to your best mate: "I'm gay. And by the way the person I want to shag is you."'

'But you should still tell him. How can you have an honest friendship if you don't?'

'No. I'm happy about who I am, but I'm not sure Luke would be thrilled. Honesty really isn't always the best policy.'

'But you don't know –'

'Yes,' William replies with a ferocity I've not seen in him before. 'Yes I do. Eight years ago I told my parents. I "came out" as they call it. After I'd delivered my carefully prepared speech about how I was still the same person and how it didn't change the way I felt about them, my mother locked herself in her bedroom and didn't come out for three days. She cried a lot, but refused to discuss it. My father was more outspoken. He called me a "fucking faggot" and punched me in the face. He told me he never wanted to see me again, and as he died last year, he got his wish. I couldn't go through that with Luke.'

'But I'm sure he'd understand. He'd be OK about it.'

'Cassandra, he's a straight, working-class, northern bloke. Believe me, you don't meet many of those at Gay Pride rallies. Do you really think he's going to say: "Oh, goodie, me best pal's a poof."' William impersonates Luke's accent with wicked accuracy.

'Now you're the one being prejudiced. He might surprise you.'

'No, it's not worth the risk.'

I sigh. Perhaps William is right. But it seems so unfair that he's forcing himself to live a lie. 'How do you cope? Doesn't it hurt to see him with women?'

'Like hell. But I manage. I was even his best man. His wedding was the worst day of my life.'

'Oh, damn,' I say. 'What a bloody, bloody dreadful mess.'

'Life's a bitch,' agrees William. 'But I'm used to it now. At least if he's not gay I can't take the rejection personally. And in the meantime, when I'm with another man, I just close my eyes and pretend it's him.'

'I tried that too. It doesn't work, does it?'

William looks at me and laughs again. 'No,' he says. 'It doesn't.'

Luke's Story

Alone in my bed at one o'clock in the morning, I sigh and turn onto my back. The room is not hot, but my skin is filmed in sweat. I'm desperate to sleep, but my mind is racing and frantic; nightmare thoughts keep me wide awake. Blinking into the darkness, I think about the bottle of vodka, unopened in the kitchen. When I bought it, I told myself that I didn't need it. That drinking myself into a stupor was no solution. But right now I have no alternative plan.

I've been drinking a lot recently. Not as much as before, but too much, and I know how easily a bottle a week can become a bottle a day – how soon I will need a drink just to get out of bed in the mornings.

Tense and anxious, I need to fuck. There are a number of girls who would be more than willing. New people I have met through work, or older acquaintances that I knew before I went to the States. But now I need more than a quick screw. I know what I want. Who I want.

I reach over to the drawer beside my bed and take out my pictures of Elizabeth. But the images that had once moved me are too familiar, and as I shuffle through the prints I feel nothing. The attractive, smiling girl in the photos has become disconnected from the real woman who had been my wife. I close my eyes tightly, but I can't remember the exact colour of her hair. I can't remember the taste of her skin.

When Lizzy died, sex provided some refuge from the pain and for a dazzling moment allowed me to forget. But a series of one-night stands was no substitute for making love with the woman I adored. So I learned how to pretend. I used sex to lock myself into some warped fantasy world, where she was still alive.

In the beginning my ability to conjure her up in my mind came as a surprise. In bed with one of many women whose names I never bothered to learn, disjointed, random thoughts formed into swirling recollections that took me to a level of pleasure I barely remembered. Sex satisfied me for the first time in months.

Then the search became deliberate. I chose partners carefully, looking for a particular tone of voice, a certain mannerism – anything that would allow me to plunder forbidden memories. I would play tricks, using a word here, a gesture there, to recreate scenes that should have been forgotten. I became a master of the art, and could reach the point where fantasy blurred into reality with ease. Callously, I would close my eyes and commit the ultimate act of betrayal.

But after the brief high always came the low. Once I'd poured myself into a nameless, faceless lover I would be left racked with self-loathing and disgust.

So I made myself kick the habit. Slowly I learned to stop clinging to the past and forced myself to live in the present. Rather than seeking them out, I avoided women who reminded me of Lizzy. Women like Cassandra.

It's been nearly five years since Lizzy died. The pain hasn't gone away, but it has faded, and sometimes I allow myself to believe I'm over her. But tonight the need is as raw and as strong as ever. I want her badly. Angrily, I press my fists against my eyes. I won't cry. Fuck. I will not cry.

I drag myself from my rumpled bed and stagger, naked, to the bathroom. Stepping into the shower, I turn the controls to low and move under the spray. The chill of the water shocks me and, for a moment, I stand gasping and shuddering. Then, I let my head fall forwards, and watch the cold liquid run from the ends of my hair to splash onto my feet in icy columns. I part my lips to let the water soothe my parched throat.

As I soap myself I am startled by a memory of other hands. Strong, manicured hands against my thighs, my stomach, my buttocks – kneading, stroking, sliding over me. The idea sends an unwelcome frisson of sexual pleasure through my body. I swallow hard. I won't give in. Fighting the thoughts that crowd my mind, I turn my fingernails into my own skin in a desperate attempt to purge myself. It doesn't work. Leaning against the wall, I press my shoulders against the cold tiles and groan out loud. Christ, what is the matter with me?

I step out of the cubicle and, still wet from the shower, walk back to my bedroom to fling myself down on the sweat-stained sheets. The warm linen seems to burn into my flesh. For a while I lie quite still, unsure of my feelings. It's been a while since I've masturbated, but tonight the powerful fantasies that swell in my brain are irresistible and the gnawing pain of desire will not be denied. With a sigh of defeat, I roll onto my stomach.

Slowly, cautiously, I press myself against the bed. It's smooth and soft, yielding to the pressure like a woman. It feels good. I sigh with pleasure as my cock begins to harden. My thoughts drift, and finally I start to relax.

For what seems like a long time, the gentle movement is enough, but gradually my need increases. Lifting myself slightly from the bed, I slide my hand down my stomach, watching my fingers curl around my aching erection. The pleasure of that first touch is intense. I groan again and close my eyes. Involuntarily, my fist begins to move, sliding slowly up and down. My cock stiffens further and, beneath my fingers, I can feel the throb of my blood. It takes all my concentration to resist the urge to go quickly, and I force myself to pause and enjoy the sensation of my hard prick in my palm. My hips begin to take up a stronger rhythm, grinding, rubbing, an ever-changing pressure against the bed and my hands.

Only now, I'm not alone. She's there, invading my mind, as she has done so many times before. Covering her body with mine, I brush my lips against her soft throat, breathing in the sweet scent of her long silky hair. Delectable underwear melts away in my fingers. I can feel her satin skin as she wraps her legs around me, her arms draw me close, her hips push up to meet me. I feel her breasts crushing against my chest. Then filling my mouth. I can hear her, moaning and crying out. I can feel her trembling pleasure.

I bury myself, deep inside her sex. Then it's her mouth. Then her anus. Every orifice of her body is mine. She's tight and hot around me.

She makes me obscene. Nothing is forbidden and dark hallucinations flare in my head. A shiver runs down my spine as I remember the threat beneath her velvet touch. She can hurt as well as heal. I feel her teeth against me, and she bites me hard, then harder still until I sob. Agony and ecstasy merge.

My desire gives her strength and she dominates me with ease. She forces me to hold my breath, and my oxygen-starved brain throbs, reflecting the pulse that pounds in my genitals. Her control over me is absolute. My pleasure, my life, rests in her fingertips. My chest strains, and I hover on the very edge of consciousness. My surrender is complete.

It's almost too good, the sensation almost too intense. I don't want it to be over, but my craving for relief is overwhelming. I need to climax. Opening my legs wider, I draw up one knee to brace myself against the bed. I thrust hard, my body captured by the need for release. My hand is moving quickly now, faster and faster, my pleasure increasing until nothing else matters. It won't take long. I know it can't take long. I have to end it. Now.

I feel the slow rising warmth and finally I can be still. Every muscle in my body knots as I wait, knowing that I've reached the point of no return. And then the first spasm grips me. I'm coming. I haul myself onto one elbow to watch myself ejaculate over the sheets – one spurt, then another and another until I'm totally spent.

When at last it's over, I collapse, panting with exhaustion, back onto the bed. Slowly, very slowly, I recover my breath, and I feel my mind returning to some semblance of sanity.

And as I lie motionless and quiet, the realisation dawns. This time it had been different. This time, when I came, it was Cassandra's name that had choked in my throat.

10

Cassandra's Story

When I get home from the party, I notice the Aston Martin parked on the other side of the road as soon as I pull up outside my flat. Even among the sleek Porsches and BMWs of Chelsea it is difficult to miss. I glance at my watch. It's three thirty in the morning. What on earth is he playing at?

'Cassandra!' he calls, his voice resonating in the still of the night.

I ignore him.

'Cassandra wait!'

Christ, he's going to wake up the whole square. I turn as he lopes across the road.

'Cassandra. You're OK.'

I eye him coldly. After the brush off he had given me there is no way I'm going to let him think I'm pleased to see him. 'Of course I'm OK.'

He follows me through the entrance hall and up the stairs to my flat. I open the front door and turn to face him again. He looks flustered. His clothes are slightly crumpled and he's breathing hard.

'Good. I just wondered.' He raises a hand to lean against the door frame, his movements oddly clumsy.

'Thank you. I'm fine.'

'Good.'

We stand staring at each other. He turns as if to go,

and then pauses. He doesn't look at me as he says: 'Has he fucked you?'

The question catches me off guard.

'Has who fucked me?'

'Simon, of course.'

'That's none of your business. I can fuck who I like.'

'Not him.' His voice is strangely quiet. 'Just not him.'

'Why? What's he got to do with you?'

He laughs – a nasty, rattling laugh without mirth. 'A lot. Just tell me. Has he fucked you?'

Something inside me snaps. 'Yes!' I exclaim in exasperation. 'Of course he's fucked me. What do you think we do together? Discuss the weather?'

For a moment he's silent, then he says: 'Before you met me? Or afterwards?'

'I don't bloody know. Before and after. What do you want? Dates and times?' Straight away I wish I hadn't said it. I see him flinch, but his pain gives me no satisfaction. I feel nothing but very sorry.

'Luke . . .' I go to touch his hand, but he steps back from my reach. 'Look,' I say, 'do you want to come in? For a drink or something?'

'No. Thank you. No.' He runs his hands through his hair. 'I must go.'

'Fine,' I say, and without a backward glance, I slip inside the flat and close the door.

I decide I will give him ten minutes.

'Nine,' I say to myself as I kick off my shoes.

'Eight.' I wander into my kitchen and take two glasses out of a cupboard.

'Seven.' I open the fridge and take out a bottle of Australian white.

'Six.' The wine is perfectly chilled, and as I pour it into the glasses they frost invitingly.

'Five.' The doorbell rings. I cross the hall slowly. Deliberately. Making him wait. I hold the glasses in one hand as I unlock the door.

But I'm not expecting what happens next. The door crashes open, banging hard against the wall, and the glasses fall to the floor, splintering against the pale wood.

'Luke!' I exclaim. He stands in the doorway, swaying slightly, and for the first time I realise that he is completely pissed. I go to step back, but he is too quick. With a swift lunge he reaches out and grabs my wrists.

Taking me into his arms, he crushes me against him, and I inhale the musky, end-of-the-day smell of him. I can't help but be aroused by the closeness of him.

'Luke what the hell –'

He silences me with a kiss, cramming his mouth hard against mine, his teeth bruising my lips as he violates me with his tongue. Any tenderness he had shown when he had kissed me in the past has now been replaced by a savage passion that takes my breath away. But startled by the sudden attack, I can do nothing but let him kiss me. He tastes of vodka and cigarettes. Of him. It turns me on like the flicking of a switch.

When he comes up for air, I wriggle out of his grasp. I try to move away from him, but stumble into the arm of the sofa, and topple over face down onto the cushions. He falls on top of me, landing heavily on my back. In fury, I thrash my arms and legs to throw him off. But there is nothing I can do. My protestations irritate rather than repel him, and he stills me by yanking my arms behind my back. He is pressed against my bottom. I feel his cock jabbing against me, hot and already huge. Beneath his weight, my legs are forced apart, and the rough fabric of his chinos chafes my naked thighs above the tops of my stockings as he scrapes against me. His lips are against my neck. I can feel his breath on my skin as he pants with lust.

'Christ,' I hiss. 'This is barbaric.'

'Yes,' he says huskily. 'Yes it is.'

Raising himself again, he pulls up the back of my skirt with one hand and rubs my bottom with his palm. He presses hard against me, sending swift pulses of desire to my sex as he handles me through my panties. Then he shoves one hand into the top of my knickers and it skims over my bare behind. I feel him trying to yank my panties down over my bottom. But I won't be taken like this. With a supreme effort, I roll him off me, and we both tumble onto the floor. I scramble to my feet, clawing out of his clutches. Slowed by alcohol, he staggers slightly as he hauls himself up, and I am halfway across the room before he catches me again. But this time, he won't let me go, and he encloses me in a tight bearhug.

'Luke. For Christ's sake! What are you doing?'

'Why? Don't you like it? Don't you like it when he pushes you around like this?' he says, tightening his grip further still.

'What are you talking about?' My question maddens him even more and he gives me a small, jarring shake.

'I know that bastard. I know this is what he does with women.'

Still advancing as he holds me, he bulldozes me against the wall, pinning me with his weight. He wraps his fingers around my wrist, and presses my hand against his cock.

'Does he want you this much?' he demands as he forces my palm up and down the length of his erection. 'Does he get this hard?' As he rubs my hand over his wonderful prick, every instinct begs me to rip open his trousers and impale myself on him. I am ravenous for it.

But he mustn't suspect. Wrenching myself from his grasp, I put up my hands and try to push him away. But as I struggle against him I am shocked by his strength. We are totally unequal.

Pressing his hips against me to keep me still, he tears open the front of my blouse like some lunatic hero in a bad romantic novel. Over his rasping breath, I hear a series of pings as the buttons bounce on the floor. He shoves his fingers into my bra to pull out my breasts and gropes at them, his hands scraping my skin.

'Careful, you're hurting me!' I exclaim, but he's indifferent to my protests. Rage has turned him into someone I don't recognise. He looks at me with unseeing eyes, and I know there is no reasoning with him. I want to be indignant, but protest would be futile.

He shoves my bra down so that I am fully exposed and bends to kiss my breasts. Taking my tender flesh in his hands, he rubs my swollen nipples against his lips, his teeth – all of his greedy mouth. Then, suddenly, he bites me – hard – just below my right nipple. I hear myself cry out. I can't tell if it is in pain or pleasure.

I reach up and twist my fingers into his hair, pulling with all my strength. It's useless. He raises an arm and takes hold of my hand, squeezing it tighter and tighter until I have to let go.

But still I won't give in. I can't wrestle him off me, so I fight dirty. As he bends again to maul my neck, I shove his shirt off his shoulders. Gripping his arms I lean forwards and press my mouth against his naked flesh. Then I part my lips and sink my teeth into his chest, biting him until I can taste his blood. He yelps in pain, but he will not be deterred.

'Bitch,' he mutters. With his palm against my cheek he simply pushes me away.

I scream in frustration and, in a last attempt to stop

him, I slap his face. Momentarily taken aback, he steps away from me. He stands still, his chest heaving as he struggles for breath. For one ghastly second I think he is going to hit me back. He looks uncertain and, in a fleeting moment, I see him fight to control himself. Then, with icy calm, he shoves me roughly back against the wall.

And I understand. It doesn't matter if I make it hard for him. The result will be the same. I want to say something, but I can't find the words. There is nothing to be said. So I cry. I can't stop myself from crying, huge sobs escaping suddenly from my beleaguered body.

Ignoring my tears, he grips my wrists in one hand and pins them above my head. The position leaves me utterly defenceless and ruthlessly exposed. Briefly he pauses to look down at my breasts. They rise and fall unsteadily as I pant with exhaustion. With his free hand, he pushes my skirt up my thighs, and yanks my panties to one side, pulling the fine lace away from my mound. I feel myself colouring as he fingers my wet knickers. I've been fighting him as hard as I can, but now he has touched my underwear, he will know. He will know how much I want him.

He pushes two fingers into me, rubbing me roughly. My wetness surges onto his hands. Deep inside me, he pauses. I feel the muscles of my sex contracting involuntarily against him, seeking sensation. But he is oblivious to my need – my pleasure is not an issue. He knows I am open for him and that's all he wants. Without ceremony, he takes his fingers out of me.

He reaches down to undo his flies, but his hand is shaking and he can't do it. Backing away from me slightly, he uses both hands to unfasten his trousers and release himself from the confines of his boxer shorts. Now would be the time to escape, but something in his eyes holds me, and I stand motionless, my legs trembling, my skirt hitched up around my waist. Waiting. There is no fight left in me.

He advances again, putting a firm hand on my shoulder to press me against the wall. He kicks my feet apart and wedges himself between my legs. When I look up into his face it scares me. I see the hardness of his expression. I register the brutality that's clouding his eyes. But I'm still not prepared when he rips into me. Holding his cock in his fist like a knife, he lunges, penetrating me with one forceful drive and lifting my feet from the floor. I gasp in shock.

His lips are close to my ear when he snarls: 'There. That's real cock. That's what you need. Not his limp dick.' I haven't the breath to answer.

He is caught in my panties on one side, and I can feel the fabric dragging against my sex as he shoves into me. But nothing will stop him. With his hands braced against the wall beside my head, he thrusts up inside me in long, tearing strokes, grunting with each powerful and deliberate movement. His hard stomach bangs against me, his chest squashes my breasts. Lust has stripped him of any manners. He is rough and potent as he takes what he needs. Christ, this would be rape if only I wasn't enjoying it so very, very much.

As desire replaces anger, I press my arms against the wall to steady myself against his violent thrusting. I close my eyes as pleasure engulfs me. I see myself being taken. By him. By another man and then another, my body bruised and battered as each takes his turn. The image shocks me and I open my eyes again to clear my head of my obscene thoughts.

I wrap my thighs around his waist, opening my legs as wide as I can to let him plunge into me so deeply that I wonder if he will tear me in two. I jerk my hips against him now, my movements as brutal as his as I seek to maximise the crude pleasure of him grinding against my clit. Using my legs to pull him to me, I clench his cock inside me, gyrating so that I'm riding the length of that fantastic column. I pull back and then thrust, once, twice. I can't help it – suddenly I am coming. I cling to him as the climax blasts through me, sending my whole body into glorious spasm.

I look up and see that his eyes are tightly closed as he focuses on his own imminent end. Words of anger and violence begin to form on his lips, only to fade before they can be heard. He pistons into me, his pace increasing as he gives way to frenzied urges. Then his face distorts and, with a howl of ecstasy, he comes. I hold him, feeling the incredible strain as he pumps into me.

When it's over, he slumps against me, his head resting on the wall. His breath comes in great shuddering gulps.

'Cas, I'm so sorry,' he groans. 'Oh God, I'm sorry.' His cock grows smaller, and finally slips from me. I feel his come gush down my thighs in a luxuriant rush.

'Don't be,' I say gently. 'Really, it's all right.' But he doesn't seem to hear me. I reach up to touch his face, but he pulls away, shaking my hand off of him.

'I must go. I have to go.'

'But you can't drive home in that state.'

'I have to.' And doing up his flies he turns towards the door. I try to stand in his way, but he pushes me aside and lumbers out into the hall, shrugging on his shirt as he stumbles away from me.

Polly, my neighbour, is coming up the stairs, rummaging in her bag for her keys as she nears her front door.

'Luke!' I call. 'At least stay until you sober up a bit. Let me make you a cup of coffee.' But he flees down the stairs, ricocheting into Polly in his haste to get away.

'Wow,' says Polly, watching his retreating back. 'I think you'd better take that as a no.'

I try to laugh, but can't.

'Oh Polly, don't you just hate men?'

'Not really. I just don't like them very much.' I look up. Polly isn't smiling. 'Do you want to tell me about it sometime?' she says.

'Yes,' I say weakly. 'That would be nice.'

11

Luke's Story

'Toby!' I yell. 'Toby, where the fuck are you?' Toby comes running, stumbling, down the corridor as he rushes towards me.

'Luke?'

'Why have these press pack corrections not been done?' I jab my finger at a pile of press releases on my desk. My red pen marks stand out like scars on the pristine paper.

'I didn't know there were any corrections,' replies Toby. A deep flush is spreading up from his neck.

'But I told you yesterday that there were changes from the PM. How can I run this fucking office if nobody does what they're told?' I spit the words as my anger mounts. Out of the corner of my eye I can see the other members of my team disappearing into offices and meeting rooms – scuttling off the corridor to avoid my rage.

'But you didn't tell me.'

'Of course I did.'

'No.' Toby is shaking with fear but he stands his ground. And suddenly I remember. I told Camilla, and she is not in the office today. I told the wrong bloody press officer.

'No, you're right. I asked Camilla.' Toby shrugs and turns away. 'I'm sorry,' I call as he walks off back to his desk. But Toby doesn't acknowledge me. The damage has been done. I've only been here a few weeks, and if I'm not careful I'll have no staff left before the end of this Parliament.

The other press officers resume their work, and I go back to my office where I try to read a draft White Paper. But I can't concentrate. My head is churning over the events of last night.

I can't believe what I did to Cassandra. I can't believe the pathetic things I said. When I think of how she had cried as I slammed her against the wall I feel sick. The fury that made me so violent terrifies me.

But I can't deny that I've never been so turned on. Never so certain that I had to have a woman – whatever the consequences.

Leaving my office again, I cross the corridor to the men's loos and lock myself in a stall, shutting out the hum of activity. I lean against the door, exhale slowly, and close my eyes.

I've already masturbated today – this morning, in the shower, spattering my semen against the tiles. And I do it again now, right here, with my back against the cubical door, coming quickly and silently into my hands.

But masturbation brings no relief. I go back to my office and take a bottle of vodka from a cupboard. I pour myself a stiff drink, splashing two inches of liquid into the bottom of a glass. I swallow it down in one, and feel the alcohol sear my throat. It settles in my stomach, warm and almost comforting. I pour another and drink it as quickly as the first. Then I slump against my desk, but the calm doesn't come.

As the press team drifts away for their lunch breaks, I change out of my suit and go for a run. I push myself until my breath burns in my chest and my right shoulder throbs agonisingly. My skin heats as I sweat out the alcohol. But the pounding rhythm of my feet against the pavement doesn't soothe me as it usually does. It doesn't stop me thinking.

Back at the office I shower, rubbing my body raw with cheap soap. I choose a clean shirt and dress hurriedly. During the afternoon I work hard, ploughing through mountains of paperwork until my head aches. Working, my mind is finally occupied and I create an illusion of control. I make countless phone calls, read every letter that is waiting for my attention, reply to every email, pausing only to switch on the lights once the sun sets.

At last I go home and collapse into my bed, sore and exhausted.

Still I can't sleep.

Cassandra's Story

I lie in the bath and sip a glass of champagne. I'm as nervous as a teenager going on a first date. But then again, I am going on a first date. When Polly invited me to her flat, she had said 'for supper'. But when I accepted, I knew I was agreeing to more than just a meal. The lust in the other woman's eyes was so obvious, I can't pretend that I had not understood the proposition.

I look down at my naked body. My nipples, already stiff with arousal, peep up from the surface of the warm water. I reach up to rub my palm languidly over the firm tips and I'm startled to feel an electric response of disproportionate strength spark in my clit. Cautiously I move my hands down my stomach and slip my index finger between my thighs. Beneath the water I can feel the thicker, oilier wetness of sexual excitement. In my head I may not be certain that I want to go to Polly, but my body is more than ready. I contemplate finishing myself off, giving myself a little tension-soothing rub, but then I decide that my sexual charge will spike the evening nicely. I won't relieve it yet.

I lift myself from the bath and walk naked to my bedroom, enjoying the tickle of the trickles of warm water that drip from me. Then I wrap myself in a towel and sit down at my dressing table. As I sweep moisturiser over my face and neck, I suddenly feel afraid. What am I doing? Another woman is offering me sex, and I'm going to accept. That would mean I'm ... a lesbian?

I do find other women attractive. I will occasionally steal a furtive glance at a pretty pair of breasts at the gym or on a beach. There's nothing wrong in that. I'll even admit that looking at women sometimes excites me. When I was younger, I found a porn mag that belonged to my brother and as I thumbed through the pages, a photo-spread of a girl with peach-pink skin and a wet, plump mouth caught my eye. I don't know what it was about her, but the pictures turned me on in that shocking, instant way something can when you're in your teens. I had taken the magazine to my bedroom to masturbate, staring at the upward tilt of her nipples as I came.

Certainly watching Camilla and Lucy making love on the DVD had aroused me as much as watching Luke. And I am curious to know what it feels like to touch a woman.

But I am not a lesbian. I'll get dressed and ring Polly with an excuse.

Then, as I shrug off the towel and begin to rub body lotion into my skin, I'm surprised at how much the feel of my own hands against my limbs rekindles the warm glow of desire that had flared in the bath. I haven't felt such a delicious buzz of anticipation since that first time with Luke.

Luke. My experiences with him have left me disorientated and uncertain, and I don't like it. I need to take control again. And how I do that becomes clear. By choosing to spend the evening with Polly, I'm proving to myself that I'm once again in charge. I have to go.

With renewed enthusiasm, I open my make-up bag and take out my foundation. I apply my make-up carefully, wondering if Polly likes a little or a lot. In the end I play it safe with a slick of mascara and a touch of sheer blusher. Finally, I sweep a translucent gloss over my lips.

And now for clothes. I choose a ludicrously expensive lilac and cream made-to-measure silk bra and G-string over which I wear the matching suspender belt. Flesh-coloured stockings complete my underwear. I pull a short, tight red dress over my head and smooth it down over my hips. Then I turn to the mirror and survey my reflection. I'm not disappointed. My body looks curvy but fit beneath the costly fabric of the dress. The outline of my underwear can be seen, and when I move I catch an occasional glimpse of the top of the bra. I would never go out looking like this, but for a night in with Polly, the pleasingly tarty effect is perfect.

'You look tense.'

After a delicious meal of lobster and far more champagne than was sensible, I'm sitting on the floor in front of Polly's fire. Polly sits next to me. Close next to me. And yes I am tense. A woman is going to make love to me. Oh yes. I'm tense.

'Are you OK?' she asks.

'I'm fine,' I reply. 'It's just I've never –'

Polly's hand slips almost by casual accident round the back of my shoulders.

'I know. But it really isn't difficult.' Beneath my hair, she caresses my neck. It feels good, and my face relaxes into a smile. The wine and Polly's touch soothe me. A seductive jazz track is playing softly in the background, adding to the calm. Polly's right, it won't be difficult. 'Just take it easy and let me look after you. You want me to look after you, don't you?'

I draw a long breath. 'Yes,' I say. 'I do.'

Polly leans towards me and kisses me, with a long lingering kiss. In spite of my nerves, my mouth opens, and I let her push her tongue inside. It turns me on more than I could have believed. My inhibitions fade, and when Polly reaches behind me and unzips my dress, I don't protest. The dress falls open, slithering down my arms.

'That's better,' says Polly, as she eases the dress down to my waist. 'You look much more comfortable now.' Polly looks down at my bra, and I see a smile of lusty pleasure cross her lips. I like the way she's looking at me. She reaches up, and rolls the lace down so that my nipples poke from the top of the bra. We both look down, and watch them harden. I don't feel tense any more, just delighted to be admired.

'You have very beautiful breasts, Cassandra.'

'I don't mind if you want to touch them.' The words spill out of me before I can stop myself. But I'm growing eager to feel this woman's hands on me.

'Oh I do.' There is laughter in Polly's voice. 'And I will. All in good time.'

I'm trembling with anticipation at Polly's next move. Her slow pace is so teasing, so seductive, that when she finally does begin to stroke me the dart of pleasure is almost too intense. I can't stop myself from whimpering. With a gossamer-light touch, Polly lets a finger float over first one and then the other nipple. It drifts, tormenting me for what seems like an eternity, and I feel my breasts grow heavy with want.

My eyes close in dreamy bliss. I sink down onto Polly's

floor and let myself give in. I hardly notice when my bra is removed. I don't feel my panties sliding down my legs. Her lips close around one nipple – she sucks me into her mouth and into oblivion.

Lulled into a trance of sensuality, I watch through misty eyes when she stands up and wriggles out of her own dress. Beneath it, she is wearing a white lace basque. She looks incredible. Touchable. Tentatively, I lean forwards and run my hands down the sides of her corseted body, feeling her slender waist and the smooth curve of her rounded hips. Polly sighs, swaying at my touch and, encouraged by her obvious enjoyment, I let my hands move up to fondle her lace-encased breasts. The unfamiliarity of a woman's softness heightens my arousal. Polly's breasts feel so wonderful, I can't take my hands off them.

She comes closer, climbing over me, lowering her chest to mine, and I watch as the space between us narrows. The sight of my bare breasts close to hers, concealed so erotically, sends a charge through me. I can't look away.

Her arms embrace me, and we lock together, breast to breast, sex to sex. I lift myself, enjoying the feel of her against my almost naked body. And she enjoys the feel of me – as she moves over me, she shudders with contented pleasure.

She reaches behind her back to undo the corset, but I want her to keep it on for a little while longer. Bolder than I would have dreamed, I lift a hand to stop her.

'No,' I say. 'Leave it on. You look so . . . feminine.'

Polly laughs. 'It's not just men who like to see women in pretty things.'

She slides her hand down my belly and gently slips it between my legs. She smiles as her fingers move easily across the wet surface of my sex. I feel slightly embarrassed, but at the same time secretly proud that my arousal is so obvious.

'Goodness,' she says. 'And you certainly do like it.' As Polly continues to caress me, I feel my excitement threatening to engulf me. Her touch is expert, and my clit is tortured quickly and efficiently into a state where I could almost orgasm. But Polly is not going to hurry over giving me my first climax.

She inclines her head towards the bathroom.

'Shall we have a shower?'

'That would be nice.'

I follow her into the bathroom. It's girlie, decorated in soft pinks and white, and the perfect setting for lesbian sex, I think. And as the word 'lesbian' floats through my consciousness again, I realise that I'm not wary of it any more. All I am is turned on.

Moving me to face her, Polly reaches down to unclip my stockings, and I bend to help her by unfastening the other. But Polly stops me. 'Let me. There's no need to rush.'

I stand perfectly still as, with the tip of one finger, Polly rolls my stockings down my legs. She slips out of her own underwear, and, taking my hand, leads me across the room and we step into a cast-iron roll-top bath.

Polly unclips the shower, and uses a warm spray to soak us both. Then she soaps her hands and leans forwards to massage my back. I rest against her, sighing softly, but soon I want more.

I soap my hands too and, turning to face Polly, I reach out to rub her breasts, feeling them slip and slide beneath my palms. Growing bolder, I knead, lift and push the heavy globes like a dirty old man groping a young girl. I don't want to give up playing with these fascinating toys, but I can tell by Polly's deepening breath and fluttering eyelids that she needs my touch in other places.

With a daring that I can hardly believe, I push a finger into her slit. I had wondered if I would know what to do. But it is instinctive, and I pleasure Polly just as I pleasure myself, increasing the pace as her excitement grows. I rub hard now, one finger working against her clit while another moves rapidly inside her sex. Polly thrusts towards me, tensing and relaxing the muscles deep inside her body.

She lets out a little gasp and reaches down to still my hand. For a brief moment, I wonder if something is wrong. And then I feel it. At first, it is the tiniest flicker against my finger, but then it builds, and I sense ripple after ripple grip my hand.

'Oh, Polly, that is so beautiful.'

Flushed with the glow of sex, Polly smiles. 'I know. Nothing beats feeling a woman come. And now it's your turn.'

Polly lifts the shower again, and moves it towards my body. The water playing on my breasts makes me moan with pleasure. Then the spray moves lower until at last Polly is spurting it up between my open legs. I crouch low, moving my sex closer towards the deliciously pleasurable jet, letting the water pound against my clit. I wriggle against it, my sex lips spread wide by the water, while she watches my clit as it trembles in the spray.

I don't want to go slowly now. I need her to bring me off. I call out for it, letting filthy words spill from my lips. I fill my head with coarse fantasies, fixing on nasty thoughts of me, so randy that I'll let myself be mastur- bated by another woman. So randy that I'd do it any- where. I see us somewhere public, in the showers at my gym, my legs wide open, my shame appalling, but my need to be masturbated so much stronger.

Polly leans over me and her lovely breasts swing towards my face. I incline forwards to kiss them. I move from one to the other, my tongue circling Polly's nipples, licking, sucking and taking as much of them as I can into my wide open mouth. And on my haunches in the bottom of Polly's bath, with another woman's breasts pressed into my face, I begin to climax.

A little later, wrapped in fluffy towels, we lie on Polly's wide, comfortable bed. The room is illuminated by candles, their strong musky scent creating an atmosphere of serenity and decadence. I feel as if I'm drifting off to sleep, but then Polly is kissing me again, her insistent little tongue flicking at my lips. And as Polly's tongue teases my mouth, I know that I am ready to enjoy more of the new pleasures she can offer.

Now we have both reached our first much needed orgasm, we can afford to take even more time. Polly lies back on a pile of plush cushions and her legs flop open. Glossy with her juices, the petal-pink folds of her sex shimmer in the candlelight. I can't resist, and I lean forwards to kiss those most intimate lips. Cautiously, I put out the tip of my tongue and taste the unfamiliar but thrilling acid tang of woman.

'Oh yes,' purrs Polly. 'I love to be licked.' Her words spur me on.

Sighing, Polly pushes up towards my face, as I probe more deeply, seeking out Polly's clit. And when I reach the spot, Polly's whimper encourages me. I lick harder, dragging my tongue against her bud. But Polly wants more.

'Cassandra,' she says, almost shyly, 'this is what I

really like.' She reaches over to a bedside drawer and takes out a huge double-ended dildo. I shudder in delighted expectation as Polly raises the soft plastic, fashioned beautifully and realistically as two gorgeous cocks joined at their bases. I can't stop myself reaching out to run my hand down its length. 'Let's see if you like it too.'

She takes a small bottle of lubricating fluid out of the drawer and begins to massage it over the dildo, but as I lie back and part my legs, I know that lubrication is the last thing I need. Gently, Polly runs the tip of the dildo over my eager sex, teasing until I push my hips up to meet the wonderfully wicked toy.

'Please,' I pant. 'Put it in me.' Slowly, Polly works the dildo into my sex, and I sigh with joy. As Polly masturbates me with the dildo, she bends her head to kiss my breasts again, and her lips tug on my nipples, sending me giddy with delight.

But then I hear her say: 'Cassandra, will you fuck me?'

I raise myself onto my elbow and see Polly on all fours at the end of the bed, offering her lovely sex for my enjoyment.

'Please Cassandra,' Polly whispers. 'I need you to fuck me now.'

I kneel behind Polly and look down at the wonderful phallus rearing up from between my own legs. It is a spectacular sight.

I cup it in my palm, feeling the unfamiliar weight of cock. My cock. I take more of the lubricating fluid and, with one hand, smooth it the length of the dildo, jerking myself like a man. Then, trembling with anticipation, I take the tip of my lovely prick between my fingers and guide it towards Polly's waiting sex. Gently I press forwards, nudging, probing to find the place. Then I feel a softness and, as I ease my hips forwards again, I feel

Polly yield and open. She shudders as slowly I penetrate her.

As I watch the dildo slide into Polly, I almost come. But like a man, I know that I have to satisfy my lover first, and I close my eyes to stop myself from looking at the unbearably arousing sight. I lean forwards and pull Polly into my lap, parting her legs so that I can massage her clit. It doesn't take long. Bucking and plunging as she pushes back onto the dildo, Polly comes, sweat running in rivulets down her opulent body.

Now I can concentrate on my own pleasure. With my hands on Polly's hips, I begin to thrust. Her soft mound bounces gently against me, its little thatch of curls tickling my skin. And all the time the magnificent dildo is sliding in and out of us both as I move.

At first, I go slowly, taking the time to rub myself languidly against Polly's bottom between each stroke. But soon, I can't stop myself from lunging hard and grinding beast-like against my lover. I hear myself grunting – a hideous, male noise escaping from my mouth with each thrust.

This is what it feels like to take a woman. This is fucking. I am fucking a woman. As I climax again, I can almost feel myself ejaculating, pumping my hot semen into Polly's soft warm cunt.

But later that night I dream of Luke. I feel his body on mine. I feel his weight pressing into me. Opening me. He flows through me, surging over me in erotic waves of pure love. I wake as I come, and I lie still, my heart pounding as my orgasm ebbs.

Then the tears start. And once I begin to cry, I can't stop the powerful sobs that rack my body and clutch at my chest.

Bastard. Bastard. Bastard.

12

Luke's Story

'How are you getting on with Cassandra?' Sitting opposite me in a bar near to his Fleet Street office, William looks at me quizzically. His question is perceptive. I know I had sounded starchy and formal when I had phoned him and asked him to meet me for a drink. He had obviously sussed that something was up.

'Cassandra?'

'You seemed to be getting quite close. I wondered how it was going?'

I shake my head. 'It's not going anywhere.'

'Why? What happened?' The question is simple, but an answer is difficult.

'She turned up at my place last week out of her head on coke. Then a few days ago I saw her with Hugo Wrighton in the Ship and Anchor.' I had tried to stay calm. I had first met Hugo just a week ago and had instantly recognised the dull eyes, the over-animated movement. His habit is a serious one. 'They didn't think I was watching them, but I saw her give him some money. A lot of money.'

'And this is relevant because?'

'Wills, the man is a complete smack-head. It was obvious what she was paying him for.' I take a final drag on my cigarette and light another. I've been smoking all day and my mouth feels like a sewer.

'You mustn't jump to conclusions. It could have been

for anything. Maybe he cleans her windows. Maybe she's paying for his dear old mum to go to Disneyland.'

'William. She. Does. Drugs.'

'So? So do a lot of people. So do I.'

'Yes, but I'm not ...' I hesitate, choosing my words carefully. 'Involved with you.'

'And are you *involved* with her?'

'Yes. No. Oh God, I don't know.' I trail away, unable to describe my complex feelings for Cassandra. 'But I do know I can't deal with it.'

'Luke. There's something else you're not telling me.'

William looks me straight in the eye and I understand why he is so feared as an interviewer. There is no lying to him. I take a deep breath. 'I raped her.'

'You did what?' William explodes.

'I raped her.'

'Jesus, Luke. How did that happen?' I see William click into journalist mode as he takes on board the gravity of what I have said.

'The usual way.'

'But what did you do?'

'You've done your time on the tabloids. You should know what rape is.'

'Well yes, but ... Have the police questioned you yet?'

'No.'

'Do you think she's been to the police?'

I feel my flesh turn cold. 'I don't know.'

'But surely if –'

'I don't know.'

'So tell me what happened?'

William terrifies me when he takes a small notebook from his pocket and begins to write. 'What are you doing?'

'Making some notes. We'd better get our facts straight here. Tell me, what did you do?'

'I went to her flat. I pinned her against a wall, I pulled up her skirt and I . . . I forced her to have sex with me.' I think of how sex had been before with Cassandra. Exotic sometimes. Wild sometimes. But there had always been respect. The squalid act at Cassandra's flat had taken me to a new low. For the first time in my life, I had really disgusted myself, and describing what I had done is acutely painful.

'Did she tell you she didn't want to?'

'Not exactly.'

William is scribbling frantically in neat, precise shorthand. 'Did she ask you to stop?'

'No.'

'Well, did you believe at the time that she wanted you to stop?'

'No.'

William closes the notebook and leans back in his chair. 'So did you think she was enjoying it?'

'I don't know. But she came.'

'And what happened afterwards? Was she upset?' Irritatingly, William is smiling.

'No. Well, yes, a bit because she didn't want me to go. She wanted me to stay because I was pissed. But I left and drove back to my flat.'

'I see.'

'Don't laugh at me, Wills. This is serious. Don't fucking laugh.'

'Luke – that wasn't rape.' William gestures to a waiter. 'It was something else altogether.' The waiter brings our bill and William hands it to me. 'Your treat, I believe.'

When I return to party HQ, Cassandra is the only one left in the office. She is on the phone with her back to me as I walk towards her desk.

'No, Julian,' I hear her say. 'I told you. I'm desperate.' Her voice rises in an anger I remember so well. 'No. Wednesday won't do. I can't wait that long. Yes, I know I've left it late, but I thought I'd be OK until next week and I'm not.' There's a pause. 'You know what I want. I want –'

When she sees me, she jumps with a guilt I recognise. After guilty she looks furious. Really furious.

'Jesus, Luke,' she says, covering the receiver with her hand. 'I thought you'd gone home.'

'I had.' I'm finding it hard to speak. 'I forgot my car keys.' She doesn't resume her phone conversation, but watches me as I go to my office and close the door behind me.

William's words echo in my head. I tell myself not to jump to conclusions. I tell myself not to be stupid. I go to get my keys from my desk drawer, but my legs won't carry me any further. I lean against the wall, and then slowly slide down it to land heavily on the floor. Then I put my head on my knees, and wait for the shaking to stop.

The next night, I leave the office late as usual, and cross the pavement to hail a cab. My luck is in and an empty taxi slides into the kerb beside me. But as I go to open the door, a female hand passes over mine. I notice an expensive suit, a foot of pale golden hair.

'Cas?' The single word escapes before I can check myself.

'What?' The girl turns to face me and I find myself looking into dark-brown eyes. My rival for the cab is very attractive.

'Nothing. I'm sorry.' I nod towards the cab. 'Please,' I say, 'take it. I'm sure I'll easily get another one at this time of night.'

'I couldn't possibly. But we could share. My flat is only round the corner. You're Luke Weston, aren't you?'

'That's right.'

'Well, then you must share with me. I'm a great fan of yours.'

I laugh. 'How can I resist flattery like that?'

When I hold the door open for her, she lets her hand rest on mine again and our eyes meet. She smiles sweetly.

In the cab, she leans forwards and takes off her jacket. Her breasts are close to my arm. I can smell the perfume of her – designer scent and freshly washed hair. She sits, smoothing her skirt over her bottom, lowering herself to the seat with artful grace. When she turns towards me, her legs part slightly, and it's difficult not to look down at her thighs.

We chat, and she tells me her name is Lizzy. She tells me that she works in The House, but she's vague about exactly what she does. I don't care. I lean back against the seat and listen to her talk in a soft, accentless voice. And I have the distinct, but not unpleasant impression that I am being hit on. Hard.

I wake in an empty bed, and lie still for a moment, my mind working slowly as I remember where I am. We had ended up in her flat, getting steadily drunk on what had appeared to be a limitless supply of chilled champagne. Inevitably, we had moved to her bedroom. Grabbing me by the wrists, she had flung me onto her bed, and kissed me, her tongue forcing its way into my mouth.

A hard kiss, it became harder, until I felt her teeth against my lips and tasted my own blood. A lean leg snaked around my waist. Her move was sudden, and its savagery excited me. When she jammed her groin against my cock, I was already ramrod hard.

Still kissing me, she climbed astride me. She hitched up her skirt, pulled her white satin panties to one side and took my hand to shove my fingers up into her. Then she moved closer to my face, and thrust herself towards my mouth. Her clit sought my lips and fucked me, while I did the best I could to accommodate her. She held her skirt, delicately between finger and thumb, lifting the fabric from her thighs so she could watch herself. It was not long before she started to groan, the noise becoming deeper and louder with each jerk of her slim, pale hips. On her hands and knees above me, she bore down against my face, shuddering like a dog as she came.

I felt assaulted, almost degraded, but so very, very randy. My cock throbbed to be touched. I needed to be relieved as badly as she had needed to relieve herself. As she sank face down onto the bed beside me, I knelt between her spread thighs. I scrambled to unzip my flies, and took my cock in my hand.

Slipping one arm under her hips, I pulled her up to meet me, guiding myself into her pliant body. I entered her in one movement – I wanted it to be quick, like a stress-relieving wank at the end of a tense day. My climax was a necessity. With my palms either side of her shoulders, I rubbed the length of my cock inside her, pumping her at my pace. Using her. As I moved her from one position to another, her submission to my will thrilled me. She asked nothing, said nothing, just let me do what I needed to do.

I focused only on my pleasure, enjoying the anonymous wetness that engulfed my prick. This sex was not about giving – I was taking what I could. And it was good. I lunged into her, bringing myself to orgasm as selfishly as she had reached her own climax. The orgasm was deep and delicious, and I grunted with the pleasure of it. I held her against me, until the spasms weakened and finally faded to stillness.

She'd been like a fantasy woman from a letters page in a porn mag. As a young boy, I had read those letters with eager enthusiasm, burning with lust for impossibly willing women. I had wanked to countless orgasms with my mind full of insatiable girls who wanted nothing more than to make themselves available for my amusement. But unlike the airbrushed beauties whose pictures I had spoiled with my spunk all those years ago, this woman was real. Last night, I had played out the games of my fantasies, making my boyhood masturbatory dreams come true.

But that was only the beginning. I had considered myself broad minded. But she knew tricks that were way out of my repertoire. She had left me shocked, exhausted, and very satisfied.

I hear a noise through a door that leads off the bedroom. I get up, pick my discarded trousers from the floor and pull them on, then I follow the sound into a well-decorated bathroom. I find her, squatting on the floor over a long silver vibrator. It buzzes, softly, deep inside her. As she rises and falls over its length, it slips from her, sparkling with her juices. Her hands are active, thrumming against her clit.

Leaning against the door, I watch in silence as she slides one hand up to grab a full breast. Tipping it to her mouth, she spits on her nipple, and uses the lubrication to massage her spectacular curves in sweeping strokes. Her skin glistens beneath her palm and she looks lovely. But the show is not for my benefit; her masturbation is for her satisfaction and she's clearly intent on nothing but her own self-gratification. Her greed and egocentricity both amuse and fascinate me.

She opens her eyes and gazes intently into mine. There is a plea in their darkness.

I smile. 'If you wanted anything else, you only had to ask.'

'But I do want something else,' she says in a voice breathy with arousal. I raise a questioning eyebrow. 'I want you to piss on me.'

'What?' Her bizarre request takes me by surprise.

'When I come. Will you piss on me?'

I hesitate, and my heart pounds with apprehension. I've never been asked to do something like that before. I've never even thought about it. But her proposal strikes a chord and I'm intrigued. It appeals to an evil, shaming part of my psyche of which I am barely aware. I do want to do it.

I cross the bathroom to stand over her. I unfasten my trousers and take my cock into my hand, but watching her fuck herself with the vibrator has been a turn-on, and I'm not sure if I can do what she asked. I wait, trying to think about anything but what she is doing in front of me.

She looks up at me as her masturbation nears its frantic end. Bucking and writhing on the vibrator, she cries: 'Now. Please, now.' I obey, letting go, my breath coming in shallow gasps as I do it. I watch my urine soak her, spurting at first and then flowing over her bouncing breasts and down her belly. And as I urinate, she arches towards me, pushing herself into the stream. When it's over, I stare down at her spent body, too shocked to speak, too excited to turn away.

Feeling wonderfully filthy, I'm hard just seconds after she closes her lips around my prick. I come quickly, pumping thick wads of spunk into her dirty throat.

* * *

Afterwards, we share a shower, dry each other with warm soft towels, and begin to dress. I'm just putting on my jacket, when a banging on her front door shatters the calm of the flat. Hastily tugging a T-shirt over her bare breasts, Lizzy runs out into the hallway, and I follow to see three policemen push past her and into the flat. They look out of place, their large, uniformed bodies jarring with the feminine décor.

Lizzy and the chief policeman obviously know each other. 'All right, darlin'?' he says, giving her a curt nod as his men shove her out of their path and march through to the living room.

'What d'you want, Blackley? He's a friend.' She jerks a thumb at me. 'Nothing you need to worry about.'

'We're not here to check out your professional interests, love.' Blackley gives me a withering inspection. 'Mind you, he's less ugly than your usual punters. Moving up in the world, are we?'

'I said. He's a friend. That's all.'

'I know, love.'

'So what are you doing in my flat?' She backs towards me, and her fingers curl around my hand. Behind me, cushions are thrown from sofas, drawers are emptied onto the floor.

'Ah. Someone told me that you've got more here than just a client.'

Slowly, it falls into place. There had been no argument for the cab. The long blonde hair, her improbable name, were not coincidences. My pleasure had been paid for. A policeman comes out of the kitchen. A small bag of white powder dangles from an outstretched finger. There's not enough for a party. More than plenty for a good night in.

'Bingo,' he says.

'Well done, Mathews,' says Blackley with a satisfied smile.

'You bastard!' The girl makes a lunge towards Blackley and I grab her as her nails fly to his face. 'He planted that, Luke. It wasn't there. Believe me. He planted it.'

But she's wrong. Blackley and his men have planted nothing. My world crumbles. I feel as if I'm fast-forwarding through a chess match. Pieces are flying in all directions but I can't counter-move. I have been hopelessly outranked. I go quickly through the options in my head. There are explanations but none of them are credible. I want to scream, to kick out, to escape. But this time I know the fight will be useless. Blackley looks at me, challenging me to contradict.

'It's mine,' I say quietly. Lizzy stares in open-mouthed disbelief. She knows I haven't been in her kitchen.

'Luke, what are you doing –'

It's at that moment that Blackley recognises me. 'Bloody hell,' he says. 'You're that Luke Wilson.'

'My name's Luke Weston.' I see Blackley struggling to make sense of what he has walked into. He is floundering, out of his depth.

'That can't be all there is?' he says to Mathews. 'Keep going until you find the rest.' Blackley and his team wouldn't have turned out for a tiny bit of charlie. He had obviously been told that there was more.

'There's no need to trash the place,' I say, as a pile of books is swept from a shelf. 'That's all there is.'

'It's enough to bury you, mate,' Blackley replies. But not enough to look like a set-up. A gun has been held to my head. All I can do is wait for the click. 'And you're in deep shit too, Natasha,' he continues. The girl clings to my hand, shaking like a leaf. At least now I know her real name.

13

Cassandra's Story

I know exactly what he's doing. When the story breaks he's item one in every news bulletin, his face is on every front page. He resigns so quickly the news of his departure is included in the same pieces.

He gives interview after interview, going over the circumstances of his arrest time and time again. He answers every probing question, giving every minute, humiliating detail. Yes, the cocaine was for his use. He was bored, he was lonely, and yes, he paid for sex. Yes, it was wrong. Yes, it was not appropriate to his position. And no, the Prime Minister did not know about it.

His plan is calculated. By letting the press gloat over every tiny indiscretion, he is allowing the story to flare and burn out in the shortest possible time. He calmly accepts the role of court jester. He's the country's biggest loser. Scorn is poured on him. But not the party. He carefully manoeuvres himself into a position where he can be cut off like a cankered limb.

The final interview he gives is for a late-night TV news programme. I watch it with tears pouring down my face. His story is ousted from the front pages the next day by the extra-marital affair of a Premier League footballer. And by the end of the week, once the Sundays have had their say, it's all over.

I can't work out what has happened, but I know that the story is not right. I ache to know the truth. I try to phone him numerous times, but his calls are fielded, and I'm never put through. The day after the last interview, his private numbers go through to a recorded message telling me that the number I've dialled has not been recognised.

In desperation, I try his parent's farm in Yorkshire. The phone is answered after a few rings.

'Hello?' He sounds terrible.

'Luke. It's me.' There's a soft click, and the line goes dead. I don't call again.

Luke's Story

Before I leave London, I hunt down Natasha, finally finding her in a coffee shop near her flat. She is not pleased to see me. I know the press have been hounding her, and grainy pictures of her have been splashed all over the newspapers. The more cerebral publications called her a high-class call girl. At the lower end of the spectrum, in stories with headlines such as WESTON'S BANG FOR BUCKS, the descriptions used by the Red Tops have been less subtle. The quotes that featured in the stories were all attributed to her 'close friends'. She, bravely, said nothing. I buy us both an espresso and sit down opposite her.

'I am so sorry,' I begin, the words sounding inadequate. She is wearing no make-up and her hair is tied back from her face. She looks very young, and very vulnerable. And nothing like a prostitute.

'So you should be. I've never been so embarrassed in my life.'

'I was framed, Natasha.'

'I know. A man rang me and told me where you would be that night. He told me it was your birthday

147

and he said you needed cheering up. He paid in cash. I should have guessed it wasn't kosher.'

'Did he tell you his name?' I didn't need to ask.

'Simon something. He didn't give me his last name. I only spoke to him on the phone so I can't even tell you what he looked like.' She sips her coffee and looks at me with suspicion in her world-weary eyes. 'Why did you tell them that you gave me the money?'

'Because I knew I would never be able to prove what had really happened. And I wanted to get the focus off you. I was going down anyway. There was no point in taking you with me. If they thought you were just one of many, I knew they'd try and get a few gory details from you. But if they knew the truth, they'd never leave you alone.'

'The truth is you did nothing wrong. Why aren't you fighting to clear your name?'

I shake my head.

'I can't. Like the best lies, it's not completely unfounded. I'm no saint. I've taken some stupid risks and there are things in my past I'm not proud of. I wouldn't be comfortable masquerading as the innocent victim in all this.'

'So you'll let yourself be written off as a whoring coke-head?'

'Whoring coke-head maybe. But not a hypocrite.' I push a brown envelope across the table.

'What's that?' Natasha asks.

'It's ten thousand pounds.'

'To keep quiet?'

'Shit no, I've nothing left to hide. But I know they're still pressing you, so call it compensation for the hassle. It's not over yet. And the quickest way to get them off your back is to give them something good. Have your revenge. Make up something juicy. Tell them I liked to dress up as a Marie Antoinette or sing the 'Hallelujah Chorus' when I came.' I take a business card from my jacket pocket and hand it to her. The name on it is a famous one, and she looks impressed.

'This guy's a publicist. He's also a mate of mine and I've told him to expect your call. He'll help you get your story out. They're going to tell it anyway, and you might as well make sure they hear your side.' I take her hands and force her to look at me. 'This isn't the most chival-rous deed I've ever done. But it's the only thing I can think of to make it stop.' She laughs. The situation is too ridiculous to do anything else.

'No,' she says at last. 'You spoke to the press because you had no choice. I don't have to give them any more crap to dump on you.' I am touched. She owes me nothing. 'And I don't want your money.'

'Take it. It's the least I can do.' Her eyes are steady on mine. 'Take it. Please.' Still she makes no move, so I reach under the table and push it into her handbag anyway.

Something I had read in the more salacious versions of our story had intrigued me, and I am interested to find out if what they were saying was true.

'The fee they're quoting is two thousand quid. Do you really charge that much?'

'Not quite, but they're in the right ball park.'

I whistle in admiration at her impressive rate. 'Blimey, no wonder it was so good.'

She manages a weak smile.

I decide to spend the following week on my parent's farm in Yorkshire. My dad and my brother Ben are busy with autumn drilling, and I help, trying to pretend that driving a tractor and loading bags of seed is taking my mind off the pile of shit my life has become.

'Never mind, lad,' Dad says. 'Nothing's broken, is it?'

'Only my heart,' I reply.

Dad calls me a daft bugger and punches me in the arm.

On the second night of my stay in Yorkshire, Ben takes me to the Bull's Head, a pub in the village that had been the centre of our very limited nightlife when we were teenagers. In the car park, my Aston looks absurdly out of place, and I pull up between ranks of muddy Land Rovers with a degree of apprehension. These days I don't belong.

Farm workers in heavy jackets and strong boots stop talking and glance up from their glasses of lager as Ben and I walk into the bar. Obviously my hopes that my mistakes had been forgotten had been optimistic. There's a copy of a tabloid on an empty table, and I see the name 'Weston' in a headline. My heart sinks. Eyes travel from me to the paper and back again as Ben and I cross the room.

The silence is oppressive, and I hold my breath in anticipation of the clever remark. It doesn't come. With a scrape of a chair, an elderly man I vaguely recognise gets up and walks to the table. He picks up the paper, folds it neatly and then drops it onto the logs that smoulder in the large fireplace. I smile my thanks, and he grunts back an acknowledgement. A murmur of conversation begins again, and I am ignored. Accepted. Once more, I'm the boy off the Weston farm rather than the idiot from London who got caught with his dick out.

Ben frowns as I order a pint of beer for myself as well as one for him. But I glare at him and he bites back the comment that I know is on the tip of his tongue. The old pecking order still stands, and my little brother still does what he is told.

The girl behind the bar pulls the two pints with a

strong right arm. An inch of attractively rounded stomach is bare beneath a T-shirt that strains over high, full breasts. A small jewel glitters in her navel. Low slung jeans accentuate curvy hips and a shapely backside. Her long auburn hair is scrapped back in a ponytail from a face that is pleasant, and somehow familiar. I hand over a note in exchange for the drinks.

'It's Laura, isn't it?' I ask. 'Laura Holcolm?'

'Laura Baxter now.' Her smile is friendly.

'You're married?'

'I was. Till he pissed off with one of our barmaids. Left me the pub though, so I can't complain. And you're Luke Weston.' A memory strikes her. 'I let you kiss me once.'

I smile and for some reason I feel embarrassed. 'Yes. You told me I was the best-looking boy in the school.'

Beside me, Ben splutters into his beer. 'You told me *I* was the best-looking boy in the school,' he protests with mock indignation.

'Well, maybe later I'll have to have a proper look at you both and come to a final decision.'

We take our pints of beer and find a quiet table. Ben does most of the talking, and I am grateful to do no more than listen. He tells me about a TB infection on a neighbouring farm, how difficult it is to get spare parts for the combine and the ever decreasing size of his milk cheque. Somehow sharing his problems helps me to forget about mine. He asks me no questions. He has no interest in my career and no desire to discuss what happened to me. I'm happy not to explain.

As we talk, I'm aware that Laura is watching us, and when I return to the bar for more drinks, her attentiveness verges on the flirtatious. She accepts my offer of a drink, smiling broadly and looking me straight in the eye as she pours herself a very large vodka and tonic. She takes a gulp, tipping her head back in a movement that makes her breasts point towards me. It's a practised gesture, and when she looks at me again, I catch a glint of triumph in her eyes. She knows she has caught my attention.

The evening passes quickly and it seems like no time before we are the last customers left in the pub. As we get up to leave, Laura, who stands behind the bar polishing glasses, calls to us.

'Wait,' she says, 'I haven't decided which one of you is the best looking yet.' Ben and I exchange amused glances as Laura comes round from the back of the bar.

'That's right,' she says, positioning us next to each other in a patch of slightly brighter light beside the fire. We stand, like the schoolboys we had once been, awkward beneath her gaze. Ben and I are alike in many ways. We have the same blond hair, the same green eyes, but there are differences. This competition will be interesting.

'Weston major or Weston minor?' she asks herself. 'I've always found it hard to decide which I prefer. But I can't really tell much when you're both wearing so many clothes. Let me have a look at you without your shirts on.'

Sniggering, we strip to the waist, throwing shirts and jackets to the ground and wait for her verdict. The firelight throws deep and dark shadows on Ben's fairer skin. Mine it gilds with a warm glow. I wonder which will appeal to Laura. Ben's body has been thickened by years of working on the farm, and his arms and legs are bigger than my gym-fittened limbs. But I am slightly taller, and I find myself pulling myself up to my full six foot one inch in a childish attempt to impress her.

'Mmm,' she says, eyeing us each in turn. 'Smooth?' She moves towards me and sweeps an appraising hand over my chest. My stomach tightens at the unexpected intimacy of this relative stranger. 'Or hairy?' She turns to

Ben and reaches to tweak his left nipple. I see Ben's eyes widen with obvious sexual interest. My naughty little brother is dirtier than I realised. 'But I think what's below the waist is most interesting. Why don't you both let me have a look at the rest of you? Let's see how you compare where it really matters.'

Ben drops his trousers, and then hurriedly pushes his boxers down his legs. Hesitating slightly, I unbuckle the belt of my jeans, and then let them fall to the ground. I see Laura run her tongue over her bottom lip, her eyes narrow in concentration as she watches me slip my thumbs into the waist of my boxer shorts and bend to take them off.

Ben and I stand with our clothes around our ankles. It's been many years since I shared a bedroom with my brother, but a quick glance confirms what I dimly remembered from the last time I saw him undressed. To my relief I see that we are both about the same size – now would not be a good time to find out that Ben had developed a phenomenally enormous knob. I try not to laugh, but I'm not the only one who finds the situation funny. The farcicality of our positions is not lost on Laura, and I see her struggle to conceal a smile.

But beneath the smile, there is lust, and I feel it too. It's strangely erotic to be standing, exposed, naked, in a pub that just moments ago had been teaming with people. Laura sashays towards us and my breath begins to deepen as my excitement grows. I glance at Ben and notice that his cock is already semi-erect. My own is also well on the way, and when Laura cups my balls in her hand to give them a gentle squeeze, it lifts further. Still holding me, she reaches over and fondles Ben, who lets out a little groan of pleasure.

'Both very nice. But I'd like to see how they shape up when they're properly hard.' Laura takes my right hand

and guides it to my cock. Then she does the same to Ben, who can't resist the rather perverted invitation to fondle himself in front of her, and sets about giving himself a full hard-on with gusto. I need it equally as badly, and have to follow suit. Kicking away my clothes, I move my legs a step apart and, encircling my cock in my hand, begin to wank. Suddenly, it's no longer a game, my arousal is very serious indeed. Laura watches, her pretty features set in a mask of sexual fixation. But when Ben lets out a deep, pre-orgasmic moan, Laura places a firm hand over us both.

'Not so fast,' she scolds. 'I don't know what you both taste like yet.'

She drops to her knees in front of Ben, and I watch her take him into her mouth. As she moves against him, my own cock aches unbearably, greedy for the same attention. As if Laura can read my thoughts, she moves back and turns Ben so that he faces me, the tip of one erection bouncing against the under-surface of the other. I'm slightly alarmed by the touch of another male body, but as Laura runs her tongue between our two pricks, all concerns are shoved aside by a growing need for any touch at all. I can't push either of them away. With consummate skill, Laura treats us both, her mouth moving seamlessly from one to the other. Our slippery cocks play in and out of her mouth, weaving together like charmed snakes.

Suddenly, it's too much. Almost roughly, I pull her away from me, just quickly enough to halt the orgasm that threatened.

'Shit,' I say, as I manage to catch my breath. 'That was nearly "game over" for me.'

Laura looks slightly put out. 'That was the idea.'

'Oh no. Surely you remember the school rules? It's the boys who are in charge.'

'That's right,' says Ben. 'It's our game.'

Taking her hand, I pull Laura onto her feet and, standing behind her, I turn her to face Ben. Slowly, teasing all three of us, I slide my hand over the planes of her stomach. Her belly is so soft and luscious, I can't wait to feel it pressed against mine. But I will take my time. I lift her T-shirt, sliding it over her naked breasts, exposing her to Ben, who nods in appreciation.

I think of how I had fantasised about doing this when I was at school. I picture myself as a self-conscious teenager, unbuttoning her school blouse, lowering the cups of a sensible white bra. And as she pushes her tits into my hands, I think of how I would have reacted then. I see myself, jammed against her back, my cock jerking as I come in premature spasms I can't control, and the thought gives me a perverse jolt of excitement.

I lean forwards to unzip her jeans and let them tumble down her thighs. Pink cotton panties follow and, finally, I can run a hand over her mound. She is shaved, and the plump little dome of flesh is perfectly smooth, her inner lips clearly visible between the voluptuous outer curves. I slip a finger between the folds, and find the hard bead of her clit.

She parts her legs as I begin to stroke her, her head slumping against me as her arousal builds. My brother gazes in captivation at her open sex. I can only imagine how her exposed core must look to Ben as I masturbate her.

But whatever he sees, he wants it. Ben moves towards her and, taking his cock between his fingers, guides himself to her. I slip my arms beneath hers and support her weight, while he lifts her hips and, in one smooth stroke, plunges into her willing body. He thrusts, and her breasts wobble in my hands.

I see a familiar expression on his face. He looks so like

me it's almost as if I am watching myself. His eyes close and for a moment I think he is going to climax. But like me, he is keen to delay the moment, and he pulls out before his orgasm overtakes him. He draws Laura to his chest, and her bottom pokes towards me in a clear invitation. I hear her mutter: 'Fuck me too, Luke,' and I don't need to be asked again. Sinking to the floor, I turn her around and pull her onto me to take my turn.

Deliciously wet from already being fucked, she is easy to enter, and I slip inside her in a single movement. For a while, she rides me, and I let her use me as she wishes. Above my face, her large breasts hang over me, her hair, now yanked from its ponytail, trails across my chest.

Ben is silent, but he's obviously enjoying the spectacle. Kneeling beside us on the floor, his eyes flick from her to me, as he slowly strokes himself. And being watched is deeply dirty. I've never regarded myself as an exhibitionist, but now I love the thought of him seeing my prick up a woman. I love the thought of him watching her cunt engulf me. I want him to watch me come. But Ben can watch no more.

'Why make do with just one of the best-looking brothers in the school when you can have us both,' he whispers. Squatting down beside our conjoined bodies, Ben slips his fingers between us, rubbing the wetness of sex across his fingers. Gently pushing Laura down closer to my chest, he smears her juices over her exposed bottom, making her gasp as he sweeps over her. I feel his fingers skim me as they dip deep into the crevice, and my pulse surges as I realise what's going to happen.

Part of me wants to stop him – to play the big brother and tell him not to be so revolting. But a stronger part of me wants him to go on. I say nothing.

Ben straddles my legs and the thick dark hairs on his thighs brush against me as he lowers himself. Laura and

I are still as we wait for what he is going to do. With his callused hands on her hips, he eases her back towards his body. He takes his erection into his hand and his face creases, as if his own touch is almost too much to bear. Still deep inside her, I feel his cock nudge delicately at the entrance of her anus. He nudges again and Laura flinches slightly as he forces her to open. I reach up to stroke her hair, but she doesn't need my reassurance. Her eyes blaze with a fever of want. She will not stop him. Laura stares down at me, her lips pursed in concentration as slowly he enters her.

Ben comes closer and the scent and the sweat of our three bodies mingle as we form one united whole. Finally the process is complete, and Laura dares to move. She sways towards me, and then back onto him, rocking with increasing confidence as she lets herself give way to the pleasure. Ben draws himself closer still and reaches round to lock her in a loving embrace, his large hands covering her bouncing breasts. I stretch up to join the caress, my fingers entwining with his as we both fondle her generous flesh. She enjoys the touch and she arches forwards, her erect nipples pushing through Ben's fingers to meet my palms.

Ben's gentleness surprises me. Clinched in a union that would shock many, he keeps the mood sensual. He kisses her back, her neck, her shoulders; soothes her with tender words. I respond too, and he stills the animal in me that wants to tear into Laura and bring myself to the orgasm for which my senses are screaming. I force myself to ignore the rising need and concentrate on Laura.

When I move my hands down her body and part the soft flesh of her sex she sighs and spreads her thighs further to allow me to finger her clit. There is no longer a part of her that can escape our crusade for her pleasure.

Her heaving chest and flushed skin leave me in no doubt that she is enjoying it. I carry on teasing her, until her breath deepens to a hoarse rasp. She abandons herself, her body softening against mine, as her control seeps away. Then with a few final thrusts of her hips, she pushes herself into her climax, and her whole body is convulsed as she orgasms on us.

And now I can let go. I grit my teeth as my own pleasure mounts. My head whirls with lurid images of my youth. Of pert young bottoms barely covered by short skirts, of my first girlfriend's inexperienced hands on my cock. Then I wonder how I've changed from the innocent boy whose idea of filth was a peek of Laura's nipple, into a depraved man who can share her with his own brother.

And the thought of Ben's penis so close to mine as we both enjoy the same woman is finally too much. I feel him shudder as he starts to come. And I can only join him. Our groans resonate in the empty bar, as together, we fill her.

Dawn is breaking when I'm roused from sleep by a slow and expert blow job. Laura's mouth is sliding up and down the length of my very stiff cock. She is wet, and firm around me, her pace steady but relentless. I stretch against comfortable cotton sheets and give way to the ministrations of her talented mouth.

'Good morning,' I just about manage to mutter. I come even before I'm fully awake.

After I have returned the favour, she lies next to me and we share a cigarette. Beside us, Ben sleeps, snoring softly.

'Go back to her,' she says.

'Who?'

'Your girl. Cassandra, is it?' It's only then that I remember the conversation of the previous night. We had all ended up in Laura's comfortable Victorian bed, but Ben had fallen asleep, leaving me alone with Laura and a bottle of cheap whisky. I had then given Laura an alcohol-sodden version of the story of my relationship with Cassandra. My account had been detailed. Really, horribly detailed.

'Oh God,' I say, covering my eyes with the back of my arm. 'I must have been so dull.'

'You were. But the shag afterwards made up for it.' Snatching the cigarette from my fingers, Laura takes a puff, and is suddenly serious.

'But you must go back to her, Luke. Take it from one who knows. When it's the real thing, you should hang on to it with all your strength. Being in love isn't like catching a bus. There may not be another one along later.' Then she laughs. 'Anyway you have to go back to her. I can't let you bore the tits off another girl like you did me last night.'

I can't think of a reply, so I fuck her again. Soundly.

14

Cassandra's Story

William has planned a party. A grand one. He had told me I was the only woman he would marry, but as I'd already turned him down on numerous occasions, William had given up hope of being a dashing groom. And as Luke wasn't likely to propose, he was never going to be a blushing bride either. Cheated of the wedding of which he had always dreamed, he had decided that an obscenely lavish birthday bash would have to do instead.

Tonight, as I drive towards William's beautiful house, I see a uniformed attendant waving at me, and I slow to a halt.

'May I park your car for you, miss?' the attendant asks. I step out of the car and hand over my keys.

The outside of the manor is illuminated by banks of tiny candle flames. They rise in a twinkling arch to the front door. As I walk up the steps, the doors are opened by another pair of liveried staff and I walk into William's marbled entrance hall. I pause to help myself to a glass of champagne and then I'm lured by the sound of a band into a large ballroom which is already crowded with people.

There are many faces I know at the party. The usual mix of earnest politicians and cynical journalists: two species that are rarely friends but always have plenty to say to each other. I drift from one group to another, finding it hard to concentrate on any one conversation.

Then I see him, standing alone at the edge of the room. Sipping champagne, he watches me closely over the rim of his glass. I have only ever seen him in casual clothes or the uniform that is his business dress, and I half expected him to appear out of place and gauche at a black-tie event.

But in his superbly tailored suit Luke looks fantastic. Surrounded by a monochrome sea of men in evening dress, he stands out like a Rembrandt in a village art society exhibition. His hair, dazzlingly blond against his dark jacket, is slicked back from his face, drawing attention to his perfectly chiselled features. His eyes sparkle dangerously in the candlelight. The exuberant Oxbridge political brigade often opt for the loudest, brightest ties, but he wears plain black, beautifully tied over a crisp, white wing-collared shirt. He looks like an expensively wrapped present, and I long to tear off the packaging and get to the goodies inside.

His arrival has not passed unnoticed, and I see little huddles of party aficionados nudging and nodding to each other as the news spreads. Luke has not been seen since the whirlwind round of interviews that followed his arrest. He has chosen a highly public forum to make his reappearance.

He sees me looking at him, but without acknowledging me, turns his back and begins to walk away. I watch him grab another glass from a passing waiter and leave the room. Well, fuck you, Mister Luke Weston.

Later in the evening, as the party warms up, I'm on my way to the loo when I bump into William. A little more than slightly drunk, his tie is coming undone and his eyes are crossing slightly. He catches hold of my arm and drags me onto the dance floor.

'Luke still pissed off at you I see.'

'Not as pissed off as I am at him.' I put my arms around William's waist, enjoying the feel of his big, comfortable body. 'Oh, William. Why are all the nice blokes gay?'

William laughs. 'I think you'll find all the nice blokes are straight.'

I look out through French windows onto the acres of gardens, woodlands and fields, picturing generations of little De Courcy children frolicking through the grounds, the history of the great family and the magnificent estate inexorably linked.

'This is a wonderful house, William. How long has your family lived here?'

'I've been here nearly five years.'

I'm confused. 'But I assumed the De Courcys had owned Temworth for centuries.'

'Oh no. The family pile's in Norfolk. I'm the second son, so big bro inherited the estate along with the fancy title. I just borrow this place. From Luke.'

I gasp. 'This is Luke's house?'

'Yes.'

I look around in disbelief. I do a quick mental calculation – the fabulous house, the farmland, the woods, the stables – it adds up to a fortune. 'Luke owns all this?'

'Yes. Everything. Everything from the Amigoni portrait on the landing to the Zola first editions in the library.'

'Luke really is –'

'Loaded?'

'Yes.'

'Oh believe me, Cassandra, Luke's worth millions.'

I consider asking more, but then I decide it's too late. I really don't want to know.

We are joined by Camilla, who whisks William out of my arms and into a secluded corner. She obviously does not know that she's barking up a very wrong tree, and I'm amused to think that tonight even Camilla is not destined to pull.

On the other side of the dance floor, I spot Toby, who is clearly not letting his terrible dancing ability spoil his enjoyment. His party mood is infectious and, emboldened by slightly too much champagne, I join him, dancing with wild abandon. The band is singing one of my favourite Abba songs and, a bit of a Dancing Queen myself, I let rip, my body taking up the beat of the music. I quickly gain a small audience of appreciative men at the edge of the dance floor. I lift my arms so that my dress rises to flash a hint of thigh and swing my hips provocatively.

Seeing the men watching me with growing interest, I decide I'll give them a bit more of a show, and I vamp it up, bumping and grinding like a pole-dancer.

'Go on, Cas,' shouts one. 'Let's see what you've got.'

I'm joined by three guys I vaguely recognise from party HQ. They take it in turns to whirl me round, sending me spinning from one to the other. As I dance briefly with each one, they try to make the most of the contact, pawing me and grabbing at me with eager hands. Their touch thrills me.

Then I feel a firmer grip on my hips and I turn around to see a very drunk Simon behind me. He thrusts his groin against my bottom, rubbing himself like an excited dog. I laugh as he slips the thin straps of my dress down onto the tops of my arms, and my right nipple pops out over the top of the black velvet. Pulling the dress back up, I carry on dancing, but he yanks once more. This time, he's more successful, and the dress comes right down to my waist, leaving both breasts fully exposed. Struggling back into the bodice, I put out my hands as Simon advances again.

'No,' I say. But Simon is not easily deterred. He grabs me by my hands and pulls me towards him. His moist lips slobber at my neckline.

What comes after this passes in something of a blur, and it is a while before I realise what is happening. One minute, Simon is dancing. The next, someone pulls him off me and punches him hard in the face. Simon reels across the dance floor to crash through a table of unsuspecting guests.

'Young and sweet only seventeen,' sings our Swedish sound-a-like into a deathly silence.

'She said "no".' Everyone turns to look at Luke. He stands alone in the middle of the dance floor. Slowly, he clenches and then unclenches his fists.

Simon is hauled to his feet by a group of men who had been sitting at the wrecked table, and for a moment he looks as if he is going to try and hit Luke back. But something in Luke's expression must have stopped him. Grumbling about some people not being able to take a joke, he shambles away.

As quickly as it had begun the incident is over. A team of caterers descends to clear up the mess, the babble of conversation resumes. The band picks up where it had left off and people start to dance again.

Embarrassed by the scene, still dazed and confused, I can't move. I stand helpless while the party carries on around me. But then someone grabs me by the elbow and propels me back to the dance floor. I crane round to see who it is. Luke. He pushes me into the middle of the crowd. He's still shaking with rage, but, holding me tightly, he begins to dance, forcing me to follow his unsteady rhythm.

The band, doubtless irritated at having their music interrupted, launches into 'Jealous Guy'. The sarcasm is lost on Luke. He stares down at me, his eyes dark with a fury that scares me.

'Satisfied?' he hisses.

'What do you mean?' I ask.

'Did you get the reaction you wanted?'

On the other side of the room, I can see Simon. Safely surrounded by a group of party staff who would readily stop him from attacking Luke, he's making noisy threats about teaching 'that git Weston' a lesson.

'I wasn't trying to get any sort of a reaction.' I meet Luke's gaze, trying to capture some of my usual insouciance.

'Oh, come on, Cassandra. Don't act the innocent. Men can't help getting turned on when a woman puts on a performance like that and you know it. You were a bloody disgrace.'

In his arms, I can feel his hard, fit body beneath his suit.

'Asking for it, was I? Save your Neanderthal sexual politics for someone else, Luke. I was dancing. That's all.'

His fingers on the tops of my arms press deeper into my flesh.

'You weren't dancing. You were putting on a wank show.'

'Don't be disgusting.'

I flinch as he tightens his grip further still.

'Disgusting?' He lets go of my arms and puts his hands on my bottom to jam my body against his. He holds me in a vice-like grip and as we dance, he glares down at me with something like hate. I'm startled, but strangely curious. What have I done to provoke him so? 'But you like turning men on like that. You love giving them something to think about while they jerk off.'

'No,' I snap back. 'No, I bloody don't.'

He pushes one long leg between mine, forcing my thighs slightly apart. His hands press even more firmly against my bottom now. Through my dress, the pressure of his leg against my pubis is highly pleasurable. I curse my body for its betrayal. He's being so vile to me, but I can't stop myself from being aroused by the feel of him so tight against me.

'Are you sure?' he asks.

'Yes!'

He moves his lips close to my ear as he whispers: 'Then why has young Toby got a pile of dirty pictures of you and a pair of your panties in his filing drawer?'

Now my shock is real.

'How do you know about those?'

'I found them when he was moving offices last month.' He's taking delight in my discomfort.

'My God. Poor Toby. What did you do with them?'

'I put them back where they were. I quite fancied jerking over them myself. But they were already rather ... sticky.' The thought of them sharing the pictures of me and both masturbating with my knickers makes my head spin with lust.

As more couples come onto the floor, we're being jostled slightly now, but neither of us takes notice. I let the pulse of the music wash over me, enjoying the sensation of his body rocking with mine. He moves me, slowly, gently up and down his leg. Almost in spite of my will, my hips begin to sway and I rub myself against him. I look up into his eyes, and I can see that he knows what is happening to me. But I can't help myself. I can do nothing but respond.

'Anyway,' he continues, 'why should I wank over a picture of you when I can just help myself to the real thing?'

Now he's going too far. How dare he assume so much.

'You conceited bastard. Don't be so sure.'

'It's not conceit. It's the truth and you know it, don't you?'

He pushes one hand between our bodies and covers my left breast with his palm. Jerking up my head, I look into his eyes, pleading silently as he moves his hand, rotating it slowly against my nipple. It's so good. I can feel the liquid heat of arousal sweeping me slowly, but inevitably onwards.

'Don't you, Cassandra?' he asks again. I can say nothing. He bends to nibble the lobe of my ear, and I try not to think about how nice his lips feel against me. I turn my head away, but he pulls me back. He is not rough, but there is an insistence in his touch. I have to give in.

He slides his hand down and I feel him tugging at the hem of my dress. Slowly, he pulls it up, and I sigh into his jacket as I feel the velvet inching up my stocking-clad thighs. The skirt is full, and he lifts the front without it rising at the back and revealing my bottom.

Now I can feel his hand brushing against my lace panties. He's teasing me beyond endurance. Taut with excitement, I can't contain a soft whimper as I feel his fingers curl and he slips one, then two, inside my knickers, easing the frail fabric away from my body. I push against him, unable to bare the soft, tormenting caresses, urging him to give me more. As if he can read my mind, he straightens his hand and drags his fingers between my legs, at last giving my desperate clit the contact it needs. Forwards and backwards, forceful, mechanical – his hand becomes the most important thing ever. Terrified that I will betray us both, I don't dare to take my eyes from his as his hand works.

I feel it building – that delicious, demanding congestion. The need for relief. But it has to stop. I can't let go

here, surrounded by people. I try to speak. 'Luke, I ...
Please. I can't.'

But he ignores me, and I feel him push one finger
deep inside me.

Before I can stop myself I cry out – an irrepressible
squeal that makes the couples dancing around us stop
and stare.

'Are you all right, love?' A tall man who is dancing
with a flashy blonde is looking at me with concern.
Before I can speak, Luke pinches my bottom with his
other hand, turning his fingers into my flesh in a silent
warning.

'Yes, I'm fine,' I say, my voice surprisingly calm. 'I
stubbed my toe.'

Carried away by music and alcohol, the other dancers
quickly forget the outburst, and soon we are being
ignored once more.

Luke has not taken his hand out of my panties, and
he goes on casually caressing me until all thoughts of
stopping him fade. Now greedy with lust, I push my hips
towards him, begging for more. Sliding his thumb over
my bud, he slips his finger into me again. I feel him
reach high up inside me, pause, and then slide down
again, raking against me as he withdraws. Once, twice,
three times. I let my head fall against his chest.

Now I want to climax in his arms on a crowded dance
floor and it doesn't matter who can see what he's doing
to me. I like the thought of him lifting my dress right up
so that the pale flesh above my stocking-tops can be
seen. I like the thought of everyone's eyes on my backside. I don't care about anything but my urgent need to
orgasm. I'm lost to the pleasure that is welling deep
inside me and, clinging to him, I turn my face into his
shirt to wait for the climax that I know is so close.

My orgasm, when it hits, tightens my chest and

makes my pulse surge. I bite into my own hand to stop myself from screaming out as waves of pleasure sweep through me.

Weakened by the force of my climax, my legs buckle slightly, and my breath comes in short gasps. But Luke has no sympathy. Taking hold of a handful of my hair, he pulls my head up and forces me to look at his cold, impassive face.

'You see,' he whispers. 'I can help myself. Any time I want.'

I can't argue.

We continue to dance, our feet shuffling to a rhythm that bares no relationship to the music. As he holds me close, I can feel his cock, firm and warm, against the flesh of my stomach. His arousal intrigues me. Clearly he's not as unaffected as his spiteful words would have me believe. I look deep into his eyes, challenging him to make the next move.

But he won't let me see any weakness. Keen to maintain the upper ground, he grabs my wrist and drags me, stumbling behind him through an open pair of French windows. The cool of the night air is refreshing after the stuffy heat inside, and I'm grateful to be out in the open.

We're standing on a wide terrace. A wrought-iron balustrade edges the paved area, and beyond it, Luke's beautiful gardens slope away into the darkness. Luke leads me to the far side of the terrace and, for a moment, he stands looking out into the black night, a silent, brooding presence beside me. Then he takes my hand and guides it to the front of his trousers. Beneath the fine fabric, his prick thrusts against my fingers.

'Get it out,' he commands, his voice husky and low.

I look over his shoulder to the ballroom only yards behind us. 'But someone will see,' I protest.

'Just do it,' he says and presses my fingers into him more tightly.

With our backs to the party, we will look as if we are chatting innocently. But the thought that we could be discovered at any second thrills me, and amazingly I feel my sex spasm with the first pangs of renewed desire. Ignoring the warnings that pound in my head, I move my fingers to the top of his zip.

The position is awkward, and I can only undo the zip slowly, but as I inch it down, the teasingly slow progress seems to heighten his excitement further and I hear him suck in his breath through his teeth. A tiny twitch plays on his lips as he fights for control. He leans forwards and grabs the balustrade, his knuckles white and taut. His whole body is so tense, he looks as if he'll shatter into fragments at the slightest touch.

His cock is already so hard it takes me a while to untangle it from his boxer shorts, but finally it springs free, almost leaping into my hand. I run my fingernails up the length of him, letting the shiny surface slip and then catch against his moist skin.

'Go on,' he says urgently, 'wank me.'

I take him into my hand and begin to caress him, letting the ends of my fingers swirl around the tip of his cock with each stroke. That first night in his hotel room I had learned from his sighs of pleasure and encouraging moans how he liked to be touched. Later, when he had let me watch him doing it himself, I'd noted how he held himself, how he slowed slightly before he came. And now I mimic his own movements, my hand sweeping over him at exactly the tempo and pressure he prefers. I lean over to fondle his balls with my other hand, stroking and lifting them up against the base of his prick.

'Oh, that's good, Cas.' The words come in a rush, and I realise he had been holding his breath. My hand tightens around his cock, but by now he's so stiff that my fingers make almost no impression on his iron-hard flesh. His eyes are closed in concentration as he struggles to compose himself. I can tell that he wants to thrust into my hand – the necessity of keeping still is tantamount to torture.

I work quickly now, knowing that he's close. With the heightened awareness that comes with sexual arousal I can hear his every breath, hear the rustle of fabric as my hand brushes against the front of his trousers. I can smell his need.

Then, a low moan escapes from deep within his chest and he begins to shudder. 'Christ,' he mutters. 'I'm coming.'

I look down as the first arch of semen bursts from him to splash down onto the garden below. His orgasm goes on and on, spurt after spurt cascading through my hands.

When it's over, he stands for a moment, clinging to the balustrade, breathing hard. Then he straightens his shoulders, pushes his cock back inside his trousers and does up his flies.

Another voice breaks into my oh so private thoughts. 'Luke! Hey, Luke.'

From the doorway of the ballroom, Camilla is waving frantically.

'Shit,' says Luke. His fingers close around mine in a painfully strong grip. 'Let's go.'

When I start to protest he gives me a small shove towards the edge of the terrace. Roughly twisting my arm up my back, he marches me down a flight of stone steps into the garden.

'Luke, where are you taking –'

'Be quiet.' To silence me, he covers my mouth with his hand. His orgasm has done nothing to soothe him, and I can still feel the tension in his touch.

He walks too quickly and, in my high heels, I can't keep up with him. Impatient, he pulls me to him and I slump against his chest. With one strong arm locked around my waist, he half carries, half pushes me across a series of lawns towards the stables.

I feel myself break into a sweat of terror. I want to shout out, but something stops me. I'm genuinely scared, but somehow the fear only serves to heighten my rising excitement. I want to go wherever he's taking me.

Eventually we arrive at the stable buildings. The last time I had seen the beautiful red-brick courtyard and the elegant horses that now look out from the smart loose boxes I had believed it all belonged to William, but Luke's clearly on very familiar territory. He bustles me towards a small wooden doorway and, with one hand still clasped around mine, he reaches into his jacket pocket for a set of keys. He unlocks the door and goes to push me inside, but I resist. I still haven't been to the loo since William had caught me, and now I'm bursting. It seems ridiculous to have to ask his permission, but I have no choice.

'Luke, I have to go to the loo.'

'No. I'm not letting you out of my sight.'

'Please.'

'I said no. I'm not finished with you yet.'

'Please Luke. I won't try to get away. But I really need to pee.'

'Go there then,' he says, gesturing towards a darkened corner of the yard.

'I can't! Not with you here.'

'You'll have to wait then.' And he turns back to the door. But now I'm desperate to go.

'OK, stay there. And please don't look.' To my dismay, he turns and looks straight at me. He never takes his eyes from me as I lift my dress, pull my panties down to my ankles and squat. He simply leans against the door, folds his arms over his chest and waits. But I have to do it. Even with him watching me. I look down and watch the warm puddle forming at my feet.

'Very nice,' he says, as I finally stand up and pull up my underwear. Burning with embarrassment, I can't meet his eye. I'm racked with shame at what I've just done in front of him. I'm mortified that he had apparently enjoyed watching me do it – I've always dismissed men who got their kicks from that kind of thing as total perverts. But I'm even more ashamed that I had enjoyed him watching me.

I remember how the thought of Luke watching Camilla on the loo had disgusted me. Now he had watched me and it was indeed disgusting. Disgusting and I want to do it again. I'm terrified by just how disgusting I'm prepared to be.

But Luke clearly is not troubled by such fears and, without missing a beat, he shoves me into the blackened room. The dark frightens me.

'Please,' I say weakly. 'I'll scream. If I call out, there'll be someone here in a second.' I don't know if he is looking at me.

'Go on then.' His voice comes from the darkness.

I say nothing.

'I said go on then.'

Still I remain silent.

'You don't want to do you?'

'No.' The humiliation of my confession makes me blush.

'OK, so stop being such a silly girl, and just do what you're told.'

He flicks on a light, and I cover my face with my hands as the brightness stings my unaccustomed eyes.

'I'm sorry,' he says. 'But I need to be able to see.' Briefly, he turns his back on me, and I hear him slide two heavy bolts across the door.

As I grow used to the light, I see that we're in a tack room. Around the walls are racks of gleaming saddles and bridles. Beside the door, a wooden stand supports a row of plush horse blankets, each embroidered with the name 'Weston'. In one corner, a deep bucket holds a collection of leather-bound whips. They are all different lengths: long ones for schooling, shorter ones for racing. I shudder as Luke crosses over to the whips, and picks one out – a long lunging whip with a vicious tail. For a moment, he examines it, running it through his hands, tapping it lightly against his palm. Used to training horses, he handles it capably and, when he flips the end into a precise loop, I understand the threat.

'Luke? What are you doing?' I don't need to ask the question. It's perfectly obvious.

'If you're going to behave like a tart, I might as well treat you like one.' His words send a shiver of lust through me. I want to be treated like a tart.

But he isn't going to touch me again yet. He backs away from me and sits down on a rug box at the edge of the room. The whip rests in his lap. He reaches for his cigarettes. As he lights up he watches me carefully, squinting slightly through the smoke. He runs his eyes slowly up and down my body assessing me the way a horseman judges a prized animal. Evaluating me like a client choosing a whore. Choose me, my fantasy tells me. Choose me. Pay for me. Do what you want with me. Standing in the middle of the room, I shudder with suppressed longing.

Then, as he studies me, a flicker of disapproval crosses his otherwise immobile features.

'Come here,' he orders. Not daring to refuse, I cross the tack room to stand in front of him.

'What is it?' I ask, suddenly worried that something displeased him.

'That lipstick. I don't like it,' he replies. And reaching up, he smears away my make-up with his thumb. It is an action that normally would have made me want to slap his arrogant face, but now I have to accept that Luke can do anything he wants to me – anything at all.

'That's better,' he says. 'Now. I want my own private show. You enjoyed dancing for all those poor sods earlier, now you can dance for me.'

I hesitate, feeling slightly foolish.

'Come on, Cas. Make me want to wank myself. We've already agreed you like it. Make me want to get it out and jerk off right now.' I cringe at his deliberately crude words. He sees my discomfort but he won't stop. 'Go on. Make me hard. Make me so hard it hurts.'

'I can't. I –'

'Dance,' he commands. But this time he uses a tone that I have not heard before – a tone that drives any thoughts of arguing with him from my mind. I see his fingers stray towards the whip on his lap. Not wanting to provoke him further, I begin to dance, my body swaying to the feint beat that drifts from the party.

But he his right – I do like it. As I circle my hips and run my hands down my body, I know that I had wanted to turn those men on. I do like the thought of them dashing away from the dance floor to find a deserted part of the gardens and masturbating into the bushes, as I had just masturbated Luke.

And I want to turn Luke on too. As I dance, he watches me through narrowed eyes, his face impassive. I move towards him and shimmy my shoulders. He watches my breasts shaking just inches from his face, but to my frustration he makes no move to touch me. My bottom sways, my dress inching up my thighs once more. But it's me who is aroused by my little lap-dancing act. He merely looks at me with cool detachment.

He finishes his cigarette and drops the butt onto the floor, grinding it out beneath his foot.

'Enough,' he says and I stop dancing and stand still, waiting.

'Right.' He lifts the whip and slowly runs the tip down the front of my body. I freeze as he traces the hem of my skirt, letting the whip lift the edge of the heavy fabric.

'Now, take off your clothes.'

Crossing my arms across my chest, I hurriedly reach down to pull off my dress. But he objects.

'No. Not so fast.'

I feel the whip brush against the top of my thigh. It's not a punishment – just a reminder.

'I want you to take your time. Lift it up slowly.' I take hold of the bottom of my dress again, and lift it slightly so that he would just be able to see the top of my stockings.

'More,' he commands. Meekly, I obey, raising my skirt higher so that a triangle of my panties will show.

'How thoughtful – the party colour,' he says, smiling for the first time. 'Good girl.'

I'm ridiculously glad that I've pleased him at last.

'Now, pull them to one side.'

I do so and, as my hand brushes against my mound, I can't help sliding a finger into the hot, damp crease. Almost instantly, I feel the whip crack against my hand, knocking it away, a silent but clear warning.

'Not yet,' he orders. 'When I say. Now. Try again.'

This time I only do what he tells me, and I stand

perfectly still with my panties pulled to one side, allowing him a full view of my exposed sex.

'OK, now turn around.'

Dropping my dress again, I turn my back to him and stand motionless, awaiting his next command.

'Now take off your shoes.' Without hesitating, I bend over to undo the buckles on my strappy high heels. But then he changes his mind and I hear him say: 'No, stop.'

Still doubled over, I freeze again. With a deft flick of the whip, he flips my dress up over my hips.

'That's good. Now pull down your knickers.'

I need no encouragement. I want nothing more than to expose myself to him. Pushing my thumbs into the thin strips of lace at my hips, I ease the fabric down over my bottom. I feel it slide, deliciously tight over my enflamed body. I feel the night air chill the wet, split lips of my sex.

'Very nice, now back up again.'

No, look at me. For Christ's sake look at me. But I dare not disobey.

'Fine,' he says softly. 'Now pull them right down and over your shoes. And give them to me.'

I slide the panties down my legs and step out of them. Then I bob down to pick up the scrap of lace and hand it to him.

'That's bad,' he says, his tone disapproving as he fingers the fabric. 'They're very, very wet.'

'I'm sorry.' The words are out of my mouth before I can stop myself.

'I know you are, sweetheart. But you know I have to punish you. Pull down your dress.'

I wriggle my arms out of my dress, and push it down to my hips, revealing my tits.

'Now take it off.'

I slip out of the dress and stand almost naked in front of him. His eyes are on my breasts, and I can't help lifting my shoulders so that they jut slightly towards him. They hold his attention and, for the first time, I see a flash of longing in his eyes.

'Touch them,' he says.

As he orders me, I run my hands over my nipples which both soothes and fuels the ache.

'Very good,' he whispers. He sounds so calm, but when he shifts slightly I look down and notice his erection, pushing up to distort the cut of his trousers. I'm glad, but I feel fear more than triumph. 'Now. Go on.'

My hands continue their lazy but delicious exploration of my breasts. 'What do you mean?'

'Carry on with the show.' I keep my expression blank. 'I want to watch you touch yourself between your legs.'

'No.' I won't let him know how much I want to masturbate.

He almost laughs. 'Don't come the prim bitch with me, Cas. You look so bloody randy – it's obvious you want to.'

It's true. I've never felt so desperate to frig myself. 'No I don't.' I'm finding it increasingly hard to speak.

'You do, Cas.' His voice is so quiet, but I hear him clearly enough. 'You want to stand there in front of me, open that pretty little pussy of yours and rub yourself off.'

'I can't,' I wail miserably.

'You can. You will.'

There is a set to his jaw, and the malice in his tone alarms me. I have to do what he bids. My hands creep down my belly and to my sex, and I wank myself, giving my clit a few small jerks. But as I rub, my need for relief overwhelms my sense of embarrassment. I feel his eyes on me, but I'm beyond caring about the indignity of my position. I rub harder, faster. My lids flutter closed. I'm on the verge of coming when he changes his mind again. The whip grazes against my hands, and I dare not carry on.

'Not yet,' he whispers.

Taking his time, he stands up and crosses the room. I watch, gulping air in an attempt to still my racing pulse, as he picks up a bridle and begins to undo the buckles with expert fingers. Running a length of rein in his hands, he orders me to hold out my arms. Helpless with desire, I obey. Without a word, he winds the soft, supple leather around my wrists and lashes the other end to a saddle rack in the middle of the room. I'm not held tightly and I could wriggle out. But nothing in the world will tempt me to do so.

Then, suddenly, we're both stilled as we hear a snatch of conversation outside. We are obviously not the only ones who have sought a quiet corner of Luke's estate.

I shiver. I look at Luke and wonder if he will try to cover my mouth again. I needn't have worried. He listens to the murmur of voices with his head lowered as if deep in thought. But when he looks up again, there's no concern on his face. He knows he holds me captive in more ways than one. He's standing behind me now. I can feel his breath, hot against my neck.

'Go on, call out, Cas,' he whispers. 'Just shout.'

The sound of laughter outside rises above his words. Casually, Luke runs a finger over my dry lips, daring me to cry for help. But I can't speak.

'They're only yards away,' murmurs Luke. 'They can save you.'

Still I say nothing. He understands me too well. Standing bound and naked but for my shoes and stockings, there's nothing I can do. I twist around to look up at him, my eyes widening in terror. I'm not frightened that he'll go on. I'm frightened that he'll stop.

And then it's too late. Whatever chance I could have taken passes, and we hear the crunch of gravel as who-ever is outside walks away.

Luke's voice breaks into the silence. 'What now, Cas?'

'I don't know.'

He smiles. He knows he has won the cruel game he's forcing me to play. 'Don't you? I think you do.' He pauses and I wait. 'I'm going to hurt you.'

There's a question in his voice. I lower my chin in a hint of a nod.

I hear him step back from me. I hear him draw in his breath. Then I feel the first sting as the whip cuts across my bare bottom. It's no more than a tap, but still the shock of the blow makes me gasp.

He hits me again, just hard enough to send a bolt of new, but delicious sensations coursing through my body. Now I do cry out, a single grunt as flames of pain spread from my smarting backside, and lust rips through my abdomen. As smack after smack connects with my flesh, I feel myself spinning on an unknown plane. But I'm certain of one thing – if he carries on, I'll soon climax.

'Luke!' I call his name. Please stop. Please go on. I don't know what I want.

But he does stop, and there's a light clatter as the whip drops from his hands and hits the floor. I hear a whimper and, for a brief moment, I'm unsure which one of us made the noise. But it was him. Turning my head, I see him staring down at the hand that had held the whip, an expression of incredulity etching his features. There's a fine line between the erotic and the obscene – a pivotal point where the arousing revolts. I wonder how close his behaviour is taking him to his own personal boundary.

Then with a slight shake of his head, he takes a deep breath, and appears to collect himself again. He walks back towards me and stands behind me. He's so close to me, I can feel his jacket brush against my naked back. I stand still, waiting for his touch.

I look down as he reaches around my body and rubs his palms across my nipples. The contrast of his golden skin against the alabaster whiteness of my own is compelling. The feel of his hands on me at last is wonderful. I shudder with relief and pleasure.

I almost faint with lust as slowly, tantalisingly, he smoothes his hand over my hips and between my legs, running one finger the length of my clit. I had thought he would handle me roughly. It would have been easier to control myself if he had. But he touches me softly, almost reverentially. The counterpoint between the harsh bite of the whip and his tender touch now is powerful and again I have to fight to stop myself from coming.

He knows exactly what to do to make me tremble. With languid precision he swirls one finger around the fevered entrance to my sex. I can't stop my muscles clenching against him as he moves backwards and I feel the wet tip of that finger pressing against my anus. He hardly moves but merely keeps up the pressure so that slowly, shamefully, my body draws him inside. He tickles me softly, and my body is suffused with joy so strong it is almost unsupportable. There is embarrassment, but overlying it pleasure of an intensity I have never experienced before.

'You see. I can help myself,' he whispers. 'To every tiny bit of you.'

'No,' I cry.

Then the cry turns to a whimper of frustration as he takes his hand away again.

'What's the matter, Cas? Tell me. Tell me what you want.'

'No.' I won't beg him.

Behind me, I hear him unzip his flies. I try to twist around again and, although I can't see him, I can tell by the slightest catch of his breath that he's holding his cock in his hand. He's standing so close to me now that I can feel his knuckles against my bottom as he slowly strokes himself.

'Is this it? Is this what you want?'

I feel him draw his cock between my legs, and, in total desperation, I try to push against him as he slides the tip slowly from my clit, across the lips of my sex and then up the crease of my bottom.

'Yes,' I say, my voice thin and frail.

'Look at you. You're panting for it, aren't you?'

'Yes.'

He's resting it against me now, its tip nudging at the entrance of my sex. I'm wet and open, but he holds himself just far enough away to stop me being able to grind against him and take him inside me. I'm shaking, my whole body shuddering with frustration and need. I have never been so excited.

'Ask me then.' His voice is uneven and, when he places a hand on my hip to steady me, I feel him tremble. For the first time I realise he is just as turned on, just as out of control, as I am.

'Please, Luke.' I can't stop myself. I will beg, plead – anything to make him give me what want. 'Please. Please fuck me.'

At last, inch by delicious inch, he slides into me and, as he begins to thrust slowly, I start to cry – tears of joy and relief flooding down my cheeks.

With his arm around my waist, he reaches down and strokes my clit, his fingers floating over me. He rubs me skilfully, carefully. Pushing my bottom back towards him, I work myself up and down the wonderful length of him. I'm so very close now.

Then he speaks. 'Cassandra,' he whispers. 'I want...' He trails off, choked with his own passion.

'What?' I ask. 'What do you want?'

He changes pace, and I feel him slow and finally take his cock out of me. I try to turn around, but I can't see what he's doing. Then, with a strange swirling mixture of delight and fear, I feel his cock pressing hesitantly against my anus.

'Cas?' he says in a voice thick with longing.

I want him to have whatever he wants. I want him to be selfish. He is right. Every bit of me is his. It is the dirtiest thing I can imagine. And I want it. 'Yes,' I say simply, giving him all the affirmation he needs.

With masterful care, he pushes gently against me until I feel my body yield. Slippery with my juices, he penetrates me easily, and a brief pain soon gives way to sensations so pleasurable that I feel dizzy. I squirm against him, trying to take more of him into me, trying to feel more of him. Trying to end it. Trying to do all that I can to make this bliss last.

Then, as he pushes one finger deep into my sex, I feel myself rise to the beginning of my orgasm. He has taken me so high I wonder if I will survive, and I struggle to fight the force of the climax that threatens to devastate me. But when his other hand reaches around me again to flutter against my clit, I can contain it no longer. Every nerve in my body is tuned to his touch, and I can respond to nothing but the raw call of sex.

'Oh, Luke,' I cry. 'What are you doing to me?'

My breath rattles in my chest as I come crashing

down into my climax. I yell. Telling him I hate him. Telling him I love him. I contract against him, the whole of my sex and anus rippling around his hands and his cock. I hear nothing, see nothing. I feel nothing but the blessed relief. Powerful spasms convulse my whole body, and hot pleasure explodes in my head.

When my senses return, I hear him mutter my name. I had given no thought to his own fight, but now I become aware of the desire that shakes him once more. His restraint has been astonishing – his self-control almost super-human and I feel a surge of admiration for his selflessness. He has held back for so long, but now, like the splitting of a hardened dam, he is breaking. And his wait will make the release all more powerful.

As my climax fades, his begins. He gasps and bends over me, racked with ecstasy. Heedless of being heard now, he cries out in a wordless shout as his climax overcomes him. His hips jerk against me as his come fills me. Raw and sensitive with arousal, I am perfectly pitched to enjoy his orgasm almost as much as my own.

Then at last he is still, and nothing but the sound of his ragged breath punctuates the silence.

'Jesus, Cassandra,' is all he says when finally he can speak again.

Withdrawing gently from me, he stands up and unties my arms. Taking my hands in his, he massages my wrists, rubbing away the tension that had stiffened them. He bends and softly kisses the top of my right shoulder, which is shiny with the sweat of sex. Then his mouth moves to first one, and then the other breast, and he sinks to his knees to cover my stomach, my thighs, the whole of my sated body in grateful, tender kisses.

Then he surprises me again. Standing once more, he nuzzles against the base of my neck, seeking softness. And parting his teeth he draws my flesh into his mouth, branding me as his possession. The pain of the bite triggers another ripple of orgasmic pleasure. I have never felt so loved.

When our eyes meet, I see that the anger has gone from his face. All that's left is a quiet calm I've not seen before. He picks me up, swinging me into his arms as if I'm a small child and carries me to a pile of horse blankets in the corner of the room. There he lays me down, cradling me against his chest.

And we sleep, curled in each other's arms on the floor of the tack room, while upstairs, in Luke's grand bedroom, William De Courcy dozes between Luke's Irish linen sheets.

15

Cassandra's Story

As dawn breaks, I lie on my back and stare up at the beamed ceiling of the tack room. Luke's tack room. The idea of Luke as the owner of Temworth Manor is going to take some getting used to. He's sprawled, naked, beside me, his head resting on my stomach.

'I only came to William's sodding party because he told me you wouldn't be here,' I say dreamily.

Luke laughs his wild laugh. It's a fabulous sound and I vow that from now on I will hear it more.

'And I only came because he told me you wouldn't be here,' he replies.

I yawn and stretch my arms over my head. 'He's a good mate you know, Luke.' I wonder how much Luke really knows about William's feelings.

'I know.' He is idly stroking my pubes, which are still damp with his semen.

'He really cares about you.'

Luke looks up at me from beneath his fringe, a slightly confused expression on his face. 'I know,' he says. 'And I really care about him.' William was right. Luke doesn't have a clue.

He rolls me onto my tummy and reaches out to trace the pale-pink welts that are still faintly visible on my hips and bottom. As his fingers run over my tender flesh, a thrill shoots through me as I remember the pain. What Luke had done to me hadn't been some silly S & M game played behind twitching curtains by the bored and sub-urban. His anger had been genuine. My fear had been genuine. It had all been very real indeed.

He looks concerned. 'Cas. Last night ... The thing with the whip ... I've never done anything like that before. I didn't mean to hurt you.'

'Yes you did.' His contrition touches me, but I decide I won't let him off the hook just yet. I'm not going to tell him that it had been the best sex I'd ever had.

'Perhaps I did.'

'And did you enjoy it?'

For a moment he looks thoughtful. Then he grins and says: 'Yeah. I did. Did you?'

'Yes. So that's OK then.'

'Is it still painful?' He leans over to plant gentle kisses on my bare bottom.

'Yes,' I fib. 'But that's making it feel much better.' I lie still, enjoying the sensation of his cool, soft lips soothing my skin. 'Luke?'

'What?' He moves slowly up my spine.

'About Simon.'

'What about him?'

'I've never slept with him.'

Luke pauses only briefly. 'Good,' he says quietly. 'So why did you tell me you had?'

'To piss you off.' I feel his mouth soften into a smile.

'It worked.' He carries on, dropping delicate kisses on my shoulders, sweeping my hair to one side to reach the back of my neck.

'It was Simon who started the rumour about you taking that money in the States, wasn't it?'

'Yes.'

'And he had something to do with the drugs charge?'

'Yup.'

'Shit. He must really hate you.'

'It was in his interests to get me out of the way.'

The kisses are distracting, but I won't be fobbed off this time. 'So,' I say into the silence. 'Are you going to tell me why?'

He stops kissing me and sits up, wrapping his arms around one leg and resting his chin on his knee. 'Yes. I've been behaving like a complete wanker. I guess I owe you an explanation.'

'You do.'

'OK.' He speaks softly, his voice hardly above a whisper. 'How much do you know about what happened to Elizabeth, my wife?'

I shrug. 'Not much. Only that she overdosed and you found her dead on the bathroom floor.'

'Yes,' he says. 'She was found dead on a bathroom floor. But not mine. And not by me. I want to tell you about it, but not here. Can we go back to London?'

'If you like.' I look down at his bruised fist. 'And I guess we'd better clean up those fingers.'

He holds out his damaged hand and smiles. A row of teeth marks is still imprinted on his knuckles. 'If Simon tries to sue me for assault, do you think I'd get away with saying the bastard bit me?'

'I don't think even William could make a story like that stand up,' I say laughing. 'Come on. Let's go home.'

On the road back to London Luke drives fast and aggressively. I try not to flinch as he overtakes in country lanes, pulling in and out of the traffic with heart-stopping recklessness.

At first he chats with a forced joviality. Then, when the traffic starts to slow as we near London, he slips into tense silence and his face sets in concentration.

He lets me into his flat, and we go to the kitchen where he busies himself making coffee, sloshing the viscous strong liquid into plain white cups. I sit at a stainless steel breakfast bar, watching him move around the room. He's still wearing his now badly creased white shirt and the trousers of his dinner suit. His tie hangs loose around his neck, a shadow of stubble shows on his jaw and his hair is appallingly tousled. But he still looks superb.

He searches in two drawers before he finds a spoon and uses it to stir the coffee. Then he opens the door of an obviously empty fridge and peers in.

'No milk,' he says.

'Black's fine.'

'Good.'

He plonks my coffee onto the bar and offers me a cigarette.

'Yum,' I say, peering into the pungent blackness whirling in the cup. 'Coffee and a fag has always been my favourite breakfast.'

'I really can cook a pretty funky eggs Benedict,' he says, attempting a smile.

'Not without any eggs you can't.'

He shrugs and looks sheepish.

'Don't worry,' I say. 'You can owe me.'

Then he leans against the glass-topped kitchen units, lights a cigarette for himself and begins his story. He speaks without emotion, his voice level and calm.

'She was everything I ever wanted – beautiful, great fun, sexy. Very sexy. Both her parents had died when she was in her teens and left on her own she'd grown up a little wild. But she wasn't bad. Really, she wasn't bad.

'The four of us – Lizzy, William, Simon and I – met when we were at Oxford, and for a while we were great friends. We came from different backgrounds, but were all ambitious and we shared an obsession with politics. We worked hard, partied hard and talked about how we were going to change the world. My first year at university was the happiest of my life.

'I'd never believed in love at first sight, but that's what it was. There was never a time when I didn't adore her. But before I could pluck up the courage to tell her how I felt, Simon had already moved in on her.

'For a brief time, he did make her happy. Then, just before we were about to leave for our first summer vacation, he dumped her. He left her with plenty to remember him by – two cracked ribs, a broken wrist and a badly split lip.

'During that summer I stayed in Oxford with her and picked up the pieces. It was me who helped her come up with an excuse for the bruises, fabricating a story about a car accident so she didn't have to tell anyone what had happened.

'She soon got over the physical damage. Her emotional recovery was slower, but day by day she grew stronger, and gradually life drifted into a new normality. It was only as we were coming to the end of our time at university and began to make plans to go our separate ways I realised that if I didn't act soon, I was going to lose her forever.

'So I did the only thing I could think of and asked her to marry me. The night we got engaged, we made love for the first time. It was a disaster – I was too excited and she was too nervous. But the next time it was OK, and after that it just kept getting better and better. We married the week we graduated.

'I knew she was wealthy, but I had no idea quite how rich she was until after we got back from honeymoon and moved into Temworth Manor. I'd never seen it before, and I was overwhelmed. I didn't know people still lived in houses like it. There was other property too – a flat in New York, a chalet in Switzerland, a whole bloody island in the Caribbean. Just one of the paintings her family owned would have paid for my dad's farm ten times over.

'After university, my career went well. I got a job on a broadsheet, and was soon promoted. She became a reporter on a regional TV station, and William went to work on a Red Top. Simon was elected as MP for Ellisdon North and we didn't hear from him.

'For a while, life was great. I thought I'd have the whole fairy tale – kids, grandchildren. I wanted us to grow old together. I wanted it to last forever. But it didn't.

'Things started to go wrong when Simon came back into our lives. He called out of the blue and said he wanted to meet up. She wanted to see him and I didn't have the balls to stop her. So I tried to put what had happened to the back of my mind, and suddenly there we were, acting as if we were best mates again.

'By this time his private life had become dangerous. He went to the craziest parties and his sex life was off the rails. But he was careful. He surrounded himself with people who had as much to lose as he did if he was found out. Publicly, he was a picture of respectability.

'We all did drugs in those days. Coke mostly. But whatever you wanted, Simon always had it. I could take it or leave it, but she just didn't seem to know when to say no. And Simon encouraged her, getting her to do more and more until it slowly began to take over her life.

'Simon always wants what he can't have, and now that she was married, he wanted her back. He went after her as if I didn't exist. He had been her first love, and he used all the tricks in the book to remind her how power-ful those young emotions could be. Gradually, he wore her down.

'I guess it was inevitable that she would end up having an affair with him. When I found out, I was so blinded by fury I saw no alternative but to leave her. She came home just as I was packing to go and she went mad. She cried so much. I'd never seen anyone so upset. When I tried to get out of the house, she stood in front of the door and, still sobbing her heart out, she slowly undressed. She got onto her hands and knees and clung to my legs, begging me to stay. It was dreadful. She was so proud, so ferociously independent, I was truly appalled to see her behaving like that. I couldn't help but be affected. I had to forgive her.

'Then, she got out my cock and began to kiss me. Despite everything, she could still turn me on and I was hard instantly. When she took me into her mouth, the sensation was electric. She hadn't let me touch her in a long while and emotions were running so high I came almost straight away.

'After that we made love all night. If it wasn't perfect, it was as close as I'd ever been. She told me she loved me. She told me she would give up the drugs. She said she would finish with Simon.

'But she couldn't do it. Her addiction was too serious, and Simon was the easiest route to what she needed. She was so wired most of the time, she gave up trying to hide the relationship from me. Simon was too ambitious to let his career be ruined by an affair with a married woman, and he was discreet in public. But he spared me no detail. He loved telling me how he enjoyed screwing my wife.

'She would go to his house at any time during the day or night and come back days later, reeking of him. Sometimes she only stayed home long enough to pick up a change of clothes. We hardly spoke.

'Her habit started to get expensive. She was losing it

at work, and I had to lie for her more and more. I sourced background information for her stories, wrote her scripts, did just about everything apart from her pieces to camera. But her problem became obvious and eventually she was sacked.

'I realised she was in really big trouble when I found out she'd started to inject heroin. I knew our marriage was over by then, but I still cared for her and I wanted to do everything I could to protect her. I couldn't persuade her to see a doctor, so I went to talk to Simon to see if he would help. But he just laughed in my face and told me I was trying to stop her having a good time. I wasn't. I was trying to stop her killing herself.

'It was four o'clock on a Sunday morning when I got a call from him to say she was very sick. He didn't even have the guts to tell me she was already dead. He was sobbing hysterically. But he was crying for himself, not for her. He couldn't cope with the thought of a scandal. He told me to come and get her, and begged me to do everything I could to keep it out of the papers. I didn't want her name dragged through the press either, and I was so stunned myself, I went along with everything he said.

'I drove to his house and his cleaner let me in. Simon had already pissed off. It was then I found out that she was dead. He'd left her in a huddle in his bathroom. She'd choked on her own vomit. I carried her to the car and drove her home. When I got back to Temworth Manor, I called an ambulance.

'He didn't even come to the funeral. Two weeks after we buried her, he married Fiona Rogers. Only now he didn't mind the publicity and he sold the wedding pictures to a gossip magazine for a fortune.

'I wanted to tell the real story. I wanted the world to know that kind, caring, husband Simon Moore was the biggest shit ever. But I knew I couldn't ruin him without ruining the memory of her too. I didn't tell anyone what had happened. Not even William knows the truth.'

'For the next few weeks I was really out of it. I tried to carry on working, but I knew that my career as a journalist was finished. My job, which had been so important to me, suddenly seemed pointless. And so I resigned.

'I started to drink. After what happened to her, it should have been the last thing I wanted to do, but when I was drunk it hurt a little bit less. It was stupid, but I didn't care.

'And if I'd wanted to drink myself to death, I certainly had the means to do it. Of course we had no children, and she had no close family, so apart from a few trinkets she'd left to friends in her will, I inherited the lot. Two months after the funeral, I had thirty-eight million quid sitting in a current account. I bought a house for my brother, paid off the mortgage on my parent's farm and gave them enough money to retire in comfort, but apart from that, I had nothing to do with it.

'It wasn't my money and I couldn't spend it on myself. The things I have now are things that she bought for me. She had the Cartier watch you admired biked to my office when I'd left my old one at home. Aplauso and the other horses were birthday and Christmas presents. She bought me the Aston the day I got soaked waiting for a taxi in the rain. I had never been comfortable with that kind of wealth. Now it sickened me.

'So there I was with no wife, no career, a pile of cash I didn't want, a house I couldn't bare to live in any more and a rapidly escalating drink problem. It felt like my life was over.

'William managed to persuade me that I had to get another job. Obviously I didn't need the money, but I had to do something to keep myself busy. I knew if I stayed around here I'd go totally insane, so I lent the house to William and went to work in America.

'William introduced me to Paul Greenford, who was an old family friend. Senator Greenford, as he was in those days, and his wife Serena, were brilliant. Paul gave me a job in his press team as a sort of glorified tea boy. Sometimes I was so pissed I could hardly stand up, let alone talk to a journalist, but they stuck with me. They were the ones who made me get help for my drinking.

'It took a while, but eventually I began to be able to get past breakfast without a bottle of vodka. I worked bloody hard to make up for the bad times, and I slowly climbed my way up the ladder until I was one of the key people in Paul's team. Eventually I began to be able to think about something other than how much I missed Elizabeth and how much I hated Simon. I didn't cope well. But I did cope.

'After the assassination attempt I had to have a few weeks off, and it gave me time to take stock. I loved my life in Washington, but I began to realise that staying in the States was only a way of avoiding my problems, and I knew I couldn't keep running away for ever. I had to come back and face up to what had happened.

'And as part of that process, I wanted to do something to make sure that Lizzy hadn't died for nothing. I started to think about using her money to open up some sort of rehabilitation centre that would help people with addiction problems. I'd failed to stop her killing herself. But maybe I could stop someone else making the same mistakes.

'When I was offered the job at Downing Street I couldn't refuse. It was a great career move, plus it meant I could start to think about the rehab centre and finally look to the future.

'At first, everything went according to plan. And then I met you. I knew straight away that you were special and, in the beginning it scared me. But in Brighton I managed to convince myself it would be OK. I really did think I was strong enough.

'Then, when I saw you with Simon – when I thought the whole thing was happening again – I realised I wasn't strong enough at all.

'That night at your flat after Simon's party, all the rage came flooding back. I know I didn't have any right to be jealous. But I couldn't help it. I couldn't bear the thought of him in the same room as you, let alone touching you. I just couldn't handle it.

'After that I thought it was best to stay away. I tried to forget about you. I tried to tell myself that I don't care. But I do. If I lost you too, I wouldn't survive it, Cas. I wouldn't fucking survive it.'

At last he stops talking and takes a nervous drag on his cigarette. Profoundly moved by his story, it's a while before I can stand up and go to him. I put my arms around his trembling shoulders and hold him tightly.

'It's OK,' I say as he buries his face in my hair. 'It's OK now.' And as I stand holding him, fragments of thoughts are already beginning to form into a plan for revenge.

16

Cassandra's Story

They say revenge is a dish best served cold, but my scheme is definitely hot. At a hastily arranged meeting in London, I am surprised at how easily we manage to persuade all the helpers we need.

Afterwards, on the way back to Temworth Manor, Luke insists on taking a highly convoluted route out of town, and I'm not surprised when we find ourselves in a strange and totally unfamiliar backwater of West London. As we pass a vandalised phone box and a restaurant called the Star of India for the third time, I realise we have been going round in circles.

'Face it, Luke, we're lost.'

Scowling as he takes yet another right turn into a street he clearly doesn't recognise, he says: 'No we're not. I'll know where we are in a minute.' He's shouting above the Wagner he insists on playing very loudly on the car's powerful CD player. More of a pop fan myself, I'm not convinced that the music is helping us to concentrate on finding our way.

I sigh and stretch my legs. The cream leather seats of the Aston are supremely comfortable, but it's far too pleasant a day to be conducting a tour of London's less elegant suburbs and I'm suddenly desperate to get out into the fresh air.

'There's a nice looking pub there,' I say, gesturing

down the street. 'Why don't we stop and get a drink? Then we can check where we are.'

Luke shrugs. 'Good idea.'

He isn't going to admit that he's wrong, but it's the nearest I'm going to get to an apology. He slows, bumps the Aston up the pavement and comes to a halt in front of the pub.

There's nothing remarkable about the pub from the outside, but once inside, I realise that the Queen's Head is a far from traditional inn. The interior is dimly lit, but despite the lack of sunlight, it's stiflingly hot. Although it's only two o'clock in the afternoon, loud music thumps and coloured flashing lights give the place the atmosphere of a seedy nightclub. A mirrored disco ball spins from the ceiling and, in a far corner, a handful of dancers gyrate on a little dance floor.

As we stand at the bar waiting to be served, Luke fidgets and looks uneasy while I survey our surroundings, assessing the other customers.

'What can I get you, gorgeous?' I turn to the good-looking barman, a smile ready on my face, only to discover that he's addressing Luke.

Luke, now firmly back on the wagon, orders a Diet Coke for himself and a Bud for me. He doesn't raise his eyes as he hands over a ten-pound note.

As we carry our drinks out to a small and secluded terraced garden at the back of the pub I say: 'I think that barman liked you. If you play your cards right, you could have him.'

'Cas!'

'Luke, I do believe you're blushing.'

'Shut up, Cas.'

'Yes, you are blushing. You've gone all pink. It's really cute.'

'Cas,' he hisses. 'Shut the fuck up.'

'Ooo, you know you're very sexy when you go all Yorkshire. I love it when you're masterful.'

He grins. 'I know you do, you dirty cow,' he says, trowelling on the accent.

In the garden are a few wooden tables. None of them are occupied, so we choose the most sheltered and sit down to enjoy the autumnal sunshine.

Just then the pub door opens again and two men come into the garden. One is tall and blond, the other stockier and dark. While the blond, in his tight white T-shirt, is obviously gay, the dark man, who wears baggy jeans and a chain-store checked shirt, looks very conventional and almost boringly straight. But he isn't. As the two men walk down the garden, he puts a hand on his companion's arm, twists him around and kisses him on the lips. His mouth is open, and I see him push his tongue into the other man. I nudge Luke.

'Look! That's some snog.'

Luke laughs.

I watch Luke drinking his Coke, and think back to my conversation with William about Luke's sexuality.

'Have you ever been with another man?'

'No.' Luke laughs. Then, obviously registering my serious expression, adds: 'Good Lord no.'

'And you've never experimented? Not even when you were younger?'

'No. I went to grammar school. It wasn't considered normal to bugger your mates in the toilets.'

I wonder if William is right. Luke swears he's not interested in men, but I know how he feels about being fucked. Is a real cock very different to my fingers? As if he can read my thoughts, Luke laughs again and says: 'No, Cas. You're a girl. You can do what you like to me.' How true, I think, smiling at the memory.

We both watch as the two men disappear behind a

row of shrubs into another part of the garden. I stand up to watch them through a gap in the foliage. The blond leans against a table. Beneath the black leather of his trousers, his erection is obvious. He runs his palm the length of it, proudly displaying the delights he has to offer. Then slowly, tempting as a stripper, he slides the zip.

'Hell,' I say to Luke. 'Do you think they know we're here?'

'I doubt it.' If they do suspect, it doesn't faze them, and before I can say anything more I see the dark man step in front of the blond and plunge his hands into his trousers. With a groan of pleasure, the blond thrusts his hips forwards, encouraging his companion to feel whatever he wants. I'm near enough to see the blond's eyes close, and a smile curl his lips. I hear him mutter something, but I don't have to catch his words to know his meaning. His pleasure is obvious.

When he opens his eyes again and his head turns in my direction, I retreat, alarmed, back into the shadow. It would be polite to look away. But I don't do polite.

A frisson of excitement runs through me as the dark man pulls his companion's T-shirt out of his trousers and lifts it up to expose a gym-toned stomach and the magnificent swellings of tanned pectorals. He reaches out and rubs his palms against them, groping and kneading until the brown tips of his partner's nipples pucker and point in arousal.

Standing behind me, Luke is eyeing me curiously.

'My God, you're enjoying that, aren't you?'

I can't help blushing. I've never seen two men together before, and I'm unsure of my feelings. But at the same time the novel picture is undoubtedly arousing, and I can't ignore the growing heat between my thighs.

I'm shocked at what I'm seeing, but certain that I want to see more. 'Yes,' I whisper. 'I am.'

'And I'm enjoying watching you,' Luke says, reaching round my body to fondle my hardening nipples through my shirt.

Pressing himself against blondie, the dark man writhes, erect cock rubbing against erect cock, urgency now building. And his companion is going to give him what he needs. Blondie slides down the older man's body and kneels in front of him. Closing his eyes he opens his mouth wide.

I shudder as the older man unzips his trousers, and takes out a cock of such spectacularly vast proportions that I fear for the kneeling man as the huge appendage nears his lips. But his lover clearly doesn't share my concerns and, putting his hands at the sides of the blondie's head, he plunges into the willing and open mouth, sinking himself to the hilt. I'm surprised that the receiver doesn't gag, but he just groans with pleasure, and reaches down to extract his own smaller but equally stiff cock and rub it furiously.

Luke is kissing my neck, sending me wild with the lightest of caresses. I turn to meet his lips, but he pulls away.

'No,' he says. 'Watch.' And he gently turns me back to face the scene playing before my greedy eyes. Luke lifts me up onto my hands and knees on the table, pulls down my panties and I feel his tongue travel the length of my exquisitely aroused lips. He understands me better than I understand myself. To watch two men fondling each other while Luke licks me is indeed paradise and I willingly give in to Luke's command.

Suddenly, the older man pulls away, raises his lover to his feet and turns him to the table. We see him push blondie face down onto the wooden surface and yank the young man's trousers down to the tops of his thighs, exposing a taut behind. The youthful buttocks quiver and then, as the older man parts them to reveal a trembling hole, they thrust upwards inviting penetration.

The invitation won't be rejected. Drawing himself up level with the young backside, the older man aligns himself with the opening.

'Oh no,' I whisper. 'They're going to fuck.'

'Yes,' says Luke. 'And so are we.' And as I watch the huge prick disappear into the blond's bum, Luke eases himself into me.

The older man begins to thrust, slowly at first, then wildly, against the hard buttocks of his partner, and I feel my lust soaring. The sight of that tight anus clenching as the massive organ slaps into it is the most compellingly rude thing I've ever seen. Seeing it in the open air, just yards away from a crowded pub, makes it even more filthy.

But I'm just as dirty. Just as bare. Just as exposed. I think of my own bottom. How it must look, sticking up, spread wide. I think of taking a prick up it too, my own entrance stretched taut around a shaft. And as I think it, it happens. In a smooth movement, Luke pulls out and moves up. For a moment, my body tenses. But it's what I want.

'Yes, Luke. Please. Please do that to me.' I don't know if I say them out loud, but the words 'stick it up my arse' flash obscenely in my mind. I feel the tip push into me, then the rest slide slowly home, and I take all of him. Down goes my hand and I rub at my clit. I'm masturbating, being buggered and watching two men fuck. It doesn't get any dirtier.

The blond's prick is in his partner's hand, and with

firm strokes it is firmly pumped. I watch it thicken and redden, waiting for it to spasm. It doesn't take long. Soon spunk is spurting from it, slithering across the table in white streaks.

And as blondie comes, so do I, choking back a scream of delight. I squirm on Luke's cock, control slipping away as my orgasm deepens and then, before the shrieks I can no longer suppress betray us completely, mercifully fades.

The older man is nearly there too. His face contorts and finally he stiffens and moans as he finishes between the cheeks of his lover's buttocks. Then, when it is over, he turns to me, looks me directly in the eye and smiles.

'Was that good?' Mortified with embarrassment, I can't bring myself to reply. I pull away from Luke and duck down behind the hedge, where I remain crouched until I see the two men return to the pub.

Luke can't hide his mirth. 'That'll teach you. You perv.'

I don't bother to deny that I'd had a good time. 'But what about you?' Looking down at Luke's deflating cock, I'm unsure if Luke reached his own climax. 'Was it good for you too?'

Luke smiles as he adjusts his boxer shorts and does up his trousers. 'Oh, I enjoyed myself all right. You were just to busy to notice.' The thought of Luke having an orgasm up my bottom, while I'm rendered senseless by my own is a wickedly nice one. 'Now,' he says softly. 'Let's go and get another drink.'

This time, we sit inside. A cabaret has started and, on a tiny stage, a statuesque blonde is belting out Gloria Gaynor songs in a disturbingly masculine voice. Luke glances at her and then looks away, a slight frown creasing his brow.

Dressed in a blue slinky dress the blonde is stunningly

glamorous. Her well made-up face is beautiful and strangely familiar.

'She's good,' I say, nodding towards the singer.

'Yes,' Luke replies, but I hear a note of uncertainty in his voice.

The singer notices Luke and falters. Muttering something about how at first she was afraid, she was petrified, her voice fades to a hesitant whisper. As the music stops, a hush falls on the room, and everyone hears when Luke exclaims: 'Ber-luddy hell! William!'

Half an hour later, Luke, William and I are sitting at table in a quieter corner of the pub. In an attempt to diffuse the situation, I've bought yet another round of drinks. William has changed into his regular clothes, and scrubbed off most of the make-up in the men's loos, but a smudge of eyeliner remains around his eyes, blackening his already dark lashes. His hair, after being flattened under the blonde wig, droops and looks as dejected as the rest of him.

'Bloody hell, William,' says Luke.

'If you say "bloody hell, William" like that again I'm going to have to slap you,' William says.

'I'm sorry. It's just I'm a bit ... Bloody hell, William.' Luke shakes his head. 'You're gay.'

'Nooo. I just like wearing dresses and hanging out in drag clubs.'

Luke ignores the sarcasm. 'And is this a new thing? Or have you always fancied blokes?'

William is slowly shredding a beer mat, tearing it into tiny fragments with shaking hands. 'I've always fancied blokes,' he replies. William glances at me and I see a tortured uncertainty in his eyes. I nod, offering him encouragement. 'But, Luke,' says William, 'it gets worse.'

Luke looks up. I lean towards William.

'Tell him, William,' I whisper.

'Tell me what?' Luke's voice is getting louder.

William takes a deep breath and says: 'It's you, Luke.'

'What?'

'As soon as I met you I knew I was going to fall for you. I know it's useless, but I can't help it. My feelings haven't changed in twelve years. It's you that I want.'

'Oh God.' Luke leans back in his chair and shoves both his hands into his hair.

'I'm sorry, Luke.'

'So am I. But I'm not gay, William. I'm not even curious. I can't even begin to . . .'

'I know. I know.' William takes a long swig of his beer. 'So what are we going to do?'

'Do? Nothing.'

'You mean . . . just carry on. We can still be friends?'

Luke looks puzzled, as if he doesn't understand the question. 'Yes. Of course.' Then realisation dawns. 'Shit, Wills. We're mates, aren't we? I would never not . . . You didn't think I would . . . ?'

William smiles and leans over the table to cover Luke's fingers with his large hand. 'No, Luke. I of course I didn't.' William throws me a look, but the secret of his doubts is safe.

Then, suddenly, Luke begins to laugh.

'It's not funny,' says William, scowling.

'Yes it is. All this time I just thought you were really crap with women.'

Luke's Story

But later it doesn't seem so amusing. In the early hours of the morning, I find myself standing outside Temworth Manor. My house keys are in my pocket, but I can't bring myself to use them. I ring the bell. And wait. When William opens the door, he's still dressed. Like me, he can't sleep. We both know we have to talk.

There's a lot to say. Keeping ourselves awake with cigarettes and cup after cup of strong black coffee, we sit on one of Lizzy's family's George III sofas and talk long into the night.

I'm taken aback by what William tells me about his feelings. It's unnerving to be loved so much and for so long, without knowing. I struggle to understand it. As I listen to his story, whispered softly in his aristocratic drawl, and watch his intelligent eyes well with emotion, I begin to realise that what I feel for him is also complicated. When William told me he was gay I had been surprised – almost prudishly shocked. Now I am merely confused.

When finally he says: 'I've given up trying to get over you,' the sadness in his words moves me. I want, more than anything, to take away the pain. He's wearing blue jeans and a pale T-shirt, which strains around his thick biceps as he moves. Instinctively, I want to let him put those big arms around me. But I'm not brave enough to give him the hug that might comfort him.

As he pours us both another cup of coffee, I find myself staring at his hands. I wonder what it would feel like to be touched by him. I'm startled by the thought of his fingers inside my trousers, persuading my cock into the first stirring of an erection.

Misjudging the reason for my silence, he suddenly looks up at me and, with a lopsided grin, he says: 'Don't worry. I'm not going to make a move on you.'

I surprise us both when I answer: 'But maybe I want you to.'

'What?'

I can't say it again. The words rise to my mouth, but no sound comes. All I can manage is the slightest nod.

'Luke, it's OK. You don't have to –'

'I do.'

He looks at me for a long while. It's me who looks away first. I look at his lips, noticing the dark stubble below the full curves, noticing the strength of his jawline. Noticing William. His fingers run through my hair, and the caress is so warm, so reassuring, I can't stop myself from leaning against him. Slowly, he moves forward and I tense.

Then he kisses me. His lips are soft against mine, and the kiss is very tender. But the sensuality of it reaches me. When it's over, I find it hard to breathe steadily. I look down to see his hardening cock tightening his trousers beneath the studs and a ripple of emotion runs down my spine. It feels like arousal. With a small groan, I tear my eyes away.

'Luke,' he whispers, concern deepening his voice. 'Oh, Luke. Are you sure?'

What I'd told him in the pub was true. I haven't ever thought about sex with another man. But this is somehow different. With William, suddenly it's different. I want his hands on me. I want his lips on me. God help me, I want even more.

'Yes,' I say simply.

Then he kisses me again. He's unhurried, his lips gliding over mine, nipping, licking, tasting. This time I relax into the embrace, and my cock begins to stiffen. When he breaks away, I'm sorry that he's stopped. He reaches up to the top of my shirt, and he undoes one, and then all, of the buttons. My teeth graze my bottom lip as he slips one hand inside my shirt. He leans on me slightly and, pressing his palm against the swell of my chest, he lets out a little murmur of reverent admiration.

It's pleasant to feel the roughness of a man's skin against my own, and at the same time it's strange. But the desire the novelty stokes is very familiar. His hand moves across my body, exploring, gently soothing away the tension in my ribs. As he touches me, his eyes flick to my face, checking for acquiescence. There's nothing to deter him.

Then he moves down my arms, and he unfastens the cuffs of my shirt. Obediently submissive, I lean forwards to allow him to take it off all together. With the shirt removed, he looks down at me, examining the contours of my body. As his eyes travel over my arms, my shoulders, my chest, I've never felt so naked. I haven't ever considered what I look like to another man, but I'm glad when I see the smile flit across his lips and I know that William likes what he sees.

Still staring at me, he reaches forwards, and touches my neck, stroking me with a feather-light touch. He moves lower, across my collarbone and then lower still. Very carefully, he runs one finger the length of the scar on my shoulder, tenderly smoothing over each tiny inch of distorted skin. His lips follow his finger, and he kisses the pitted, damaged flesh. It's such a startlingly intimate thing to do that my heart lurches.

He is the one who speaks first. 'Jesus,' he says, his mouth still close to the scar. 'You could have been killed.'

'But I wasn't.' I reach up to touch his face, and for a brief moment I am the one who reassures.

Taking my hand in his, he lowers his head and presses a warm kiss into my palm. Then he licks me. Slowly. His tongue touches lightly against the inside of my wrist, and then floats, in one even stroke up the inside of my arm. The eroticism of his action jolts me, and my breath rushes from my chest in a low sigh. When he moves over me to kiss and lick my nipples, I struggle to breathe at all. He isn't to know how much I like that, but his touch is perfect. I know that I must have more of it. My confusion clears. The time when I could have stopped him has passed.

'Tell me what you want,' whispers William.

But I can't begin to put my needs into words. 'I don't know what I want.' I'm stammering stupidly. 'I don't know what to do. I need you to teach me.'

William smiles. 'With pleasure.'

His hands snake down my body to my waist. With no sense of urgency, he undoes my belt and then unzips my flies. I raise my hips to let him slide my clothes down my thighs in a final gesture of surrender. He pauses, staring at my now fully erect cock as it rests against my stomach.

'You're gorgeous,' he says. 'I knew you would be.' My throat constricts as I watch his hand move towards me, and I grit my teeth as, finally, I feel his touch. He strokes me, his palm brushing the length of my erection. For what seems like an eternity, he toys with me, wrapping his fingers softly around me, lifting my prick and letting it fall, gently fondling my balls, like a blind man touching to discover the precise size and shape of every bit of me. It's almost unbearable, I need more than this terrible teasing. I need more of him. Almost as if he can read my mind, William tightens his grip, and at last I feel the friction I want.

It would be enough: lying against the sofa, my cock in his hand, is paradise. But William wants to give me more. Slipping to his knees between my legs, he buries his face in my lap and I hear him murmur: 'Oh God, you are gorgeous.'

Then, wonderfully, I am in his mouth. I gasp and arch my back, my eyes closed as sensation rockets through me. I can't help – I fall still as his skilled lips slide over me and I let him control me, knowing that he has to take charge. In a haze of bliss, I relinquish any responsibility and duty, secure in the knowledge that all that's expected is for me to enjoy what's happening. The newness of what William is doing is easy to appreciate.

'William.' His name sounds strange on my lips. I force myself to look down. 'I can't believe you're doing that.' But he is. Another man is sucking my dick. And I'm loving it.

His hands are warm on my balls, the pressure carefully applied until I moan out loud. He handles me differently to a girl, his movements more sure, more understanding of where I'm sensitive to his touch. The tentative and exploratory approach of a woman has a charm of its own, but William's knowledge, his certainty about the way my body works, brings a new intensity to my pleasure. I know he could make me come in seconds.

But William's too practised to let that happen. He takes me higher slowly, leading me one careful step by careful step. I fight him, resisting the urge, my fingers twisting into his hair as I struggle to delay the moment.

But now he fights me back. Sucking, pulling, drawing me ever deeper, coaxing me to the edge. It becomes almost insupportable.

'I can't hold it much longer.' I want to say more, but words fail me. I'm disorientated. Giddy with arousal, my ability to think is swamped by my need to come.

I sense it in a moment of stark clarity – that split second when it changes, when I know that it is going to happen. A surge of pleasure washes over me, and my skin tingles, heralding the climax that is now inevitable. My jaw tenses, my hands fall away and clench at my sides. My hips lift and I press towards him, pushing as much of myself as I can into him.

And I orgasm, groaning with ecstasy as I spurt into his mouth. The explosion rips every last ounce of energy from my body, leaving me superbly, deeply satisfied. Finally, I collapse a shoulder against the sofa and draw a long, hard breath.

William looks deep into my eyes, searching for my reaction. I don't know how to react, or what to say, so I do and say nothing. And still no words pass between us as he rises to kneel over me. He undoes his trousers, and takes out his prick. Bracing one arm against the sofa, he wanks, his cock close to mine. He had handled me so tenderly, but he masturbates himself with quick, rough strokes, as if he is rushing before I change my mind. Change my mind is the last thing I want to do.

Almost immediately, he comes over my own spent cock in a series of strong spasms. We both look down as his semen splashes through my pubes and over my stomach. When it's over, we stare at each other, both still panting with the effort of our orgasms. He sinks to the floor, wiping a sheen of sweat from his forehead with the back of one hand. Neither of us speaks. Finally, I reach out to take hold of his hands, and pull him up beside me. Still half-naked, we lie quietly in each other's arms. I listen, as his breath slows to the soft sigh of sleep. I watch the muscles of his face relax as his sleep deepens and, when I'm certain he's no longer aware of what I'm doing, I kiss his mouth.

'I love you too,' I whisper. Then, as the sky begins to lighten, I close my eyes and drift into unconsciousness.

The next morning, Cassandra's eyes flash with amused interest when I tell her that I've slept with William.

'He said you would never do it!'

'Well, he was wrong.'

'What, um, exactly did you do?'

It's somewhat embarrassing to discuss details, but I want Cassandra to know. I'm not sure that what I did counts as cheating – I need to confess.

'Everything.' I can't stop grinning. 'All the way.'

We had woken, cold and stiff-limbed to collapse, laughing, into the comfort of the big bed I had once shared with Lizzy. It was then I had asked him to fuck me. Really fuck me.

'What was it like?'

I shrug. 'Nice.' Cassandra gives me a 'yeah right' look. 'OK, it was better than nice.'

Suddenly, Cassandra looks concerned. 'Will it happen again?'

I'm flattered by her jealousy, but she has nothing to fear. William's masculinity had attracted me. The weight of him, the sheer size of him, made me feel excitingly vulnerable. The length of his naked body next to mine had thrilled me. Touching a man, someone I understood so well, had come so very naturally.

But in the morning, when, so gently, he had finally entered me, I knew it would only happen once. And even when, shaking with the force of my orgasm, I had cried with the pure delight of it, I had known it would be the last time. The emotion that had crackled between us will never reach the same intensity. The circumstances that had propelled me into my first and probably my only homosexual experience had been unique.

'No.' As I say the word, I know it's the truth. 'I'm glad it happened. But no, it will never happen again.'

'Well, I obviously need to keep an eye on you to make sure you stay on the *straight* and narrow,' she says, with a theatrical emphasis on the word 'straight'. 'Perhaps you'd better move into my flat with me.'

I smile. 'Yeah,' I say. 'Perhaps I will.'

17

Cassandra's Story

'So. Your little secret's out at last.' I'm sitting in the front seat of William's car as we drive through London to Westminster.

'Oh yes,' says William with a sigh. 'It certainly is.'

'And are you OK?' He doesn't look great. His kind brown eyes are circled with shadow, his skin grayed by lack of sleep. He glances away from the road and looks at me uncertainly.

'Do you really want to know?'

'Oh, William. We were friends before all this. And I'm still your friend now. Yes, I do want to know. How do you feel?'

'I want to feel relieved. I do feel relieved.'

'And?'

'And sad. Really terribly, heart-wrenchingly sad. It's over.'

'But you knew it would be. You said yourself that nothing could ever happen between you and Luke.'

'I did. And it's the truth. But there was still a small, irrational part of me that could pretend. Now I know for certain that it's not going to be, and it bloody hurts.'

'I wish there was something I could do to help.'

William shakes his head. 'There's nothing to be done.'

'Has it made things difficult with Luke?'

'No. Luke's been great. True to his word. We still have

a laugh. We're still mates. Best mates. But it's nothing like enough. It stinks, Cas.'

William sighs again and I reach out to give his hand a comforting squeeze. 'Come on, William. It's not like you to feel sorry for yourself.'

'No. But I do feel bloody, bloody sorry for myself.' He sounds the closest I've ever heard him get to angry. 'I feel as if I've lost everything. Before, I had my fantasies. But in reality, it was so much better. He was so sweet, so eager to please. I know what he's like and it was so damned fantastic.'

'Well, that's good isn't it?'

'No. No it isn't. Now I know I've got to forget about him, because now he's real to me and that makes it wrong. I can't even think about him when I'm having a wank without it feeling like some squalid abuse of our friendship. I don't even have my fantasies any more.' William bangs his fist on the steering wheel, his teeth clenching in frustration. 'I wish it had never happened.'

'Well, they do say you can't miss something you've never had . . .'

William almost smiles. 'And now I've had him, I miss him so badly.'

'I'm sorry.'

'Don't be. He's with you and that is as it should be. I want him to be happy. He deserves to be happy.'

'But?'

'But what about me, Cas? What is fucking well going to happen to me?'

As the traffic edges towards Parliament Square William is not concentrating. He should have seen the lights change to red. He should have seen the car in front of us stop. But he doesn't. He doesn't appear to notice anything until we feel the jolt and hear the sickening crunch of metal against metal.

I see the driver getting out of his car. He glances down at his crumpled bumper and then walks towards us. William opens his window as the driver says: 'Not much harm done.'

Suddenly, it's just too much. Covering his face with his hands, William begins to cry, his shoulders heaving convulsively. Watching a big man like William break down is truly awful, and I put my arm around him, frantic for him to stop.

'No, William,' I beg. 'Please don't cry like that.'

The driver also tries to offer some comfort.

'Really, there's no need to be upset,' he says softly, and he leans through the window to place a reassuring hand on William's arm.

This unexpected kindness makes things worse, and William sobs even harder. 'Oh God,' he wails. 'This is so embarrassing.'

But the driver keeps his hand on William's arm, stroking it gently until at last, the tears stop. 'Better now?' he asks.

William takes a deep, even breath. The driver pulls a packet of tissues from his pocket and offers one to William. William blows his nose noisily. 'Yes,' he says. 'Thank you.'

William looks up into the driver's pleasant, smiling face. I'm sure that William's penchant for falling in love with straight men has dented his confidence in his ability to spot guys who share his sexual preferences. But this one looks into William's eyes for far longer than would be comfortable if he didn't fancy him like crazy.

The driver is not excessively handsome and with his wavy dark hair he is not made in the same mould as Luke. But there is something nice about him.

'Really, the damage doesn't look too bad at all,' he says.

'No.' William returns his smile. 'Perhaps it isn't.'

A long time ago, William fell for a cocky northerner with an infectious laugh and hair the colour of sunshine. I wonder if one day soon, he'll be able to fall in love again. And judging by his thoughtful expression, William is wondering the same thing.

I lean over a desk and pick up a phone. Luke answers his mobile with his usual, brusque: 'Yup.'

'Hi.'

'Hi!' His tone changes when he recognises me. His voice is warm and husky, as it is when he's in my bed.

'Where are you?'

'On the M4, heading back to London.' The throaty roar of the Aston's engine in the background confirms what he tells me. 'I'll be with you in under an hour.'

'Good. I'm dressed for our little adventure this afternoon.'

'Are you?'

'Oh yes.' I lift up my skirt and take a peek underneath.

'What colour did you choose?' He is amused.

'A truly adorable pink,' I say. 'With little bits of navy ribbon – very cute in a Moulin Rouge sort of way. French knickers, as you requested, with lovely soft lace. I'm touching them now. They feel gorgeous.'

He laughs. 'You rude girl.'

'And I remembered the stockings. Black and very, very sheer just as you wanted. My legs look fabulous in them.'

'Jesus,' he says, serious now. 'I wish I could see you.'

'And they're sooo silky, I just can't help touching them. My legs are wide open so I can feel the skin of the insides of my thighs. Can you remember what that part of me feels like?'

'You know I can.'

'I wish you were touching me now.'

'Cas. Don't. You're turning me on.'

'I know. But it's turning me on as well. I'm lifting up my jumper now, because the bra is so pretty too. It pushes up my tits into such a lovely shape, I can't keep my hands off them. I know you'd love to be touching them.'

'Cas. Don't do this to me.'

I ignore him. 'I know you'd love to be holding them in your hands. Kissing them. Licking them. I know how you adore the taste of me.'

'Oh yes.'

'And I adore your mouth on my tits. When I think about it, I have to play with myself.' I run my hand down my belly and over the satin to my mound. I let it ripple, causing a gentle throb deep inside me.

'Cas! Where are you?'

'In your old office.' Never homely, the room is eerily quiet now it is unoccupied. Luke's horrible crucifixion picture has gone, which is an improvement. But gone too is the sexy energy and sense of excitement that pervaded the atmosphere under Luke's tenure. I'm doing my best to put it back.

'Shit!' He is genuinely shocked. 'You can't do that there. What if someone tries to comes in?'

'Ah, but the risk of getting caught is what makes it such fun. What do you think would happen if some crusty old minister walks in and finds me masturbating in the communication director's office? Do you think he'd throw me out? Or do you think the sight of me would make him so randy that he wouldn't be able to do anything but fuck me?'

'Cas, that's really dirty.'

'Is it? Would you find it dirty to listen to us fucking on the phone, Luke?'

'You know I would.'

I think of him, reduced to helpless masturbation by the sounds of sex. 'And would you be jealous if you could hear him panting and moaning as he came up me? Or would it only get to you if you heard me coming too?'

'Stop it, Cas. You're giving me a bastard of an erection.'

'Then do something about it, baby.'

'I can't. I'm driving for Christ's sake.'

'Go on. Pull over. Do it, Luke. Do it for me. What else is your hands-free for?'

'Stop. Now.'

'But it's too late. I have to carry on. I'm far too turned on to stop. Here I am slumped in your chair, my tits half naked, and my skirt hitched up to my waist. And you know how good I look. If you could see me you'd be wanking yourself senseless too.'

'Oh Jees,' he groans. There's the click of an indicator. Then I hear the car slow and finally he switches off the engine. 'Cas?'

'I'm still here, babe.' There is a rustle as he unzips his trousers. 'That's it,' I coax. 'Are you holding it now?'

'Oh yeah. God I'm so hard.' For a minute he is quiet and I picture him lost in brief moment of self-absorption as he strokes his prick. 'That feels good,' he says. 'What are you doing now?'

'I'm playing with my cunt.' The 'c' word sounds wonderfully crude over the phone. I know it will turn him on even more.

'How?'

'Oh, I'm only tickling myself through my knickers. But I don't think I can restrain myself much longer.'

'Take the knickers off. I want you naked.'

I smile. Luke is good at this game. I slip the panties down over my thighs, and let them tumble into a little silky heap on the floor. As I sink into Luke's chair again, the black leather is warm against my bare bottom.

'Ah yes,' I sigh, 'that's much better.' Leaning back, I fling my legs up onto the desk, kicking away a dusty pile of junk mail with the toe of one shoe. I spread my thighs as wide as I can and feel my sex opening. 'And what shall I do now, Luke?'

'Fuck yourself,' he commands, his voice low and hoarse.

Yes. I want to so badly.

'Oh!' I gasp as I plunge two fingers up into myself. 'Oh, that is so lovely. It's just like you pushing into me when I'm wet and ready for you. Can you imagine that?' He sighs. 'Tell me what it's like.'

'Soft and warm. But tight too. You have to push hard to enter me. But once you're inside, it's easy. Oh, that is wonderful.' He knows it so well. I wonder how different his prick feels in his hand, if his imagination can really replicate the depths of me as he wanks.

'You're staring down at my tits as you fuck me,' I continue. 'At first you're happy just to watch them bouncing in their bra. Then you have to get them out, and feel them.' I let out a little mew of pleasure as my own hand sweeps over my now fully exposed breasts. 'My nipples are hard against your palms. You can't stop touching them. You can't get enough of me.' I squeeze hard, pinching my nipples until I know he will hear the pain in my voice. 'You want to be gentle. But you want it so badly you can't help being rough. Can you?'

'No.'

'And I want you to be rough.' I stab at myself with one hand. It feels so like him. 'I want you to fuck me as hard as you dare. You hold my legs apart to open me. You plunge, and then plunge again, fucking me deeper than I've ever been fucked before.' My prose becomes purple, but I know he won't care. I know he'll be jerking himself so hard now he'll be struggling to listen to anything I say.

'You want to hold back. You want to hold on until you think you'll burst if you don't climax. You know how great it feels when you do it like that.'

'Yes, I do.'

'But you need to come, don't you?'

'I'm so close.'

'Good. Because I need you to fill me with your come. I need to know that your lovely prick is spurting inside me, jerking and throbbing as your spunk pumps into me.' He exhales softly. My own breath quickens as I begin to climax, delicious waves of pleasure lapping over me. 'Do it now,' I whisper.

'Yes,' he says. And then more quietly, 'Oh yes.'

18

Cassandra's Story

'And this is where it all goes on?' The set of Simon Moore's TV show is empty. His famous interview sofa, which has been squashed by the bottoms of some of the world's most important politicians, is today only occupied by me.

'That's right.'

'Wow. It really is very impressive.'

Simon's chest swells with smug pride. *'Moore From The House* is one of Main Attraction TV's leading programmes – no expense is spared. And I think most people would agree that it's money well invested. I hear my budget will be increased substantially for my fifth series next Spring.'

I stroke the big-budget fabric on the big-budget cushions and wish Simon would shut his big-budget mouth. I'm not here to talk. 'It's so exciting to be sitting here. With you.'

I pat the sofa next to me, and Simon accepts my implied invitation, sitting close to me, his knee pressing against my thigh.

'Well, perhaps you could do it more often. You could come and work for me. I can always use another pretty researcher.'

'Gosh, really? I'd love to. The thought of working with you and all those other important people is really quite powerful.' I cross my legs, slowly, allowing Simon a good view of my thighs as I slide them together. And as Simon's face colours, my own rising desire tingles. I run a finger casually around the neck of my blouse and Simon's eyes lift to my chest. 'It's making me feel quite ... funny.' I fan myself, the little movement sending a ripple through my breasts that has the desired effect on Simon. His pupils dilate with want.

'And it's really very hot under all these lights. How do you stand it?' Simon stares at my hands as I unfasten one and then two buttons on my blouse. His eyes don't move. My hands don't move. I want him aching to see more. 'Do you think I could possibly have a drink?'

Simon leaps to his feet. 'Of course,' he says fumbling in his pocket for his phone. He keys a number and then I hear him mumble. 'Sandra. Get a bottle of Dom Perignon sent down to Studio A right now.' Please is obviously a word that is beneath the mighty Moore.

'Perhaps I'll be more comfortable if I take off my blouse. Do you mind?'

Simon shakes his head. What else is he going to do? I carry on unbuttoning, while Simon follows my every move. The blouse falls away.

'And more comfortable still if you take off some more?' Simon really is pushing his luck. His eyes bulge as I slip my skirt down my legs.

'Oh yes,' I say. 'That's much better.'

And the growing swelling in Simon's trousers, suggests that he agrees. I lean back and let my legs fall open, knowing that the sight of my satin-covered crotch will drive him wild. And true to form, he lets out a little sigh of longing as he gapes at the now dampening patch of fabric between my thighs. He looks as if he's won a general election and the lottery all on one day.

'God, Cassandra, you have got a fantastic body.'

I give a little catlike stretch, basking in the appreciation. 'I'm sure you have too, Simon. You know it really is very kinky to be almost naked in your studio. Why don't you join me?' He hesitates. 'Come on. I bet you've stripped off in here loads of times before.'

'Well. No. Actually I haven't.'

'Then perhaps now's the time to try.'

Simon needs no more persuasion. He tugs off his shirt. His shoes, socks, trousers and underpants follow, and he stands naked in front of me.

'Oh yes. That really is very kinky.' Simon's erection waves in agreement. 'Just think how much you're fans would love to see you like this. I bet many of them fantasize about it every time they watch your show.'

'Do you think so?' This man's conceit knows no bounds.

'I bet they do. And probably play with themselves as they're thinking about it too.' Simon looks on longingly as I slide my hand between my legs and begin to stroke myself absently. 'I know I do.'

'Really?' Egotism stiffens Simon's cock further still.

'Oh yes.' I put my now moist finger to my bottom lip – the little girl that will appeal to Simon's outrageous vanity. 'But I don't just think about you naked. I think about you wearing other things . . .'

'Like what?' Simon is groping himself as he talks, his hand moving in little jerks against his erection.

'Like my underwear. What I really love to think about is you doing one of your wonderful interviews in my knickers.' His eyes widen. It's a thought that appeals to him too. For a moment, I let him watch me stroke myself, then I give a little jump as if a very clever idea has just occurred to me. 'Simon, please can we do it now?'

'Do what?'

'Please would you put my knickers on?'

'My, you are a naughty little thing. That's a very

wicked idea, but I like it. Get up and let me take them off you.' I stand and I look at my feet. 'Don't be shy,' he says, tugging the knickers down over my hips. 'I like a girl with interesting tastes.'

But I have lowered my head to hide a smile, not my blushes. I maintain a coy silence as Simon peels on the pink knickers.

'And my stockings?'

Simon is just as keen to get into these, and they are rolled down my legs and up his with no hesitation. He sits next to me, his thighs spread, rather suspiciously at home in women's underwear.

The sight of him is both shocking and exciting. My stockings transform his well-shaped legs, and when I run my hands up his thigh, I'm surprised that it feels as smooth as silk. At the top, the hairs on his legs curl over the nylon. Simon shudders and takes a deep breath as I caress him here too.

The pink knickers, bought a couple of sizes too big for me, stretch over Simon's hips but only just contain his prick. They strain over his large erection. One ball protrudes from beneath the lace edging. I can't resist sliding my hand higher and giving it a little tickle.

Simon lifts his hips, pushing his cock towards my hand, and, not wishing to be too heartless, I caress it for a brief moment, running my palm firmly up and down the thick shaft. I feel it grow larger still until the tip peeks out at me from the top of the knickers. Simon looks down at himself and I see a smirk of delight cross his face. He is clearly enjoying the sight as much as I am. Idly I wonder what it would feel like to be fucked by a man wearing my knickers, but then, remembering that is not on the agenda today, I pull my hand away.

'Simon. There's something else . . .'

Squirming in anticipation, Simon says: 'What? Tell me what you want, doll.'

'Well. Would you mind awfully if I tied you up?'

'No. Oh no. You go for it girl,' Simon replies.

With a degree of trust that nearly makes me feel guilty, Simon holds out his arms and I bind them to the back of the sofa with his belt. Then he spreads his legs wide for me to strap his ankles to the feet of the sofa with some ribbons that had been artfully tied into my hair earlier. As I move over him, I'm careful to let the best bits of my body brush almost accidentally against him, giving him tempting previews of what he thinks he's going to get. He holds his breath as one nipple scrapes over his chest. Shudders again as the soft down of my mons tickles his thigh.

It is then that the drink arrives. It is not carried by Sandra, but our waiter is as familiar to Simon as his much-maligned secretary.

'Weston!'

'Hello, Simon. Don't get up. Oh, sorry. It doesn't look like you can.'

'What the fuck are you doing here?'

'Sandra said you wanted some champagne.'

At Luke's arrival, Simon's cock shrivels slightly. A little tweak on the tip soon gets it twitching again, but that's all the attention it is going to get – I've got better toys to play with. I walk over to Luke and kiss him, full on the mouth, showing both men how pleased I am to see him.

I begin to undress Luke, making a show of removing his clothes. I run my hands over his chest as I slip his shirt off his shoulders, letting my fingernails graze his nipples. Simon snarls in frustration as I unfasten Luke's trousers and push my hand inside. My fingers find Luke's cock, and I stroke him softly, teasing his flaccid flesh into the first hint of an erection. Then I run my hands over his bum, and let his trousers and boxer shorts drop to his ankles. Sliding my hand back up the inside of his thigh, I take his balls in my hand and give them an affectionate squeeze. Simon and I watch, one in envy, one in admiration, as Luke's cock lifts. His eyes flicker closed, but Luke won't let himself give way yet. He has not forgotten his job as barman. Gently moving me away, he picks up the champagne bottle again and eases out the cork.

'Silly me,' he says. 'I didn't bring any glasses.'

'That's OK,' I reply, taking the bottle from Luke's hands, 'I'm sure we can improvise.' I smile at Luke and let the bottle tip.

He gasps in shock and throws back his head as the chilled liquid runs over his chest and down his body. I bend forwards to catch a wave as it flows over the taut muscles of his torso and I feel him tense as I lap it from his skin. The scent of Luke and the taste of the champagne are a delicious combination. I have created a powerful cocktail.

'Hey, that's expensive champagne,' protests Simon. But I will not waste a drop. I lick it from Luke's nipples. I sink to my knees and my tongue moves down his stomach, over his hips and finally to his cock. The warmth of my mouth after the cold of the wine startles him and he lets out a gasp. This turns to a growl of lust as I fill my mouth with more wine, and take his cock deep into my throat. I pause, letting his stiffening prick bathe in the bubbles. He takes my hair into his hands, and I look up to see him staring intently at me.

'You . . .' he begins. But pleasure robs him of words. As I gulp down the wine and begin to slide up and down his erection, his eyes close again and he says no more. But as Luke loses himself to his arousal, my mind is still focused on the task in hand. I make sure that Simon sees what he is missing. As I reach the tip of Luke's prick, I meet Simon's eyes, closing my own in hammed-up delight as I once again take the rigid organ way past my lips and into the depths of my mouth, letting Luke go where Simon so badly wants to be.

Simon moans as he realises that he has been cut out of the game. He struggles against his bonds, but his hands stop inches short of his lap. He can't even touch himself to make up for not being able to touch me. Unlike Luke's, Simon's erection bobs unloved as he writhes in his seat.

'Come on, guys' he whines. 'Let me in on the action.' But we ignore him.

I hear a catch in Luke's breath, and I know his end is near. I want Simon to know it too. I pull away and, folding my fingers around Luke's cock, I let him come over my face in a series of strong pulses. He lets out a wild cry of joy as he orgasms.

'Ah shit,' he calls. 'That's incredible.' I'm not sure if he's faking or not, but I enjoy the act.

I stand and smile into Luke's eyes. But when he bends his head to lick his own spunk from my cheeks and my mouth, the smile fades. Luke's uninhibited and decadent act turns me on a degree too far, and I suddenly know that I will struggle to keep up the show. There is nothing feigned about my arousal now.

Luke turns me so that I have my back to Simon, and whispers an order to bend over. I do as I am told, and hear a whimper from Simon. Luke's slips a hand between my legs and spreads my thighs.

'Isn't she beautiful, Simon?' says Luke, but I can tell by the hushed tone of his voice that he doesn't need an answer. Luke kneels, and leans forwards to tease me with little dabs of his tongue. And as he probes deeper, I feel myself yielding to his expert touch. Closing my eyes, I put my hands to the floor to steady myself.

A fantasy kicks in, and I see myself, tormenting not just Simon, but his audience too, exposing myself to a full studio. I imagine men watching me on the stage of Simon's set, turned on by the sight as Simon is turned on now. I see them all: the beautiful, like Luke, but also the ugly. I see the fat and the plain, the sort of men who can only ever dream of touching something as lovely as me. Unlike Simon, they will be masturbating as they watch me, relieving themselves into their hands as they look at my perfect pink pussy. And the fantasy throws me, shaking and shouting into my climax. Luke supports my weight as my body sags with the release.

When I've recovered, I turn to see that Simon is trembling, a damp patch spreading across the front of my knickers. He is ejaculating over himself – coming in my pants like a pubescent teenager.

It is only then that Simon notices the pair of technicians busy working in a dark corner of the studio on camera one. William is not an expert cameraman, but unfortunately for Simon, Chaz, William's new boyfriend, is. His cheery smile confirms that he has captured all the footage we need. Simon groans and closes his eyes as the full horror of his predicament begins to hit him.

But there's worse to come. I take my mobile out of my bag and tap a number. Upstairs, in an oak-panelled office, a phone will be ringing. John Steadman, the chairman and chief executive of Main Attraction TV, will be leaning across his vast desk to answer the call.

'Hello, Mr Steadman,' I say. 'It's Simon Moore's temporary secretary here. Mr Moore has something he'd like to discuss with you urgently. He was wondering if you could meet him in Studio A ... Oh good, thank you. I'll tell him you'll be there right away.'

'Cassandra, you bitch!' yells Simon. 'You won't get away with this.'

I smile sweetly, a convincing impression of the devoted secretary. 'Sorry, Simon,' I say. 'I think you'll find I already have.'

Luke and I dress quickly, and make our way to the door.

'Bye, Simon,' I call over my shoulder. 'I hope you get your fifth series. But I have a sneaking suspicion that you won't.'

And sitting on his famous sofa in my underwear, Simon Moore begins to cry.

19

Cassandra's Story

Camilla flings open the door to Luke's office and bellows: 'Cassandra, what are you doing in there? You know we're not supposed to use offices meant for senior staff.' Sitting at Luke's old desk I look up and sigh.

'Not normally, but the PM said I should use whatever room I wanted until I leave next month.' This is a huge lie, of course, but Camilla is too thick to suspect, and she backs out of the office muttering something about nepotism. Her bitchery doesn't unnerve me. I really do believe that I am entitled to serve the last few weeks of my notice in comfort.

When I resigned, a few people had kindly said they would be sorry to see me go. Camilla was not one of them. But it is obvious that I'm not right for this job. I see myself for what I am – a silly cuckoo in the sensible nest that is Westminster – and I know that I don't belong. My political career is over.

And so is Simon's. Poor old Simon has made too many enemies. Enemies who were more than willing to provide me with the right names, the right phone numbers and dodgy studio passes. There had been an army of volunteers happy to check diaries, fake appointments and guard the doors of the studio to ensure that William, Chaz, Luke and I had not been disturbed. It had been like putting together a jigsaw puzzle. Once the first pieces were in place, the rest tumbled after them in an irrepressible rush. It had all been so easy.

I look at the disc in my hand and smile. Simon was already on the way out. But the pictures are our little insurance policy. Slotting the disc into the computer on Luke's old desk, I click through the images again. An arm here, a leg there. Only one of the participants in the little orgy William and Chaz had so carefully filmed is identifiable. Simon's scarlet and bulging features are easy to recognise. No one will know who or what had created the huge erection that pokes from Simon's lingerie. No one will care.

Some sexual exploits are acceptable, even in the hypercritical world of UK politics. Some even add a patina of roguish allure to an otherwise sterile image. But Simon had made the fatal mistake of playing the family card, and if you tell everyone you're whiter than white, you'd better make damned sure you are. The British public is prepared to forgive many things, but not hypocrisy. Mr Moore has wobbled off his pedestal.

John Steadman of Main Attraction TV, a man well known for his strict moral views, had sacked Simon on the spot when he discovered him in the TV studio. And Simon's demise as a TV star was quickly followed by his departure from politics.

I had assured Simon that I had no intention of letting the pictures reach the PM's desk, but things had a way of getting out. No secret was ever really safe in Westminster. Simon's own devious nature meant that he would never believe that I wouldn't spill the beans. In an undignified scramble to stop the humiliating pictures from ever seeing the light of day, Simon had, for the first time in his life, done the decent thing and resigned his seat, citing 'a long-term health problem' as the reason for his early departure.

But there is one outstanding matter. I almost feel sorry for Simon as I dial his mobile number.

'Simon, thank you so much for such a lovely time last week. Did you get the little memento I sent you?'

He is not thrilled to hear from me. 'You know I fucking did.'

'Oh good. It's not a flattering film, is it? I think Chaz caught my best angles. But you really do look shit.'

'What do you want, Cassandra? I've already resigned.'

'I know. I was so sorry to hear the news. And Luke was distraught.'

'I'm sure. But there's no point in you threatening to make that video public now.'

'Simon! How could you suggest such a thing. I would never show it to anybody. Not even your wife.'

'My wife! Don't you dare send it to her. Now I've lost my job, I can't afford some fucking expensive circus of a divorce.'

'Of course I wouldn't do such a thing to dear Fiona. But it might be a good idea if you explain to the police that Luke was set up that night at Natasha's flat. Just to make sure.'

'Do I have any choice.'

'Nope. It's called blackmail. Clever isn't it?' I hang up.

Almost immediately the phone rings again and I pick it up to hear Toby, his voice shrill with excitement.

'Cas, Luke's here! He's on his way to your office.'

I look up as Luke's handsome head appears around the office door. 'Thanks Toby,' I say, and carefully replace the receiver.

'Hi. Am I interrupting?' he asks. Striding into the office, he obviously doesn't care if he is.

'Yes,' I say. 'You are.' But seeing him standing in front of the desk, I decide that I don't mind the distraction. He's dressed in a wonderfully cut linen suit, and looks –

as usual – beautifully, effortlessly sexy. He has just been to the first board meeting of his new charity, the Elizabeth Weston Foundation. And judging by his broad grin, it had gone well.

The charity is based at Temworth, which will soon be home to a number of addicts, all at various stages in the process of rebuilding their lives. The elegant reception rooms, furnished at great expense by Lizzy's family, will be turned into day rooms and rest areas. Upstairs, the bedrooms will be transformed into functional dormitories and staff flats. The best of the paintings and furniture will be sold to pay for staff wages. An unhappy chapter in the history of the house has come to a close. Maybe one day it will again be a home – filled with a family who will love it as much as Lizzy once had. But not while Luke owns it.

'A good morning?' I ask.

'Great,' he says, helping himself to an apple from a bowl on the desk. Still high from the buzz of the meeting, Luke can't stand still, and he paces around the office.

I've heard a rumour that the PM is planning to offer him his job back once the dust kicked up by Luke's arrest has settled. But ferociously protective of the Government he once served, Luke will not accept. His high ethical standards will not allow him to take on the role of managing someone else's reputation when his own is tarnished – no matter how unjustified the allegations against him. And passionate about his new project, his life has moved on to a new phase.

'So,' I ask. 'When do I start as your publicity manager?'

'Soon as you like,' he says, talking through a mouthful of apple. 'Your little black book will be invaluable. But I'll work you hard. You won't be able to doss around like you do here.'

'I work like a Trojan,' I protest, knowing it isn't quite

the truth. But somehow, I think it will be easy to put in the effort for the charity. For the first time in my life, I feel I'm going to be doing something that really matters. 'Anyway,' I continue, keen to change the subject, 'in case it had slipped your mind, you don't actually work here any more. How did you get past security?'

'Blagged it,' he says, taking another bite of apple. Luke has evidently lost none of his powers of persuasion. Dropping into a chair, he looks at the apple as if he's tasting it for the first time and screws up his nose. 'This is horrible. You know you really shouldn't eat all this healthy crap.' He tosses the half-eaten apple into the bin and raises his eyes to the ceiling to check for smoke detectors before taking out his cigarettes and lighting up.

'And you shouldn't smoke.'

Luke shrugs. 'I've given up a lot of vices in my time. The only pleasures left to me are cigarettes. And outrageous sex. And high-fat food. Which reminds me. I'm hungry. Let's go for lunch.'

'OK.'

'The Ivy would be nice,' he continues. 'I thought you could pay.'

'Cheeky sod,' I say, closing the files on the computer and removing the disc for safe storage. 'I'll only pay if tomorrow you cook me that eggs Benedict you owe me.'

'Done.'

'Yes.' I laugh. 'I have been.'

As I stand go, my arm catches the handle of my briefcase, and it tumbles to the floor, its contents spilling out onto the carpet. My heart skips a beat.

Luke's Story

I bend down to pick up the case. But Cassandra, falling to her knees, beats me to it. She quickly stuffs everything back into the bag, and something about the alarm in her reaction unnerves me. On her face is an expression I've never seen before. She looks embarrassed.

'Cassandra? What's in the bag?' The fear that rises in my chest is sickeningly familiar.

'The usual girlie stuff.'

'You're hiding something. Show me what it is.' I can't keep the desperation out of my voice.

'There's nothing there that would interest you.' She isn't telling the truth.

'Then why can't you –'

'Christ, Luke, you already know what brand of tampon I use. There really is nothing.'

My terror flaring into fury, I grab her shoulders.

'Show me then.' I find myself shaking her hard, making her scream in rage.

'Get off!'

'Show me what's in your bag!'

'No.' Her cheeks are glowing with shame. She's guilty as sin. Shocked and deeply disappointed, I let her go and stagger backwards. Slowly, I close my eyes. I suddenly feel very, very tired. My happiness slips away like a tide.

I've tried so hard to believe that it wasn't happening. I had almost persuaded myself that the night she came to my flat coked was a one-off. That there was an innocent reason why she gave the money to Hugo. That I was mistaken when I thought I heard her on the phone to her dealer. And when I've woken in a sweat of panic after a nightmare that I know so well, I've tried to dismiss my worries as paranoia. I thought it proved that

I was coming to terms with the past. Now I see it only proves I'm stupid.

'Cas, I can't stop you, but I can't go through it again. I can't be with you if you're going to do that.'

'Do what?' Cassandra's blank expression is very convincing. I have to hand it to her, she's a great liar.

'What is it? Coke?'

'Coke?' She looks genuinely bewildered. 'You think I'm hiding cocaine? But you know I don't —'

'I know you do. I saw giving Hugo Wrighton money. I saw you scoring off him.'

'No. You didn't. Hugo deals in art, Luke – not Class As. I gave him some money to find an antique political print. It was going to be a surprise present. For you.' She pushes her hands into her hips in a coquettish gesture. 'I wanted to buy you a picture for your office so you could get rid of that ghastly dead bloke.'

I still don't get it. 'Saint Sebastian?' I'm incredulous. 'You wanted to replace Saint Sebastian?'

She pouts, looking like a petulant and very pretty little girl. 'Yes.'

'But it's an El Greco.' Lizzy had taken the picture from her family collection and given it to me for my twenty-first birthday. It's the one painting I'd never sell.

'Well, I didn't know. Anyway, then I found out you already owned half of Tate fucking Britain, so I kept the print for myself. It's in the loo at my flat. But I don't suppose you notice such things when you've already got a house stuffed with Turners.'

I can't help smiling. 'Only the one Turner actually.' She is smiling too. Thank God she's smiling. I think back to the telephone conversation that had so terrified me.

'And Julian isn't your dealer?' I already know the answer to my question.

'Julian is my hairdresser. He does my highlights. I'm

not as natural a blonde as I might have led you to believe.' She winces as she speaks, her confession obviously painful.

'And you don't –'

She presses one finger to my lips to silence me. 'No. Oh, Luke,' she whispers. 'I wouldn't do that to you.'

Suddenly I know she means it. 'Then what . . .'

'I'll show you what I was trying to hide if you promise you won't laugh at me.'

I promise.

'And you won't tell anyone else?'

'I won't tell anyone else.'

She opens her bag, takes out a magazine, and holds it up to me. From a front cover flagging articles with titles such as 'Perfect make-up for your perfect day' and '10 things your best man needs to know' beams a self-satisfied looking woman with flowers in her hair. For a moment I stare uncomprehendingly.

'It's a wedding magazine,' I falter.

'Ever the on-the-ball PR man Luke,' she says sarcastically. 'Your knowledge of the British press is phenomenal.'

'You want to get married?'

'Well . . . Yes.' It's an idea I hadn't considered. I think it's a good one, but she doesn't need to know that yet. First I'm going to have some fun.

'Who to?'

'You. You doughnut.'

I start to laugh. 'So there's me thinking you're a modern man-eater who wouldn't be seen dead in a big white frock, and really you're just a sweet old-fashioned girl who can't wait to say "I do".' I try, unsuccessfully, to suppress what is now becoming a massive fit of the giggles.

'And you are an utter, utter bastard,' she yells, and I duck as she throws the magazine at my head.

'And you're –' But I'm unable to finish the sentence. Cassandra launches herself at me and, wrapping her legs around my waist, brings me to the ground in a spectacular rugby tackle. Straddling my body, she sits down heavily on my stomach.

'No, Cassandra!' I scream. 'Don't tickle me! Toby'll hear and call security. No! Not there!'

And as I howl in protest, she tugs open my flies and thrusts one hand into the front of my trousers.

I will ask her to marry me. Properly.

But not right now.

Visit the Black Lace website at
www.blacklace-books.co.uk

FIND OUT THE LATEST INFORMATION AND TAKE ADVANTAGE OF OUR FANTASTIC FREE BOOK OFFER! ALSO VISIT THE SITE FOR ...

- All Black Lace titles currently available and how to order online
- Great new offers
- Writers' guidelines
- Author interviews
- An erotica newsletter
- Features
- Cool links

BLACK LACE — THE LEADING IMPRINT OF WOMEN'S SEXY FICTION

TAKING YOUR EROTIC READING PLEASURE TO NEW HORIZONS

BLACK LACE

LOOK OUT FOR THE ALL-NEW BLACK LACE BOOKS – AVAILABLE NOW!

All new books priced £7.99 in the UK. Please note publication dates apply to the UK only. For other territories, please contact your retailer.

PAGAN HEAT
Monica Belle
ISBN O 352 33974 8

For Sophie Page, the job of warden at Elmcote Hall is a dream come true. The beauty of the ruined house and the overgrown grounds speaks to her love of nature. As a venue for weddings, films and exotic parties the Hall draws curious and interesting people, including the handsome Richard Fox and his friends – who are equally alluring and more puzzling still. Her aim is to be with Richard, but it quickly becomes plain that he wants rather more than she had expected to give. She suspects he may have something to do with the sexually charged and strange events taking place by night in the woods around the Hall. Sophie wants to give in to her desires, but the consequences of doing that threaten to take her down a road she hardly dare consider.

LORD WRAXALL'S FANCY
Anna Lieff Saxby
ISBN O 352 33080 5

The year is 1720 and Lady Celine Fortescue is summoned by her father, Sir James, to join him on St Cecilia, the turbulent tropical island which he governs. But the girl who steps off the boat into the languid and intoxicating heat isn't the same girl who was content to stay at needlework in a dull Surrey mansion. On a moonlit night, perfumed with the scent of night-blooming flowers, Celine liaises with Liam O'Brian, one of the ship's officers to whom she became secretly betrothed on the long sea voyage. When Liam falls victim to a plot that threatens his life, the debauched Lord Wraxall promises to intervene, in return for Celine's hand in marriage. Celine, however, has other ideas. Exotic and opulent, this story of indulgent luxury is stimulation for the senses.

Coming in September 2005

PASSION OF ISIS
Madelynne Ellis
ISBN O 352 33993 4

Adie Hamilton is young, ambitious and wants to make a name for herself in Egyptology, but when Killiam Carmichael invites her to join his prestigious research term at the desert necropolis of Saqqara it's not all dusty tombs and broken pots. Whilst Adie is drawn into the search for the vital missing fragment of an erotic mural, Dareth Sadler, the charismatic leader of a cult hooked on sex magic, and Killiam's bitter rival, arrives to threaten the future of the project. Sadler knows a whole range of erotic dirty tricks, so it's up to Adie to keep one step ahead. The result is a sultry journey of discovery and naked ambition set in the stormy desert landscape of Egyptian monuments and ancient sybaritic secrets.

CONFESSIONAL
Judith Roycroft
ISBN 0 352 33421 5

Faren Lonsdale is an ambitious young reporter, always searching for the scoop that will rocket her to journalistic fame. In search of a story she infiltrates St Peter's, a seminary for young men who are about to sacrifice earthly pleasures for a life of devotion and abstinence. What she unveils are nocturnal shenanigans in a cloistered world that is anything but chaste. But will she reveal the secrets of St Peter's to the outside world, or will she be complicit in keeping quiet about the activities of the gentleman priests?

Black Lace Booklist

Information is correct at time of printing. To avoid disappointment check availability before ordering. Go to www.blacklace-books.co.uk. All books are priced £6.99 unless another price is given.

BLACK LACE BOOKS WITH A CONTEMPORARY SETTING

☐ SHAMELESS Stella Black	ISBN 0 352 33485 1	£5.99
☐ INTENSE BLUE Lyn Wood	ISBN 0 352 33496 7	£5.99
☐ ON THE EDGE Laura Hamilton	ISBN 0 352 33534 3	£5.99
☐ LURED BY LUST Tania Picarda	ISBN 0 352 33533 5	£5.99
☐ THE NINETY DAYS OF GENEVIEVE Lucinda Carrington	ISBN 0 352 33070 8	£5.99
☐ DREAMING SPIRES Juliet Hastings	ISBN 0 352 33584 X	
☐ THE TRANSFORMATION Natasha Rostova	ISBN 0 352 33311 1	
☐ SIN.NET Helena Ravenscroft	ISBN 0 352 33598 X	
☐ TWO WEEKS IN TANGIER Annabel Lee	ISBN 0 352 33599 8	
☐ PLAYING HARD Tina Troy	ISBN 0 352 33617 X	
☐ SYMPHONY X Jasmine Stone	ISBN 0 352 33629 3	
☐ SUMMER FEVER Anna Ricci	ISBN 0 352 33625 0	
☐ A SECRET PLACE Ella Broussard	ISBN 0 352 33307 3	
☐ THE GIFT OF SHAME Sara Hope-Walker	ISBN 0 352 32935 1	
☐ GOING TOO FAR Laura Hamilton	ISBN 0 352 33657 9	
☐ THE STALLION Georgina Brown	ISBN 0 352 33005 8	
☐ SWEET THING Alison Tyler	ISBN 0 352 33682 X	
☐ TIGER LILY Kimberly Dean	ISBN 0 352 33685 4	
☐ RELEASE ME Suki Cunningham	ISBN 0 352 33671 4	
☐ KING'S PAWN Ruth Fox	ISBN 0 352 33684 6	
☐ SLAVE TO SUCCESS Kimberley Raines	ISBN 0 352 33687 0	
☐ SHADOWPLAY Portia Da Costa	ISBN 0 352 33313 8	
☐ I KNOW YOU, JOANNA Ruth Fox	ISBN 0 352 33727 3	
☐ THE HOUSE IN NEW ORLEANS Fleur Reynolds	ISBN 0 352 32951 3	
☐ DRAWN TOGETHER Robyn Russell	ISBN 0 352 33269 7	
☐ VIRTUOSO Katrina Vincenzi-Thyre	ISBN 0 352 32907 6	
☐ FIGHTING OVER YOU Laura Hamilton	ISBN 0 352 33795 8	

☐ ALWAYS THE BRIDEGROOM Tesni Morgan	ISBN O 352 33855 5
☐ COMING ROUND THE MOUNTAIN Tabitha Flyte	ISBN O 352 33873 3
☐ FEMININE WILES Karina Moore	ISBN O 352 33235 2
☐ MIXED SIGNALS Anna Clare	ISBN O 352 33889 X
☐ BLACK LIPSTICK KISSES Monica Belle	ISBN O 352 33885 7
☐ HOT GOSSIP Savannah Smythe	ISBN O 352 33880 6
☐ GOING DEEP Kimberly Dean	ISBN O 352 33876 8
☐ PACKING HEAT Karina Moore	ISBN O 352 33356 1
☐ MIXED DOUBLES Zoe le Verdier	ISBN O 352 33312 X
☐ WILD BY NATURE Monica Belle	ISBN O 352 33915 2
☐ UP TO NO GOOD Karen S. Smith	ISBN O 352 33589 O
☐ CLUB CRÈME Primula Bond	ISBN O 352 33907 1
☐ BONDED Fleur Reynolds	ISBN O 352 33192 5
☐ SWITCHING HANDS Alaine Hood	ISBN O 352 33896 2
☐ EDEN'S FLESH Robyn Russell	ISBN O 352 33923 3
☐ CREAM OF THE CROP Savannah Smythe	ISBN O 352 33920 9 £7.99
☐ PEEP SHOW Mathilde Madden	ISBN O 352 33924 1 £7.99
☐ RISKY BUSINESS Lisette Allen	ISBN O 352 33280 8 £7.99
☐ CAMPAIGN HEAT Gabrielle Marcola	ISBN O 352 33941 1 £7.99
☐ MS BEHAVIOUR Mini Lee	ISBN O 352 33962 4 £7.99
☐ FIRE AND ICE Laura Hamilton	ISBN O 352 33486 X £7.99
☐ UNNATURAL SELECTION Alaine Hood	ISBN O 352 33963 2 £7.99
☐ SLEAZY RIDER Karen S. Smith	ISBN O 352 33964 O £7.99
☐ VILLAGE OF SECRETS Mercedes Kelly	ISBN O 352 33344 8 £7.99
☐ PAGAN HEAT Monica Belle	ISBN O 352 33974 8 £7.99

BLACK LACE BOOKS WITH AN HISTORICAL SETTING

☐ PRIMAL SKIN Leona Benkt Rhys	ISBN O 352 33500 9 £5.99
☐ DARKER THAN LOVE Kristina Lloyd	ISBN O 352 33279 4
☐ THE CAPTIVATION Natasha Rostova	ISBN O 352 33234 4
☐ MINX Megan Blythe	ISBN O 352 33638 2
☐ DIVINE TORMENT Janine Ashbless	ISBN O 352 33719 2
☐ SATAN'S ANGEL Melissa MacNeal	ISBN O 352 33726 5
☐ THE INTIMATE EYE Georgia Angelis	ISBN O 352 33004 X
☐ SILKEN CHAINS Jodi Nicol	ISBN O 352 33143 7
☐ THE LION LOVER Mercedes Kelly	ISBN O 352 33162 3

☐ THE AMULET Lisette Allen	ISBN 0 352 33019 8
☐ WHITE ROSE ENSNARED Juliet Hastings	ISBN 0 352 33052 X
☐ UNHALLOWED RITES Martine Marquand	ISBN 0 352 33222 0
☐ LA BASQUAISE Angel Strand	ISBN 0 352 32988 2
☐ THE HAND OF AMUN Juliet Hastings	ISBN 0 352 33144 5
☐ THE SENSES BEJEWELLED Cleo Cordell	ISBN 0 352 32904 1
☐ UNDRESSING THE DEVIL Angel Strand	ISBN 0 352 33938 1 £7.99
☐ THE BARBARIAN GEISHA Charlotte Royal	ISBN 0 352 33267 0 £7.99
☐ FRENCH MANNERS Olivia Christie	ISBN 0 352 33214 X £7.99
☐ LORD WRAXALL'S FANCY Anna Lieff Saxby	ISBN 0 352 33080 5 £7.99
☐ NICOLE'S REVENGE Lisette Allen	ISBN 0 352 32984 X £7.99

BLACK LACE ANTHOLOGIES

☐ WICKED WORDS Various	ISBN 0 352 33363 4
☐ MORE WICKED WORDS Various	ISBN 0 352 33487 8
☐ WICKED WORDS 3 Various	ISBN 0 352 33522 X
☐ WICKED WORDS 4 Various	ISBN 0 352 33603 X
☐ WICKED WORDS 5 Various	ISBN 0 352 33642 0
☐ WICKED WORDS 6 Various	ISBN 0 352 33690 0
☐ WICKED WORDS 7 Various	ISBN 0 352 33743 5
☐ WICKED WORDS 8 Various	ISBN 0 352 33787 7
☐ WICKED WORDS 9 Various	ISBN 0 352 33860 1
☐ WICKED WORDS 10 Various	ISBN 0 352 33893 8
☐ THE BEST OF BLACK LACE 2 Various	ISBN 0 352 33718 4
☐ WICKED WORDS: SEX IN THE OFFICE Various	ISBN 0 352 33944 6 £7.99
☐ WICKED WORDS: SEX ON HOLIDAY Various	ISBN 0 352 33961 6 £7.99

BLACK LACE NON-FICTION

☐ THE BLACK LACE BOOK OF WOMEN'S SEXUAL FANTASIES Ed. Kerri Sharp	ISBN 0 352 33793 1
☐ THE BLACK LACE SEXY QUIZ BOOK Maddie Saxon	ISBN 0 352 33884 9

To find out the latest information about Black Lace titles, check out the website: www.blacklace-books.co.uk or send for a booklist with complete synopses by writing to:

Black Lace Booklist, Virgin Books Ltd
Thames Wharf Studios
Rainville Road
London W6 9HA

Please include an SAE of decent size. Please note only British stamps are valid.

Our privacy policy
We will not disclose information you supply us to any other parties. We will not disclose any information which identifies you personally to any person without your express consent.

From time to time we may send out information about Black Lace books and special offers. Please tick here if you do not wish to receive Black Lace information. ❏

Please send me the books I have ticked above.

Name ....

Address ....

....

....

....

Post Code ....

Send to: Virgin Books Cash Sales, Thames Wharf Studios, Rainville Road, London W6 9HA.

US customers: for prices and details of how to order books for delivery by mail, call 1-800-343-4499.

Please enclose a cheque or postal order, made payable to Virgin Books Ltd, to the value of the books you have ordered plus postage and packing costs as follows:

UK and BFPO – £1.00 for the first book, 50p for each subsequent book.

Overseas (including Republic of Ireland) – £2.00 for the first book, £1.00 for each subsequent book.

If you would prefer to pay by VISA, ACCESS/MASTERCARD, DINERS CLUB, AMEX or SWITCH, please write your card number and expiry date here:

....

Signature ....

Please allow up to 28 days for delivery.